ALSO BY SARAH READY

Stand Alone Romances:

The Fall in Love Checklist

Hero Ever After

Once Upon an Island

Josh and Gemma Make a Baby

Josh and Gemma the Second Time Around

French Holiday

Soul Mates in Romeo Romance Series:

Chasing Romeo

Love Not at First Sight

Romance by the Book

Love, Artifacts, and You

Married by Sunday

My Better Life

Scrooging Christmas

Stand Alone Novella:

Love Letters

Find these books and more by Sarah Ready at:

www.sarahready.com/romance-books

EVERYTHING IS ABOUT TO CHANGE

Gemma Jacobs has life figured out. She's upbeat, positive to a fault, and the master of her own destiny.

She has a wonderful career in social media marketing, lives in a trendy apartment with her fiancé Josh Lewenthal, and is pregnant with their much-loved baby.

Her life is wonderful. Absolutely perfect.

Except...

What really comes after the happily ever after?

Josh Lewenthal is laid-back, fun-loving, and always finds the humor in life. He writes a wildly successful web comic series, and can't wait to marry Gemma—the woman of his dreams.

His life is amazing. Terrific.

Except...

What happens when everything changes?

Suddenly Josh and Gemma's lives are turned upside

down, and their love and their future together are at risk. They realize their happily ever after isn't the end, it's just the beginning—and now they have to fight for it.

They confront a devastating separation, the return of world-infamous Ian Fortune, and the question of whether or not their love can truly survive when everyone says...it's already gone.

Josh and Gemma
the Second Time Around

SARAH READY

W.W. CROWN BOOKS
An imprint of Swift & Lewis Publishing LLC
www.wwcrown.com

This book is a work of fiction. All the characters and situations in this book are fictitious. Any resemblance to situations or persons living or dead is purely coincidental. Any reference to historical events, real people, or real locations are used fictitiously.

Published by W.W. Crown Books an Imprint of Swift & Lewis Publishing, LLC, Lowell, MI USA
Cover Illustration & Design: Elizabeth Turner Stokes
Interior Illustrations: Sarah Ready

Library of Congress Control Number: 2022914482
ISBN: 978-1-954007-42-0 (eBook)
ISBN: 978-1-954007-43-7 (pbk)
ISBN: 978-1-954007-44-4 (large print)
ISBN: 978-1-954007-45-1 (hbk)
ISBN: 978-1-954007-46-8 (audiobook)

Hi Mom! This one's for you.

Josh
and
Gemma
the
Second Time
Around

PROLOGUE

When I said that Josh and I would live happily ever after, I believed that love would never die.

I was wrong.

Or maybe I was wrong in that I never thought about the moment I would die. For thirty-three years I galloped through life without ever considering the moment of my own death.

A hot tear slides down my face.

Does love die when you die? I think it must. It feels like it does.

There's a heavy, dark silence smothering me and the world frays apart at the edges, unraveling at a frightening pace. The color leaches away, like threads pulled from a cloth. Soon, I'll only be left with black.

Would I do it all again? Knowing that I'd end up right here, my breath gone, my life leaking away?

Yes. I'd do it a thousand times again. And each time I'd make the same choices that led me here. To this place.

I focus on the bright sky above. The blur of Josh's bone-white face. He begs me not to leave him, not to leave, don't go, don't go, don't go.

I want to tell him a million things, a million and one, but most of all I want to tell him to take care of our baby.

To love him. To save him. To care for him.

But I can't. I can't talk. I can't breathe.

Instead.

I go.

I think...I die.

This has to be death.

Because the love, it's gone.

1

*"Everything is about
to change."*

"I WILL NEVER UNSEE THIS," JOSH SAYS, HIS FACE IS PALER THAN usual.

I bet he's regretting those two lox bagels he ate on the way to class. I warned him, but did he listen? No. He presses his hand against his stomach and moans.

"Look away," I whisper.

We're sitting next to each other on a maroon velvet floor cushion, facing a large flat screen television. He shakes his head, and a lock of black hair falls across his forehead. His eyes are wide, and a look of horror flickers across his face.

"Can't...can't look away."

I'd laugh, but I can't look away either. Every time I try, my eyes are pulled back to the graphic scene. My hand rests on Josh's thigh and I squeeze his leg.

It's the last day of our birthing class and today we get to

watch a full, explicit, should-be-rated-R close-up of a live birth.

Our instructor, Tillie Bloom, is a short, round woman in her sixties. She has a spray tan, wears dozens of plastic bangles on each arm, and likes lilac-colored lipstick.

Every Saturday morning for the last eight weeks, we've crowded into the patchouli-scented living room of her Brooklyn Heights townhouse with eight other expecting couples.

Tillie's tastes run to the eclectic. She has beaded curtains, enough indoor plants to fill a greenhouse, and floor cushions instead of couches. Hannah recommended her because she teaches pain-free birthing using hypnosis and on a whim I signed up. Pain-free sounded good.

For eight weeks now I've practiced putting myself in a deep relaxed state so that not even a baby ripping my vagina will faze me. Speaking of, the video shows the baby's head crowning, and yup, sure enough, there's tearing.

Josh leans closer and grips my shoulder.

"Gemma. Do you remember that scene from *Alien*? The one you had to close your eyes for?"

I turn and Josh is so close our noses almost touch. His eyes are brimming with self-deprecating laughter at his own unmanly horror. I get it. It's all that fluid, and blood, and that big, fat baby's head.

"I remember," I say.

His nose rubs against mine and I think he's about to drop a kiss on my lips. But then he says, in a serious voice, "This. Scene. Is. Worse."

A laugh spills out of me and Josh smiles in appreciation. He must realize this movie is freaking me out too (in six weeks this will be me!) and he's trying to make it better.

See, this is why I love him.

I drop my head into the crook of Josh's arm. He makes a happy noise and sets his free hand on my stomach. Then he starts a slow, rhythmic circle rubbing over my belly. The baby is lodged over on my right side, nearest Josh. When he shifts and pushes against me, I imagine he's trying to get closer to Josh.

I know how he feels.

I take a deep breath and draw in the comforting smell of ink and laundry soap. Josh was up early working and there are black ink blotches on his fingertips and staining his gray t-shirt. He's hurrying to finish his latest installment before the baby's born.

He has a month-long publicity tour coming up for the miniseries *Grim,* which is based on his web comic, our wedding and honeymoon, and then the baby. He wants to be finished with the latest episodes and the publicity tour before the baby's born so that he can take a month off to be with him.

Or her.

Josh says her. I say him. We'll find out soon.

We have six weeks to fit everything in.

Wedding, honeymoon, tour, then baby.

I sigh and lean further into Josh.

Tomorrow we'll be married. I try to imagine what it'll be like to be Mrs. Gemma Lewenthal. What it'll be like to stand in my parents' backyard, under the wedding gazebo that Josh, Dylan, and my dad built and say "I do."

I even try to picture what Josh will do when he finally sees me in my wedding dress, walking down the aisle.

I lift my head up and peek at him.

He looks down at me, and when he sees my expression he lifts his eyebrows.

"What?" he mouths.

"Just thinking about tomorrow," I whisper.

A slow smile spreads over his face and he pulls me closer until I'm resting against him.

Then he drops his lips next to my ear and whispers, "Tomorrow day, or tomorrow night?"

I elbow him and he lets out a whoosh of air.

"How can you say that while we're watching this?" I nod my head at the television screen.

He chuckles and his laughter tickles my ear. "I'm compartmentalizing. It's a skill."

I grin at him.

The live birth is coming to its gory conclusion.

And it is not pretty. After the baby comes the placenta. Why didn't I know you also have to push out the placenta? AKA, the afterbirth.

Tillie's bracelets jangle as she claps her hands, "Isn't it beautiful, class? Look at the miracle of life! Your body is miraculous. You too will expand and flow and stretch until your baby makes its way out. Your canal starts the width of a quarter and then expands to the width of a melon."

She makes a small hole with her fingers and then makes a little *whoooop* noise as she expands her hands in front of her face. Then she pops her smiling head out of her finger hole, ending the whole scene with a smacking noise.

I flinch and Josh pats my shoulder reassuringly.

The video fades to black.

I'm not sure what everyone else thought about the movie. Josh and I have front row seats. The others, veterinarian Ramesh and his dog walking wife Angelie, surgeon Lee and her calligrapher boyfriend Carl, Type-A couple Vera and Tucker, and all the rest, have been quiet throughout.

There's silence as Tillie walks to the front of the room and pulls the gold silk sheet back over the TV. The large flat screen doesn't mesh with her beaded curtains, or potted plants and floor cushions, so she likes to keep it covered.

She takes a moment to smile at each one of us, her lilac-colored lipstick stretching across her face.

"Before we close our session," she says in her soothing, hypnotic voice, "I want to remind all of you that you won't be able to enjoy sexual relations for six to eight weeks after delivery. Your body needs time to heal."

Josh's hand stops moving on my belly. He blows out a long, woe-is-me breath. When I scowl at him, his eyes crinkle up in a smile.

"But that is the least of your worries," Tillie says.

Then she opens her arms wide, gesturing at all of us, and her bracelets clatter. "Be aware, your relationship post-baby will change drastically. Dads, partners, you may feel left behind, unloved, possibly abandoned. Moms, you may feel overwhelmed, confused, exhausted, consumed by your new responsibilities. Many couples fall apart, or their love fades, all due to the strain of parenthood. It's easy for relationships to play second fiddle to being a parent. I'd caution each of you—everything is about to change."

She takes a moment to give each of us wobbly lilac-colored smile. "I hope it's a good change, not a bad change. But it will be a change. Good luck."

I stare at Tillie, shocked by her downer announcement. Up until today she's been all "your body is a miracle, go into the relaxation of your mind, sink into the space where you feel no pain." I wasn't expecting her latest announcement. From the uncomfortable silence around the room, no one else was expecting it either.

Josh squeezes my arm. When I look over at him he lifts an eyebrow at me in question.

"Are things going to change between us?" I whisper.

He shakes his head, a look of pure confidence on his face. I love him for that confidence.

"Not a chance, Gem." He points between us. "You and me. As long as there's a sky above, we'll keep on loving each other. Guarantee it."

"That's what I thought."

Things may change for some. Love may fade for some. But not for us.

Josh pulls me in between his legs and settles his arms around me. While Tillie gives her closing speech, reminding us about the power of our cervixes, and our uteruses, and our minds, Josh leans close and whispers, "We're getting married tomorrow."

My smile stretches so wide across my face my cheeks ache. This is what happiness feels like.

2

"Everything's better the second time around."

MY MOM MISSED HER CALLING AS A DICTATOR.

She'd be perfect as the ruler of a small country, directing how all the citizens should stack towering, jiggling, fruity-flavored Jell-O molds into national monuments. For instance, a Jell-O version of the pyramids of Giza or the Colosseum.

"To the right, Gemma. Move it to the right. No left. No. A little to the right. Up. I said up."

My mom paces behind me. I think being the mother of the bride has finally made her crack.

When Leah married Oliver, they had a traditional church wedding, then reception at a country club. There was a wedding planner, and caterers, and florists. At the time, I thought it was a lot of work.

Josh and I figured we'd make our wedding easy. A simple

backyard ceremony, folding chairs, a gazebo, easy homemade desserts for after, spring flowers from the garden. Easy.

No.

I laugh at the naïveté of my past self.

My mom took the challenge of a backyard wedding and decided it was going to be like our annual New Year's party, but bigger. Like the Fourth of July picnic, but better. Like any party she's ever hosted, but more.

More baby gherkins, but this time the toothpicks would have wedding bells.

More barbecue wieners, but this time the barbecue sauce would have champagne.

More Jell-O, but this time, inspired by the monumental Jell-O art making rounds on the internet, we'd have a three-foot-tall Jell-O sculpture. A jiggly, wiggly, lime green replica of me and Josh standing in front of a massive, fruit-filled heart.

It's possibly the most disturbing thing I've ever seen. And that's saying something since this morning I witnessed a fat-headed baby ripping that poor woman's vagina open during labor.

"Down, Gemma. Move it down. To the left!" My mom wrings a kitchen towel in her hand, pacing back and forth.

We're in the kitchen, at my parent's place, putting the finishing touches on all of the desserts for tomorrow.

My older sister Leah rolls her eyes. Then she says under her breath, "Forget bridezilla, we've got momzilla."

I hold back a laugh. I don't want to mess up the delicate task of lining up the Jell-O sculpture with near surgical precision.

My mom had detailed plastic molds created from CAD drawings—she enlisted a former engineer from her crafting club to design it. This project has been in the works for more than a month.

Out in the living room, I hear Sasha and the twins laugh and their puppy Chase bark excitedly.

There's some thumping, and then Colin shouts, "Leave my fire truck alone!"

"Go play outside," Leah yells.

My mom crowds closer to me and I carefully shift the Josh-shaped slab of Jell-O closer to the big lime-flavored heart that's full of chopped apples, carrots, and strawberries. Josh's Jell-O person wiggles precariously.

"Gemma, don't push so hard, his head will fall off! Look at his head."

His head wiggles up and down like the bobble head on the dash of a speeding car.

"I see it. He's fine. It's not going to fall off."

Leah snorts.

"Be careful. This sculpture is the metaphor of your married life," my mom says.

"Wobbly and fruity?" Leah gives me a cheeky grin.

She's in overalls, a hot pink apron, and her hair is in a high slick ponytail. It's her baking uniform.

"No. Delicious," I say. "Something I love."

Another yip sounds from the living room.

"Take Chase outside," Leah yells.

Then she glares toward the high-pitched barking. "I swear, potty-training a dog is harder than potty-training a kid."

My mom makes a distressed sound, although she already has the plastic runners down covering the white carpet in the living room.

Then she says, "No, girls. I mean this sculpture is a work of love, it'll withstand all the trials of life. It may wobble, but it won't break." Her eyes go misty and she waves a hand in front of her face.

I take a second to wonder why everyone keeps talking about marriages falling apart the day before my wedding.

But Leah, ever practical, says, "It'll break when all the guests carve into it and eat it."

Well, that's true.

I blow out a breath and give the sculpture one final nudge. The whole thing wiggles and then finally settles into place.

"How's that?"

We all take a moment to stare at it. The bright day-glo green gelatin glistens under the kitchen lights. The heart is two and a half feet tall and loaded with chopped fruit and vegetables. The Jell-O Josh is wearing a tuxedo and the Jell-O Gemma is in a poufy wedding dress.

The figures look a lot like that green stretchy Gumby toy, or some weird alien from one of those sci-fi movies from the 1950s that Josh loves.

"Perfect," my mom says.

Leah grunts and then smacks her hands against her apron. A little cloud of flour and sugar fills the air around her.

I take another second to stare at the metaphor of my marriage. I guess if anything had to be a metaphor, my favorite dessert was a good choice. But honestly, all I want from my marriage is to be able to love Josh. To love our baby.

If I have that, then I'll be happy for the rest of my life.

"Do you love it, Gemma?" my mom asks.

I breathe in the sugary kitchen air. The house smells like it does when you rip open a packet of Kool-Aid and all the fruit-flavored sugar dust floats up and tickles your nose. Grape. Lime. Cherry. Sugar.

"I do."

I give my mom a quick squeeze.

We're nearly finished with all the desserts. My mom wanted to keep with Jacobs family tradition, so we have chocolate mayonnaise cupcakes, rainbow salad (a concoction of Jell-O, cottage cheese, and marshmallows), chocolate balls rolled in pink-dyed coconut speared with toothpicks, church window cookies, key lime pie, mile-high lemon meringue pie, tomato cake (made with canned tomato soup, of course), and more.

Everything is in crystal dishes covered in plastic wrap. The dishes are on the countertops, the kitchen table, chairs, and in the fridge.

The back door bangs shut and then we hear the voices of my dad, Dylan and Josh. Dylan leads the way into the kitchen, when he sees all the desserts he greedily rubs his hands together and grins.

"They're for tomorrow," my mom snaps.

She waves her kitchen towel at him in a shoo-shoo sort of gesture. Dylan will hoover up anything in his path if you don't watch him carefully.

My dad wanders into the kitchen and heads straight for my mom.

"How about some coffee?" he asks as he bends down to kiss her cheek.

I don't hear my mom's answer, because...Josh.

He's in a long-sleeve flannel, muddy jeans, and leather boots. His cheeks are red from the biting spring wind and his black hair is messy.

He looks around the kitchen until he finds me. When he does he leans against the wall, crosses his arms over his chest and smiles.

That smile is like a heat-seeking missile that hits me right between the legs. A low throb starts up and I hold back a noise. Of course, Josh knows exactly what he's doing. When I squeeze my thighs and then cross my legs, his dimple deepens and the right side of his mouth kicks up.

On the trip up, he said, "Gem, I've been thinking...six weeks is a long time. We should have sex maybe, three, four times every day until the baby comes. Starting today."

"We're going to be at my parents' house," I said. "It's the day before our wedding. Do you know how busy we'll be setting everything up? Plus the house will be full of people."

"We still haven't had our date in the garage," he said.

Mmmm. The garage.

Josh watches me from the kitchen entry. I can tell he knows exactly what I'm thinking about because he gets a happy, my-dreams-are-about-to-come-true look on his face and then he nods his head back toward the garage.

My cheeks flush hot, and I uncross my legs.

Could we?

Should we?

No one notices the silent exchange going on between Josh and me.

Yes? No? Yes?

"Did you get all the folding chairs set up?" my mom asks.

"Yes, dear," my dad says. He roots through the cupboard, pulling out coffee mugs and a bag of ground coffee.

"And the gazebo? Why did you leave it for last? You finished the construction?"

"Yes, dear."

I shake my head no at Josh, so he nods his head yes and gestures to the garage again.

Could we?

"And you set up all the ceramic pots with the pillar candles? And the folding tables? And the—"

"Yes, dear."

"And...Dylan Michael!"

Dylan pokes the lime green heart with his pointer finger, watching it jiggle like a vibrating bed in a Las Vegas honeymoon suite.

"Yeah, Mom?" He's enthralled by the wiggly mass, he pokes the heart again.

"Dylan! Take your finger away from the Jell-O sculpture this instant. I brought you into this world, and I can take you out."

Dylan snatches his hand back like he's been burned. "Sorry, Mom."

Josh finally breaks our gaze, shaking out of our should we/could we debate. He looks down at the crystal platter holding the two-and-a-half-foot-tall lime green sculpted monument to matrimonial bliss. I press my lips together, waiting for his reaction.

He stares at the Jell-O for a moment, scratches his chin, looks up at me, then back to the Jell-O, then back to me again. He didn't know about my mom's ode to internet pop art, the Jell-O wedding sculpture. Surprise!

I watch his expression alternate between dumbfounded amusement and horror. He's trying to hold back his isn't-life-hilarious smile, and I don't know how long he's going to make it.

"Gemma?"

His low voice sends another pulse through me. Good thing no one else in the kitchen knows what he does to me.

"Yes, Josh?"

He slowly walks over to the counter where the Jell-O stands. Everyone is watching now. I smooth my face out and regard him seriously.

Josh sees my expression and covers a snort. He knows me

well enough to know that I find his consternation hilarious. He points at the green humanoid sculptures that are supposed to be us in our wedding finery.

"What is this?"

I grin up at him and flutter my eyelashes. "Lime Jell-O."

He nods and I catch the scent of the spring breeze still clinging to his shirt and the smell of the cedar planks that he and Dad built our wedding gazebo with.

He's waiting to see if I'll say anything more. So I do.

"It's also the symbolic representation of our marriage. Jiggly but unbreakable."

His back is to everyone, so I get to see his mouth twist and his eyes crinkle as he tries to hold in his laughter.

"Isn't it wonderful?" my mom says.

There's no way that anyone will ever convince my mom that Jell-O molds aren't the best thing to happen to mankind since the invention of the wheel.

Josh knows this, so he nods stiffly, keeping his back to everyone. His eyes water from the effort not to laugh.

I grin at him.

"Cool. Can I have some tomato cake?" Dylan asks, drifting toward the bright orangey-red cake.

"No," my mom snaps.

"Come on, Mom, I hauled chairs, I toted planters, I built a gazebo with my bare hands, I—"

My mom interrupts him. "Josh and Gemma, would you take the Jell-O sculpture out to the garage refrigerator? I cleared the whole thing for it."

A huge smile spreads over Josh's face and he nods his head at me. He gives me his life's-my-playground smile, which I now call Gemma's-my-playground smile, and I try really, really hard not to blush in front of my family.

"We'd be happy to," he says.

"Yup," I say. We'd be really, really happy to.

He leans closer and puts his mouth next to my ear, "I have to tell you something."

My ear vibrates at the deepness of his voice and I reactively lean closer to him. His voice is earnest, and I can tell it's important.

I glance up at him. His eyes have shifted from laughter to serious.

"Alright." I don't know why I suddenly feel like I've been called to the principal's office, it's not like Josh could ever have anything bad to tell me. But still, my mouth is dry and my hands shake.

"Pick it up on three," my mom says. "One, two, three."

The platter is heavy. Nearly three feet of Jell-O stuffed with fruit and vegetable chunks weighs *a lot.*

I nod to Josh and we both start to side shuffle toward the kitchen entry. That'll lead down the hall, through the living room, to the garage.

"Slowly," my mom says.

Josh stares at our Jell-O figures and his brow wrinkles.

Then he looks up at me, half-appalled, half-confused, "Why do we look like mutants?"

I snort and the whole Jell-O tray wobbles precariously.

"Careful," my mom calls.

Josh and I stand still and wait for the Jell-O to stop shaking. Looking closely, I can see why my mom thought Josh's head might fall off—it *is* a little off-kilter.

"And why are my eyes so close together?" Josh frowns at his replica. "Is my nose really that big?"

I bite my tongue to keep from laughing.

He looks at me to see how I'm taking his critique. When I don't answer, he sighs and shakes his head.

"All this time, I thought you were marrying me for my looks. But now I realize that's not it at all."

"Then what?" I ask.

He lifts his eyebrows up and down suggestively and nods toward the garage.

I'm about to say something about garage floors when there's a loud crash. We both look back to the kitchen entry. A kitchen chair has toppled over, knocked down by Colin's new radio-controlled fire truck. The fire truck skids across the kitchen, its lights flashing and the siren whining.

"Colin," Leah calls, "not inside."

But Colin isn't listening. There's a noise of stampeding feet coming down the hallway. Chase is on the loose. He lets out a long, mournful bark, mimicking the siren. His puppy paws slap against the tile as he bounds into the kitchen, chasing after the fire truck.

"Noooo!" Colin cries, running after Chase. "Leave my truck alone!"

"Colin, stop," Leah cries.

But Colin is determined to keep his fire truck out of the jaws of Chase. He steers the fire truck across the kitchen, directly at Josh and me.

"Watch out!" my mom cries.

Josh and I hold our ground. If we don't move, we won't spill the Jell-O.

The fire truck speeds through my legs.

"Thank God," my mom says.

Then I close my eyes as Chase sprints after it, knocking against my legs. The Jell-O wobbles, but Josh and I hold tight, and it doesn't fall. I open my eyes just in time to see Colin skid, baseball style, between Josh and me.

My mom shrieks.

"Colin, Chase. No!" Leah yells.

I hold my breath. But Colin makes it through without hitting either of us. He jumps up and runs after Chase, keeping the fire truck just ahead of the puppy.

The puppy senses a game and keeps letting out its high, siren-pitched howl. Colin isn't the best at steering, so the fire truck knocks against my mom's ankles, ramming her.

Chase is so excited he squats at my mom's feet and pees on her shoes. She shrieks and jumps up onto the kitchen chair next to Josh and me.

"Stop!" she cries from on top of her chair. "The Jell-O!"

Dylan sees a problem he can fix. And because he really is a good brother, he chases after Colin. But that means my parents' small kitchen now has a speeding toy fire truck, a howling, peeing, skidding puppy, a shouting, running five-year-old, a shouting, running thirty-five-year-old and my mom, shrieking on a chair.

I look at Josh and we both realize at the exact same moment that there's no way we're getting out of this unscathed.

Bless him, he looks really worried. I'm worried too, this Jell-O sculpture is the metaphor of our marriage. It can't be destroyed before we're even at the altar.

"Stop!" I cry, joining the chorus of voices.

"No, Chase!" Colin shouts.

He steers the fire truck under the Jell-O platter, in the space between me and Josh.

"Oh no!" my mom wails.

The wet, pee-covered puppy dashes under us, missing both our legs.

Then Colin executes another slide, skidding across the floor after Chase. I squeak as my nephew knocks against my legs and I stumble over him.

"Hold it steady!" my dad shouts.

Dylan's on his hands and knees. He crawls under us, charging after Colin, Chase, and the truck. I avoid him, and Josh and I tilt the Jell-O platter back and forth.

The sculpture slides from one side of the plate to the other, and our fruity heart and bride and groom replicas jiggle in some sort of macabre wedding dance.

"Steady!" my mom calls from the chair.

The sculpture wobbles and leans far, far to the side of the platter.

I look to Josh. He's concentrating like we're in the last inning of the World Series, and we have to keep this wedding Jell-O safe. Or else. His eyebrows are puckered and there's hard determination on his face.

Finally, we tilt it perfectly to the left, at a slight angle so that the Jell-O stops shaking.

I let out a long sigh and Josh shakes his head at me, like *is this for real?*

"Watch out!" my dad shouts.

I look down. They're back.

"Whhhhy!" my mom wails.

The firetruck zooms under us. Chase skids after it, his tongue hanging from the side of his mouth. Colin races through after Chase.

They don't hit us. The Jell-O sculpture is fine.

I look at Josh, my eyes wide.

He grins at me.

We did it.

"Colin, give me that remote! Now!" Leah says in her firm, mom voice.

Colin stops and turns to his mom.

A wave a relief runs through the room.

Dylan dashes around the island.

"Got you, dog!" he crows.

He lunges after the barking, prancing puppy. But instead of catching Chase, he slips on the puddle of pee. He dives forward, arms outstretched, and slides on his stomach across the tile floor like he's riding a slip n' slide.

I brace myself for impact.

But he misses us. He misses!

There's a moment of sweet, sweet relief. Until Dylan keeps sliding, right past us, into the chair that my mom's perched on. He rams into the chair legs and the chair flips over him.

My mom catapults into the air.

She lets out a high-pitched shriek, her arms flap around in the air, like she's trying to fly, and then she dives straight into Josh and me.

My legs knock out from under me. I land on top of Josh. My mom crashes into Dylan.

I watch, as the Jell-O heart, the Jell-O Josh and the Jell-O Gemma somersault through the air. The platter hits the ground first, clanging against the tiles.

Then the Jell-O splatters over Josh and me, globs of lime gelatin, fruit and vegetables slopping against our faces, into our hair, all over our bodies.

Our wedding heart is broken, the metaphor of our marriage is shattered.

I roll off of Josh and shift tenderly, making sure nothing is bruised. Luckily, I'm fine. Josh sits up and shakes his head like he's coming out of a pool of water. Jell-O sprays off of him. But still, he's covered in oozy, sticky green. A chunk of goop falls off his cheek and hits the tile with a wet, sucking plop.

Chase runs over to it and laps it up, his pink tongue darting frantically. Then he starts in on a bigger pile.

The lapping of Chase's tongue and the whine of the toy fire truck are the only sounds in the kitchen.

When Josh sees me, smeared in lime Jell-O, he tilts his head with interest and his eyes light up. I bet you anything he's thinking about his high school graduation.

He leans forward, drags his finger across my cheek and then pops his finger in his mouth.

He sucks for a moment, then pulls his finger out and says with a grin, "Tastes good."

At that, the stunned silence is broken.

My mom cries, "Oh noooo!" She shoves off of Dylan, then swats him in the back of the head.

"What did I do?" He holds up his hands in an I'm innocent gesture.

Leah is in full mad mom mode. She drags Colin and Chase out of the kitchen.

"Time out," she says. "Time out for both of you."

Josh takes another swipe of Jell-O, this time from my chin. I shake my head at him.

"There goes the metaphor of our marriage. I wonder if it's an omen." I drag a finger through the massive pile of fruit and gelatin. The kitchen looks like a Jell-O wrestling match gone wrong.

Josh pauses, his finger halfway to his mouth. He wrinkles his forehead.

"We'll rebuild it. Easy."

I look around, then lift a gob of gelatin-suspended fruit from the floor.

"You can't rebuild this."

My mom and dad have kitchen towels and are pushing the Jell-O into a big pile in the center of the room.

Josh takes my hand. For some reason, I'm feeling a little teary about the whole thing.

"Then we'll make another," he promises. "Everything's better the second time around."

"Who says?" I ask.

People always talk about firsts. First love, first kiss, first time riding a bike, first airplane ride, first job. No one has ever said the second time is the best. It's always the firsts.

He shakes his head at me like he can hear what I'm thinking.

"I say it. Me. Josh Lewenthal. Your future husband. Everything's better the second time around."

I pretend to take a moment to consider this. I tilt my head and study him. There's a bit of shaved carrot dangling from his ear, and lime green goop dripping down his cheek. He has a serious, earnest expression on his face, completely at odds with his appearance.

"We'll see," I finally say.

When I say this he smiles at me. "I still have to talk to you," he says quietly. "In private."

I nod. "Okay."

But my stomach feels a little queasy. "We're still getting married right?"

He snorts and flicks Jell-O at me. "You aren't superstitious, are you?"

He kisses me, and when his lips meet mine he makes an appreciative sound at the taste of lime.

The backs of his fingers drift over my cheek and his other hand strokes my abdomen. But his touch doesn't reassure me. The beginning of a headache hammers at my temples.

SATURDAY MARCH 15
2 p.m.

.   .   .

THE SHOWER'S HOT WATER RUNS OVER JOSH AND ME, RINSING bright artificial green Jell-O out of our hair and off our skin.

We're in the upstairs guest bathroom, letting the steaming water wash all the sticky, goopy mess away. Josh drags a washcloth down my back, the terrycloth fibers scratch over my skin. He leans forward and presses a kiss to the place where my neck and shoulder meet.

"This is almost as good as the garage," he says.

"You think so?" I look over my shoulder at him.

His wet hair falls over his forehead and his skin glistens with water drops. There's still some Jell-O smeared on his shoulder and I have the strongest urge to turn around and lick it.

Josh studies my face.

"Definitely," he says, voice low and taut.

Water runs down his chest, trailing over the muscles of his abdomen, drawing my eyes to the evidence of just how much he likes this moment.

The bathroom is warm and full of steam. It's the same bathroom that I used as a kid, and it's still decorated with sailboat wallpaper and an anchor shower curtain. Never in all of my teenage fantasies did I imagine Josh and I would ever make love in this bathroom. It gives a whole new meaning to the word *steamy*.

"I like what you're thinking," Josh says.

"How do you know what I'm thinking?"

He nods at me, "You're an easy read, Gem."

I lift an eyebrow. "I don't believe you."

He gives me a cocky smile.

"Let me finish." He holds up the washcloth. "Turn around and put your hands on the wall."

"Kinky."

He laughs. "It's to keep steady."

I'll bet it is.

I press my hands against the blue shower tiles and lean forward. Josh reaches around and draws the washcloth over my breasts. At thirty-four weeks pregnant, those babies are sensitive.

I hear Josh let out a ragged breath. I concentrate on the sound of his breathing, the beating of the hot water, and his hands, running over my skin. He pulls the washcloth to the sides of my breasts, down my abdomen to my hips.

His hands pause at my thighs and then his fingers grip my hips and for a moment I think he's going to drop the washcloth, push me forward, and enter me from behind. I hold my breath.

Waiting.

But then Josh lets out a long breath and moves the washcloth down my legs. He kneels behind me and drags it over my calves, down to my ankles.

The sound of Josh's breath, the sharp staccato of the water drops, and the dragging of the washcloth over my skin draw me higher and higher until I can only think one thing.

"I need you." I press my hands into the tile and look over my shoulder.

Josh is still on his knees. He presses a kiss to my inner thigh. "Not yet. I don't want this moment to end."

Then he starts up again, the slow, torturous dragging of his hands across every inch of my body. Everywhere, except the one place I want him to be.

I can't take it anymore. I look over my shoulder, his cheeks are red and his eyes are heated.

"Josh, if you don't make love to me this second, you and I are going to have problems."

He grins when I pull him up off his knees, so I turn around and put my hands back on the tile. I feel the thick ridge of him press against me. His hands draw down my back, grip my hips.

Thank goodness.

Finally.

Suddenly, there's a loud bang at the bathroom door.

I jerk straight and Josh yanks away.

The banging sounds again.

My heart pounds and all that aching need and liquid warmth vanishes. Mortified, I turn around and look at Josh. His eyes are wide and he's staring at the door, appalled.

Bang, bang, bang.

Josh rubs the back of his neck, and his face flushes.

"Who is it?" My voice comes out squeaky and embarrassed.

"Auntie Gemma, I gotta go bathroom! Please! Auntie Gemma, I gotta go bad!"

Colin.

I squeeze my eyes shut, and Josh makes a noise, half choke, half laugh.

The door handle rattles. It's locked. Thank goodness. But the kid's really trying to get in.

"Go use the downstairs bathroom, Colin. The one by the kitchen," I call. I wrap my arms around myself. If he goes away, maybe Josh and I can pick up where we left off.

"Can't. Mary's in there, she's pooping. It'll be hours. Mom said she ate six cheese sticks."

Josh buries his face in his hands and his shoulders shake with laughter. Colin said six cheese sticks like a newscaster would say "pile-up on the George Washington Bridge."

The door handle rattles again. "Please, Auntie Gemma!"

"Go to Grandma and Grandpa's bathroom. The one in their bedroom."

"Can't! Grandpa had too much coffee, his rotstate's unhappy."

Rotstate? Ohhh, he must mean prostate.

Gah.

Josh can't keep it in, he lets out a long, choking laugh.

I fling water at him. "This isn't funny! My five-year-old nephew is going to witness our shower walk of shame."

Josh shakes his head. "There's no shame. We're adults. We're getting married."

I frown at him.

"Besides, he's five. Last year he was still taking baths with the twins. He'll just think it's a shower party. No big deal."

Okay. He has a point.

"Auntie Gemma, please! I'm doing the pee-pee dance."

I climb out of the shower. Water sluices off of me onto the linoleum.

"Hang on, kid."

I grab a towel and wrap it around me. Josh turns off the shower and I toss him a towel from the rack.

When he has it wrapped tightly around his hips, I yank the shower curtain shut, blocking Josh from view, and then unlock the bathroom door.

Colin races in.

"Thank you!"

He proceeds to empty what sounds like five gallons of pee. I face the curtain and wait for him to finish. When the flush sounds and the sink turns on, I turn back around. Maybe if he leaves without incident, Josh and I can turn the shower back on.

But then, Colin looks me square in the eye and says, "Why's Josh hiding in the shower? Are you playing a game?"

I hear a snort and then Josh drawls, "Hey Colin. Yup. Gemma and I were playing a game."

"Oh." Colin sticks his tongue out the side of his mouth and looks deep in thought. "What kind of game?"

There's silence from the other side of the curtain. I can only imagine the mental hurdles Josh is jumping through trying to come up with a kosher answer. So I think fast.

"Hide and Seek. Josh is counting. Go hide! Quick!"

Colin jumps up and down, "I love hide and seek!"

He does. After chess, it's his favorite game. He sprints from the bathroom. I wait until I can't hear the thumping of his feet on the hardwood stairs, then I pull open the shower curtain.

Josh's smirk greets me.

"We have about five minutes to get dressed and find him, or else he'll come looking for us again," I say.

Then I take in the water drops on Josh's chest, the low-slung towel over his hips, and I wonder if maybe we have enough time to kick the door shut and start up where we left off.

Josh shakes his head, his eyes rueful. "I'd say three minutes."

I blow out a breath, he's probably right. I rub at my neck, trying to dislodge the headache that's taken up residence. "My family's crazy. We should've eloped."

He steps out of the shower and places a kiss on my lips. "Nah. You know you love them."

I do.

And so does he.

"How about we go to the garage after we find Colin?"

"Perfect. We still need to talk."

～

SATURDAY, MARCH 15
4:30 p.m.

WHEN EVERYONE'S DISTRACTED BY THE MOLDING OF THE NEW Jell-O heart, Josh takes my hand and pulls me into the garage.

He pushes me against the door of the garage refrigerator and kisses me. I'm dizzy and short of breath. His tongue rubs over my lips and black dots swim in front of my eyes.

"Tomorrow..." he says, then he starts to kiss me again.

Another wave of dizziness hits.

"Yes?" I ask, when he pulls his mouth away.

"When we get married..." He bites my bottom lip and his hands start to move over my arms and down to my thighs.

"Yes?"

"We have our church vows."

"Mhmm." I'm distracted by his teeth nibbling at my lip.

"I wrote my own vows," he says.

He kisses down my throat and starts to unbutton my blouse. I stop kissing him, my hands rest on his shoulders.

"They're not for everyone. Just you." He continues kissing down my chest. "I wanted to share them, before tomorrow."

When I don't say anything, he stops unbuttoning my shirt and looks up. I squeeze his shoulders and he gives a hesitant, boyish smile. I had no idea. Even though my head hurts and I'm dizzy, I feel so happy. The stress of my "easy" wedding is getting to me, but it's worth it.

"I didn't write anything for you," I say.

Josh shakes his head, "That's okay. I just want you to say yes. That's enough for me."

I stand on my tiptoes and lean forward to kiss him.

The garage door swings open. "Gemma, phone's for you."

Dylan holds out my parents' ancient cordless phone. It's baby blue, and probably one of the last landlines left in New York State.

I glare at Dylan. Then Josh slowly steps back from me. He clears his throat and quirks an eyebrow at my brother.

"What?" Dylan thrusts the phone toward me.

Finally he seems to realize he was interrupting a moment, because he looks between Josh and me, then shakes his head and sends a beseeching look to the ceiling. I'm pretty sure he's sending up a prayer for patience, because his best friend is marrying his sister and while he's fine with it, he doesn't want to witness any hanky-panky.

"The phone," he says, waving it in the air.

Josh grabs it, then shoves Dylan back through the door. He closes it and hands the cordless phone to me.

I hold it up to my ear. I'm guessing it's about the wedding. We're having almost a hundred guests. Plus Hannah, Carly, Brook and their husbands are all coming up from the city tomorrow morning. It could be anyone.

"Hello?"

"Is this Gemma Jacobs?" a woman with a raspy voice asks.

Okay, it's not regarding the wedding. I don't know this woman. "Yes?"

"This is Jane Matthews, reporter for *New Vision Magazine*, I'd like to ask you a few questions about Ian Fortune."

As she's speaking, Josh straightens and moves closer to me. He can tell that this isn't a conversation I want to have.

"No comment."

"I have a few questions. Our readers deserve—"

"No comment," I repeat firmly. Then, for good measure, I say, "Don't call again. I have no comment."

I hit the end button. Josh takes the phone from me and kisses the top of my head.

"I thought they'd stopped calling."

I rub my temples. It feels like there's a vise clamping down on my skull. "They had. Don't worry about it."

It's been nearly a month since the last call. After Ian's business went down the drain and he became the most hated man in America, everyone wanted to chat with the woman he'd verbally abused on air. I'd refused every interview.

That didn't stop the speculation, but I had nothing to say. That day was private, my relationship with Ian was private, and I didn't feel any need to join in the feeding frenzy of ripping apart Ian Fortune's character. There were plenty of stories from former staff and former girlfriends circulating the media outlets.

His reputation as an enlightened self-help guru has been gleefully destroyed and replaced with a new reputation of egotistical, unenlightened, self-centered, employee-abusing conniver who misled millions. It's not pretty.

"They need to stop bothering you," Josh growls.

I shrug. "They will. I feel worse for Ian."

Josh gives me a sardonic look and a lock of dark hair falls over his eye. I reach up and brush it aside.

Dylan opens the door again. He looks at the garage ceiling instead of us.

"Sorry to interrupt, but Dad needs Josh. Apparently, the gazebo's tilting."

Well, that constitutes a wedding emergency.

Josh's vows have to wait.

"Later," he whispers.

～

MARCH 15
Later

. . .

I PULL MY QUILT UP TO MY CHIN AND TRY TO GET COMFORTABLE. It's not happening.

I'm in my childhood bedroom, and the springs in my twin bed squeak when I shift. It's nearly eleven and I can't sleep.

I spent the rest of the afternoon and evening in a frenzied blur with Josh and my family, prepping food, setting up decorations, and triple checking that everything would run smoothly tomorrow.

My wedding dress is pressed and steamed and hanging on a satin coat hanger from my closet door.

The bodice is delicate white lace and has the sweetest empire waist. The white chiffon fabric flows down to the ground like a frothy waterfall.

My mom says it's stunning, Carly says it belongs on the cover of *Vogue*, and Leah says Josh won't be able to keep his hands off me.

I smile at the thought. That's the hope, isn't it? He hasn't seen the dress yet, and I can't wait until he does.

My mom shoved Josh out the front door at eight, telling him that he wasn't allowed to see me again until I was walking down the aisle. He's staying at Dylan's tonight. Unfortunately, it was so busy we never got a chance to talk.

We tried again, slipping upstairs, but the twins were having a shrieking, jumping, somersaulting pillow fight.

Then we escaped to the backyard, but my dad was still there tinkering with the gazebo.

We fled to the garage, but my mom came out with the freshly poured Jell-O molds. So, we gave up and finished all the pre-wedding tasks.

I kick at the sheets on my bed and push my thumbs to my temples, trying to rub the tension headache away.

I refuse to believe that I'm coming down with anything hours before my wedding, nothing's going to stop me from marrying Josh, especially not some annoying headache.

A light tapping sounds. I hold still and listen.

Another tap.

This time, I know what it is. A pebble just hit my window, making a sharp plink.

There it is again. Another plink.

I grin up at my ceiling and then kick the quilt off and jump out of bed. Sure enough, when I look out the window, Josh is standing in the front yard, about to lob a pebble at the glass.

Plink!

When I yank back the curtains he drops his handful of pebbles and grins up at me. I feel like Juliet on her balcony. I grab my phone.

I type: *Why are you throwing pebbles at my window? You're not supposed to see me before the wedding.*

Josh pulls his phone from his pocket and reads what I wrote.

He lifts an eyebrow at me, then he types: *Why are you so superstitious?*

I open the window and lean out. The brisk air bites at my cheeks.

"I'm not," I say in a loud whisper. "I'm a traditionalist."

And tradition says that it's bad luck for a groom to see his bride before the ceremony. Who am I to question tradition?

A dog starts to bark down the block. The porch light shines on Josh's face as he looks up at me.

"We still have an hour before our wedding day," he whisper-shouts back.

I think about this for a second. That's actually true. Our wedding day doesn't start until midnight. Which means...

"I'll be right down."

Josh seems really happy about this, I mean, even happier than when we found that popup comic shop in Midtown. He hitches up his shoulders and nods toward the backyard.

I pull a sweatshirt over the long t-shirt I threw on for bed and grab a pair of sneakers that I'll slip on at the back door.

I tiptoe down the steps and out the back. My parents are heavy sleepers, but as a thirty-three-year-old woman, I really don't want to have to answer questions about why I'm sneaking out to make out with my fiancé the night before my wedding.

The backdoor creaks as I slowly click it shut.

It's a dark night, the clouds are heavy and low-hanging and a chilly wind crackles through the leaves. The clouds are too thick for the moonlight to break through, so the only illumination comes from a security light in the neighbor's backyard.

I rub my arms, trying to keep warm in the chill, and step off the deck.

"Josh?" I look around.

The backyard is kind of spooky with the skeletal outline of the gazebo, the rows of empty chairs, and the unlit candles. The leaves of the big maple tree hiss as the wind whips through them.

"Over here," he calls.

I search the darkness and finally see the dark smudge of his form under the gazebo. I hurry across the grass, past the empty chairs, and climb up the steps into the gazebo.

When I'm there, Josh grabs me, pushes me back against one of the beams, and swoops down. He kisses me. Hard.

And even though my head hurts, and I'm dizzy, his kiss makes me even dizzier. I reach up and grab him, and kiss him back.

"I wanted to tell you my vows," he says.

Then he must decide that they can wait, because he starts to kiss me again. I don't mind, because his hand plays with the hem of my long t-shirt, and he's inching it up my leg, dragging his fingers up my thigh, and his mouth is so sweet. He tastes like wintergreen toothpaste and need.

When I reach for the button of his pants, he breaks off our kiss and pulls back. "Wait, I have to tell you."

I sigh, then nod and take his hands.

"Okay." Then I remember. "We only have fifty minutes now."

His eyes glint with humor. Then he turns serious, "Tomorrow..."

I swallow down the fluttering in my throat. "Tomorrow."

"We have the traditional vows."

I nod. Then say, "For better, for worse, for richer, for poorer, in sickness and in health."

He squeezes my hands. "I want to add my own promise. I love you, Gemma. I'm not the best at expressing my feelings, I don't always have all the words..."

He reaches up and touches my face. His fingers shake as he strokes my cheek.

"But even if I don't always have the words, I don't want you to ever doubt that I love you. I promise you, as long as you're here and there's a sky above, I'll love you. If you ever doubt it, just look up."

He pulls me off the cedar planks of the gazebo, back to the lawn. The cold grass tickles my ankles as we walk to the center of the yard.

He points to the sky. "Look up."

I tilt my chin up and look at the low-hanging clouds. Josh's hand is warm in mine. He pulls me closer and tucks me into his side, then he lifts his chin and looks up at the sky too.

"Does this mean you'll always love me?" I ask.

"Always."

Then a raindrop falls and lands with a plop on my nose. I blink, as another hits my cheek. Then I laugh as the sky opens up and a spring rainstorm begins.

Josh kisses me, and I stop laughing and start kissing him back.

He moves his hands to grasp my back and pull me closer, then he starts to sway, and I say, "I've always wanted to dance in the rain."

"I know," he says.

So we dance.

He spins me around and around, and the cool spring rain drenches our clothes, plasters our hair to our heads, and makes puddles in the grass.

I laugh as water pours down and splashes up.

Josh swings me around, and I laugh as a spray of water arcs out from us. Then Josh grabs me and picks me up, holding me behind my knees and under my back.

"I'm too heavy," I protest.

He scoffs. "Hardly."

Then he says, "Gemma, I'm going to take you to that gazebo, lay you down and make love to you. And after that you'll have exactly two minutes left before midnight, so you can run upstairs before you turn into a pumpkin."

"The carriage turns into a pumpkin, not Cinderella."

He merely gives me a wolfish grin and then does exactly what he promised to do.

At 11:58 p.m. I tiptoe back up the stairs to my bedroom, leaving puddles of water on the steps as the only evidence of the magic that happened.

3

"I'll keep it locked up like a treasure in my heart, and I'll take it out whenever I want to feel happy or loved."

MARCH 16

WHEN A WOMAN MAKES THE MONUMENTAL DECISION TO WALK down the aisle, she'd better be one hundred and ten percent certain she wants to spend the rest of her life with the man waiting to marry her.

There can't be any doubt.

Not a smidge.

I clasp the ribbon-wrapped bouquet of white gardenias in my hand and take a deep breath of their velvety floral and spice scent.

My dad takes my arm, and when he leans close I see a sheen of tears in his eyes. Aww, Dad.

"You sure about this Gemma?" he asks in a gruff voice, tugging at his blue silk tie.

I nudge him with my elbow. What kind of a question is that?

"I love Josh. If I can be sure of only one thing in life, that's it."

Josh stands underneath the wooden gazebo. He's in a formal tuxedo and he shifts nervously on his feet. I smile. My Josh, all nervous on his wedding day.

His hands twitch, and I can tell he wishes he had a pencil right now. I wonder if he's going to draw this scene later. Him nervous, me in my dress. I smile at the thought. I can barely hold in all the happiness I feel.

I try to memorize this moment. The domed gazebo painted ivory and pink, the scent of roses and gardenias, the soft spring breeze. All our friends and family here. Leah in a rose-colored silk dress. Dylan in a dove gray suit. Josh, waiting at the altar, nervous.

He hasn't seen me yet. He doesn't know I'm here.

The harpist begins to play, and I take a small step forward, down the satin-lined aisle. My dad squeezes my arm.

Josh turns toward me. But instead of smiling like I thought he would, his shoulders stiffen, his hands clench, and the corners of his lips turn down.

I quickly look behind me, sure that he's seen something to make him react like that. But there's nothing there. When I look back at him, I realize that he's staring at me. And he's frowning.

"Do I look alright?" I whisper to my dad.

We take little mincing steps up the aisle, in time to the slow, trilling harp.

My dad pats my arm and says in a quiet, proud voice. "You look beautiful."

But something's not right. Because when we make it to the gazebo, I see that Josh's eyes are closed-off, almost cold.

Something's happened.

My dad kisses my cheek and leaves me at the altar.

My mouth is suddenly dry, and a slippery, niggling foreboding travels over my skin.

"Josh?" I whisper. "What is it?"

"Dearly beloved," Father Gibbly begins.

I don't hear a word he says. Something's wrong. Something's wrong with Josh. He isn't smiling. His eyes aren't smiling. Coldness washes over me.

"Joshua and Gemma," Father Gibbly continues. "have you come here to enter into marriage without coercion, freely and wholeheartedly?"

I swallow down the foreboding, the rising panic the look in Josh's eyes is giving me.

"Yes, I have," I say firmly.

I smile at Josh, then nod at him, urging him to say, "I have."

But he doesn't. He's quiet.

A cold, prickly sweat lines the back of my neck. The silence stretches on.

Finally Father Gibbly asks, "Josh?"

Josh stares at me, and I see the answer in his eyes before he says it.

"No."

The ground shifts, almost like an earthquake. It's like being on a swaying boat, riding a wave, disoriented and dizzy, but in an earthquake it's the building moving, and the land is the wave. Nothing makes sense in an earthquake. Buildings shouldn't sway like boats, paintings shouldn't fall off walls, vases shouldn't slide off shelves and shatter. But they do.

Josh's "no" is like an earthquake. It doesn't make sense. It shouldn't happen.

But it does.

"No?" I repeat.

"No?" Father Gibbly asks.

From the front row, I hear my mom gasp. "No?"

Just like an aftershock, Josh says in a firm, hard voice, "No."

"But...but..." I clasp my bouquet and the metal pin holding the flowers together digs into my palm. The pain makes me ask, "Why?"

Josh's eyes go hard and flinty. So un-Joshlike. It scares me.

"I don't love you anymore," he says.

My stomach clenches into a tight, frightened ball. *What?* "You don't...."

"I don't love you anymore," he repeats. Then he steps forward, lifts my veil, and presses a cold kiss to my lips.

I JOLT UPRIGHT IN BED AND COME FULLY AWAKE WITH A GASP.

My head pounds and my heart hammers in my chest. Just a dream, it was just a dream.

The thin gray morning light streams through my bedroom window, and I squint at the clock on my nightstand. It's six a.m. I'll be walking down the aisle in four hours.

I try to shake off the foreboding. It was just a dream. Even though it was right in the sense that I am getting married today, it's wrong because Josh would never say anything like that.

He wouldn't.

For the next four hours I let my mom, my sister, and my friends feed me, primp me, and squeeze me into my dress. My feet and ankles are swollen too much to fit into my shoes so Hannah rushes to the shoe store and picks up a pair sparkly flip flops.

I'm dizzy, tired, and convinced that I'm coming down with the flu, but it doesn't matter, because I'm getting married.

"Should I tell Josh not to kiss me?" I ask my mom as she's spraying my French twist with another half-liter of hairspray. Final touches and all that.

Brook scoffs. She's lounging on the living room couch breast-feeding her daughter. "Let him kiss you, marriage is all about sharing."

My mom puts a hand to my head and frowns. "You're not hot. I'm sure it's nerves. Of course Josh should kiss you. What are you thinking?"

"I have a sachet of chamomile tea if you want it." Hannah digs through her purse then holds up a pouch of tea.

"No thanks," I say.

Leah, my mom, Brook, Hannah and I all turn as Carly walks into the living room. "Darlings, Josh is at the gazebo. It's time."

Suddenly, I'm short of breath and nervous. I wipe at the line of perspiration on my forehead. Everyone hurries out to the backyard.

My friends take their seats, my mom walks down the aisle, then the harpist begins to play. I stand just out of view, watching Josh.

Just like in my dream, he's in a formal tuxedo. But in real life, he doesn't look nervous, he looks confident, happy.

When Sasha, Mary, and Maemie walk down the aisle, throwing pink rose petals from white baskets, Josh smiles.

Then Colin walks out, our wedding rings on a white silk pillow. Leah told Colin that if he lost our rings, he would never ever be allowed to eat ice cream again. So, he's taking special care to walk slowly and carefully. Josh pats Colin on the shoulder when he makes it to the gazebo.

"Thanks, kid," he says and Colin sets the rings down at the altar.

All one hundred guests sitting in the mostly dry chairs go *awwww* when Colin bows.

My dad walks over to me and I smile at him when he takes my arm and then pats my hand.

"All set, Gemma?" he asks.

I nod, "Absolutely."

When my dad and I walk out from the side yard, I keep my eyes on Josh.

He goes completely still when he sees me, and there's a stunned look on his face. He blinks a few times and I think he mouths the word *beautiful*.

I flush. Who says he isn't good with words?

I keep my eyes on him, and he watches me. I don't want to look at anyone else. I just want to look at him. I think if I keep my eyes on him, then I'll remember this moment forever.

I'll get to keep it locked up like a treasure in my heart, and I'll take it out whenever I want to feel happy or loved.

My dad kisses me and leaves me next to Josh.

I give Josh a small smile through my veil, but for once he doesn't smile back.

It's not bad, like in my dream, it's more, he's so consumed that he can't look away from my eyes, not even to notice my smile.

A little bubble forms around us, and it's just Josh and me, even though there are a hundred people here, friends and family, and Father Gibbly is only five feet away, clearing his throat and starting the ceremony.

"Dearly beloved..."

Finally, Josh lifts the corner of his mouth and his dark brown eyes warm until the color reminds me of the coffee we drink together in the mornings, the trees we picnic under in Central Park, the leather couch we cuddle on while he sketches and I read a book. His brown eyes remind me of all that and more.

"You okay?" he whispers.

I nod, but when I do, my head throbs and the gazebo spins, almost like it's a carousel and we're circling round and round. I focus on Josh, if I focus on him, the spinning almost stops. Focus, Gemma, focus.

The breeze ruffles Josh's hair, and the dark strands brush across his forehead. The corner of his mouth pulls down and he frowns at me.

"Joshua and Gemma," Father Gibbly says. His voice is like a spike to my skull. It pierces my temples and I wince.

Josh lifts his hand toward me but then stops and lets his hand fall. He studies my face, his brows drawn with concern.

I focus on the vee of his neck where his throat dips and meets the pristine white of his shirt collar. I know his skin is salty and sweet, the stubble on his neck tickles when I brush my lips over it, and right now, I know he wishes he could unbutton the tight collar, pull free the restrictive tie and take off his jacket.

He looks beautiful in a tux, but I bet he wishes he was in jeans and a t-shirt. He swallows and his Adam's apple bobs.

I look up to Josh's eyes, and he gives a slight shake to his head.

Focus, Gemma.

I blink and try to concentrate on what Father Gibbly's saying.

"Have you come here to enter into marriage without coercion, freely and wholeheartedly?" he asks.

"I have," Josh says. His voice is firm and deep.

"And Gemma, have you come here to enter into marriage without coercion, freely and wholeheartedly?"

I want to say yes, I do, obviously I want to say yes, but I

can't. There's something heavy on my chest, it's pressing down on me, and I can't pull in enough air to say anything at all.

I grasp my bouquet. For some reason I feel like if I hang on to the bouquet I'll stay standing.

"Gemma?" Josh asks.

His voice sounds far away.

The vise-like feeling suddenly explodes, and it's no longer a clamp, it's an explosion going off in my skull. Sharp, biting teeth crash and rip through my head.

My hands fly up and I grasp my temples, trying to push the pain out. My bouquet drops to the cedar planks, hitting with a loud, hard thud. I try to yank in a breath, but I can't. There's no room for air. None.

The pain. It's too much. Too much.

Fireworks go off, flashing across my eyes, bright white explosions, blood red aftershocks.

Suddenly, I'm not standing, I'm in Josh's arms. I grasp the silk of his lapel with my hand, and I think, *that's lovely, it's so soft.* Which is a stupid thought to have when you can't breathe and your head is exploding, but there you go.

"Gemma, talk to me. Are you okay?"

Josh looks scared. No, terrified. And the fact that Josh looks terrified should *terrify* me. I should be scared. I know I should. But I can't...I can't feel anything.

Even the pain is gone.

He peers down at me and whatever he sees has him yelling, shouting something to Dylan. I can't hear, there's a whooshing, thumping in my ears, and the world is leaking away.

Josh looks down at me, horrible desperation on his face. "Gemma?"

I can't hold on to his lapel anymore, my hand drops, too heavy to hold up.

Numbness falls over me, and as I'm pulled inexorably away from myself, like a thread tugged through a needle, I suddenly have the thought that I'm dying.

This should fill me with terror, but it doesn't.

The only thing I feel is hope that Josh will be okay, that our baby will be okay, that this won't hurt them too much. Please don't let this hurt them too much.

When I said that Josh and I would live happily ever after, I believed that love would never die.

I was wrong.

Or maybe I was wrong in that I never thought about the moment I would die. For thirty-three years I galloped through life without ever considering the moment of my own death.

A hot tear slides down my face.

Does love die when you die? I think it must. It feels like it does.

There's a heavy, dark silence smothering me and the world frays apart at the edges, unraveling at a frightening pace. The color leaches away, like threads pulled from a cloth. Soon, I'll only be left with black.

I focus on the bright light of the sky above. There's a sliver of blue, just visible behind Josh's shoulders. I catch the blur of Josh's bone-white face.

He begs me not to leave him, not to leave, not to leave, don't go, don't go, don't go.

I want to tell him a million things, a million and one, but most of all I want to tell him to take care of our baby. To love him. To save him. To care for him. To not hurt too much.

But I can't. I can't talk. I can't breathe.

Instead.

I go.

It happens more quickly than I thought possible, one minute I'm there, the next, I'm not.

I think...I die.

The world is black and empty.

This has to be death.

Because I can't feel my baby.

Because Josh isn't here.

Because the sky has disappeared.

Because the love—

it's gone.

4

He said, "We're getting married tomorrow."

5

He said, "Don't go."

6

He said, "As long as there's a sky above."

7

*"As long as there's
a sky above,
I'll love you."*

I WAKE UP.

One moment it feels as if I'm still chained to the bottom of the dark, deep, silent pool and the next, I've kicked off the bottom and I'm shooting to the surface.

Speeding up, up, up.

Red and orange light filters through my closed eyelids, creating a flashing pattern that looks like the sun's rays. It promises sunshine and sky, so I try to kick to the surface faster, come awake faster.

I'm not dead. That much is clear.

If I can make it to the light, see the sky again, then everything will be okay. All I have to do is open my eyes.

It's just...I can't.

I become aware of my body in increments. My toes are cold, even though I can feel the rough fabric of scratchy wool socks.

My legs are heavy, they feel as if all my blood has stopped running and they've frozen in place. There's an uncomfortable pressure on my abdomen. My throat is on fire and my mouth is dry.

I'm still swimming to the surface of consciousness. I feel like I did when I was eight years old, at the public pool, floating underwater in the deep end. I could see my friends standing on the ledge, they were distorted and I couldn't hear what they said, and if I shouted underwater, they couldn't hear me. I had to swim up to see them, to talk.

There's a rustling noise beside me, as if someone is turning the pages of a magazine.

Then the person, a man, chuckles wryly, and the magazine pages rustle again.

Then the pressure on my abdomen eases and I smell the pungent fragrance of sweet pickles, sourdough bread, onions, and cheddar cheese. There's a loud crunching noise, and then the pressure is back on my stomach.

The man set something on me.

A sandwich?

The scent of onions tickles my nose.

And finally, finally I shove open my eyes. The bright light stings, and I blink rapidly. I'm awake. I'm here.

I'm...looking at Ian Fortune?

I turn my head, and for a second, I wonder if I was wrong. Maybe I did die and this is a twisted version of hell, some weird level of Dante's inferno where I have to spend eternity with Ian in a hospital room.

Definitely. This is definitely hell. Because nothing makes sense.

First, the room I'm in isn't right. It's a hospital room, sort of. I'm hooked up to all manner of needles and tubes and monitors, and yes, there's an uncomfortable pinching between my legs where I think there must be a catheter to collect my urine.

But beyond that, it doesn't look like a hospital. The ceiling is popcorn white, and the walls are papered in textured pea-soup-green wallpaper. There's a row of windows on the far wall with heavy, maroon curtains.

Next to my bed is an ugly baby blue and orange striped couch. There's a low oak wood table with an assortment of flowers, teddy bears, and get well cards strewn on top. There's a tall wardrobe containing an old tube TV. It's playing an episode of *The Price is Right*, circa 1980.

I close my eyes against the colorful flashes of the spinning wheel on the TV. Watching it makes my brain feel like it's being scraped with an electrified metal comb.

Or maybe the feeling is coming from the fact that nothing makes sense.

I look down at my stomach. I was right. The pressure I felt is a twelve-inch submarine sandwich, a bag of sour cream and onion chips, and a celery soda—all balanced on a beige plastic lunchroom tray on my stomach.

My flat stomach.

I'm not pregnant.

Last I knew, I was thirty-four weeks along. And now, my stomach is flat. There's a sandwich on top of me. And Ian Fortune is reading a magazine in a pea-green plastic chair pulled up next to the bed I'm lying in.

This is a dream. This has to be a dream.

Ian chuckles again, and a cold chill scrapes up my spine. Without looking at me he picks up the sub, takes a crunching bite, and sets it back down again.

I can't breathe. I can't breathe again. The weight on my chest is back, my throat goes tight, I can't breathe. What is going on? What is this?

Where's Josh? Where's my baby? Where...

The image on the front of the magazine catches my attention.

Like I called him into existence, Josh stares at me from the cover of the magazine.

He's in a tuxedo, similar to the one he was in for our wedding, but this time his pocket square is white, not blue.

His brown eyes gleam at me from the cover, and his smile —it's that charm-the-undies-off-a-nun smile, that the-world-is-my-playground smile—the one I thought I'd deciphered. But I don't think I have, because the cover of the magazine says, *Josh and Lisa: Our Favorite Couple.*

And that smile Josh has, he's giving it while he has his arm around the woman (Lisa?), as she plants a big kiss on his cheek. She's just as glamorous as he is, in a tight, sparkling gold dress.

I blink, because if I do, I think the image on the cover of the magazine will change.

It doesn't.

Josh is still there, gorgeous, happy, smiling his smile.

"I did die," I say out loud.

"Jeez! Holy jeez...you're awake! What the shit!" Ian jumps up from his chair and swipes the tray of food off my stomach.

He shoves it onto the table with the teddy bears and one falls to the ground.

"Dang it. Gemma. Give a guy some warning. Jeez. You're all *Night of the Living Dead* on me. Jeez." He swipes his fingers through his thick dark hair, his hand visibly shaking.

The magazine he was reading is on the ground now, and he's giving me an appalled, Frankenstein's-monster-has-come-to-life kind of look.

What happened to the smooth, suave, silver-tongued Ian? This version of Ian can't string two sentences together, and he looks haggard, and not quite as magnetically handsome as he once was.

Case and point, he's unshaven and wearing ratty gym clothes.

This can't be reality.

Even so, I lick my dry lips, and say, "Where's my baby?"

When I talk it feels like gravel scraping my throat, and I sound like the love child of Darth Vader and a bullfrog.

I cough and try again. "My baby."

Ian's face loses most of its color. He shakes his head. "I didn't think you were going to wake up. Gemma, what the hell?"

My heart pounds in my ears and even though my stomach feels empty, I think I might vomit. He isn't answering me.

"Where. Is. My. Baby."

He blinks, then starts to back away, "With your mom, I expect. I'm going to go get..." He gestures at the door to the room, then vaguely says, "Someone."

A flood of relief consumes me. My baby's alive. My baby's with my mom. In whatever weird version of reality I'm in, my baby's alive.

I try to sit up, I lift up on my elbows, but I feel weak and sluggish and even sitting up a few inches is exhausting.

Ian pauses at the door, a funny look on his face, his cheeks red. "Could you maybe *not* mention that I was using you as a table for my lunch?"

I push myself harder and move so that I'm half propped up against the bed's plastic headboard.

Even though it hurts to talk, I ask, "Where am I? Where's Josh? Where's my mom?"

I want to say *why the heck are you here*, but I don't. I'm still going with the dream theory.

Ian pauses, looks at the door, like he wants to go, then back to me. "You're at The Whittcombe, a care facility for..." He stops and runs his fingers through his hair again, unwilling to go on. His mouth has white tension lines around it and all that Ian Fortune charm is gone, it's completely deserted him. He looks like himself, but not like himself. Almost as if he's taken off the veneer that drew millions to him.

He shrugs. "I expect Josh is in California..." He waves his hand at the magazine on the floor. "Enjoying his moment of fame."

He dismisses the magazine and says, "Your mom should be here in a couple hours. She comes every day in the late afternoon."

Every day?

I want to ask more. As the sunlight fills my mind, and my body and brain come awake a jagged panic starts to fill me.

"I'm not dead?"

Ian shakes his head.

"Dreaming?"

He shakes his head no again. "You were in a coma."

My heart stutters and I let out a small, gasping noise.

Ian ignores the noise and shrugs. "Sorry about the sandwich. I eat in here because the cafeteria smells like Brussel sprouts and dirty socks. Nothing personal."

With that he walks out the door. Leaving me alone.

I should've asked Ian what happened to me. I should've asked why Josh is in California, why he's on a magazine cover with another woman. I should've asked Ian why he's here at The Whittcombe. I should've asked what I'm doing here. I should've asked a million things.

But as I look down at the cover of the magazine that Ian

dropped, I realize the one thing I should've asked was the date.

Because it's not March 16 anymore, or March 17, or even March 25. It's not even March.

Or April.

Or May.

No, it's June.

I was in a coma for three months.

I stare at Josh's smiling face on the cover of the glossy magazine. I stare at the gorgeous woman kissing his cheek. I remember Josh's vow. *As long as there's a sky above, I'll love you.*

Apparently, when I collapsed, so did the sky.

I stop thinking about it when a woman in scrubs and a white coat runs into the room.

I DESPERATELY WANT TO KNOW WHAT'S GOING ON. WHY THE world flipped on its axis and I'm now living in upside down land.

In the end, the medical side is very simple. The headache leading up to the wedding, the dizziness, the shortness of breath, was pre-eclampsia. The seizures that I didn't realize I had, the coma, that was eclampsia.

If I had gone to the doctor for the headache, the dizziness, the excess swelling in my legs, the shortness of breath, if I had gone in when I started to feel unwell, they would've found severely raised blood pressure and protein in my urine.

But I didn't go in.

And between my checkup at thirty-two weeks and my wedding day, I developed pre-eclampsia that went straight into life-threatening eclampsia.

It's really that simple.

All the warning signs were there, I just didn't know the signs to recognize them. They tell me I'm lucky to be awake, lucky to be alive, lucky the baby made it, lucky, lucky, lucky.

After being poked, prodded, tested, analyzed, and tested some more, the official conclusion is that I'm going to be alright. I have neurological trauma, a consequence of the eclampsia.

"What does that mean?" I ask.

"It means you suffered a traumatic brain injury," Dr. Matsos says.

I guess she's right, because ever since I got a proper handle on being awake, I've felt like I'm watching myself from outside my body. It's like I've detached from myself.

My body is a floating balloon and I'm holding onto the string, dragged along, watching myself and what's happening to me from afar. Thoughts come slowly, and no emotions travel down the string.

The only emotion I can feel is panic, and I try to shove that down as much as possible.

Plus, in the tests, my short-term memory was terrible. I failed at simple sequencing tasks, because I forgot what I was doing.

Whenever a loud noise or a flashing light happened, my mind felt like a can of soda shaken up, fizzing, and about to burst. My skin itches from the overstimulation and I want to crawl outside of myself and join my absent emotions, wherever they've run off to.

"Your prognosis is good. With proper rehabilitation, rest, and therapy it's likely you'll return to normal activities," Dr. Matsos reassures me.

I lie prone in the same bed that I occupied for months. My arms and legs ache and my head hurts. Apparently, my muscles deconditioned while I lay immobile for months and all this sitting up and talking has worn me out.

The staff at The Whittcombe called my mom as soon as I woke up. Then they assured me my family was on the way. It's been nearly four hours.

I close my eyes and try to draw a picture of exactly what my baby will look like.

I've finally decided that he has black hair and brown eyes just like Josh, when there's a loud shrieking and my family rushes into the room like commuters stampeding the subway platform at rush hour.

"Auntie Gemma! Auntie Gemma!" Mary and Maemie scream.

Sasha jumps up and down, her red pigtails flying around her head. She squeals and I can't understand a word she's saying.

Colin rushes me and shoves his little body into my side, jabbing me with his elbows. He buries his head against my chest and starts to sniffle.

Leah runs in, pulling Oliver after her, "Thank God. Gemma, thank God you're awake."

She looks me over and bursts in tears. Even Oliver, usually calm and happy-go-lucky, wipes at his eyes.

My dad rushes past the kids and grabs my hand. His hold is tight and anguished.

"There's my girl," he says. "There she is."

His voice catches, and he can't seem to say anything else, he just rubs my hand with his calloused fingers.

Dylan shoves into the room and looks me over. I think he didn't believe I was awake until this very moment, because after he looks at me from head to toe, he seems to relax and a huge look of relief comes over his face.

He shakes his head and says, "Man, Gemma. If I had

known you'd be this much trouble, I'd never have asked Mom and Dad for a little sister."

I try to respond, but it's all too much.

The shrieking twins, Sasha jumping up and down, Colin burrowing into me, my dad tugging on my hand, Leah crying, Dylan being cheeky.

My skin itches and I want to slip under the sheets and close my eyes and plug my ears. The shrieking is like bores drilling my ears, all the movement makes my brain feel like it's an electric wire shorting out, and everyone is staring at me, waiting for me to say...something.

I feel like I'm watching the whole scene on a screen and I know that I should be laughing, hugging, rejoicing, that's what should be happening. But instead, I pull within myself and try to shrink away from all the noise and the panic that's boiling hot inside me, about to erupt.

Then my family shifts, and I look to the opening, where my mom pushes a bright red stroller into my room.

The world stops.

I was wrong. Every time I tried to imagine what my baby would look like, or what I'd feel when I finally met him, every time I tried to predict anything about the future, I was wrong.

"Gemma," my mom says, her voice thick with tears. "Say hello to your daughter."

8

"Everything's going to be alright."

MY DAUGHTER IS A SOLID WEIGHT IN MY ARMS, WARM AND SOFT and real.

I hold her tightly against my chest and gobble up her features, like I've been starved my whole life and I'm finally allowed to eat my fill. I breathe her in, the brand new baby scent of her.

She's dressed in a yellow polka dot dress and has a little ribbon and bow in the fine down of her wispy baby hair. She has a round, button nose, chubby cheeks, and a little red strawberry birthmark on her temple.

She looks like Josh, so much like him.

Her fine black hair, the oval shape of her face, the upturned edges of her lips, creating the appearance of a smile, even when not smiling.

Everything about her comes from Josh except her eyes. Those are mine. They're a changeable blue gray, the color of the Long Island Sound on a stormy day.

Right now, her eyes are misty gray and solemn, and she stares up at me as if to say, "Who are you?"

I thought I was numb, but at that curious stare, the lack of recognition on my baby's face, my heart cracks open and all my longing and hope and wishes spill out and crash to the floor.

She doesn't know me. She's been in this world for three months, had her first smile, her first bath, her first cry, was fed, changed, held, rocked to sleep, and I wasn't there for any of it.

Hesitantly I reach up and draw my finger along the chubby line of her cheek. Her skin is soft and delicate. I've never felt anything so soft in my life. Her lower lip wobbles and her brow furrows. I snatch my hand back, feeling ashamed and uncomfortable. She doesn't know me.

She wiggles in my arms, arching her back and kicking her feet out, but when she catches sight of my mom, hovering close by, she relaxes.

Because she knows my mom. And she doesn't know me.

And I don't know her. Do I?

I blink, the pressure at the back of my eyes hurts. Everyone left the room except my mom. They went to the cafeteria to give me some space to meet my daughter.

"What's her name?" I whisper.

Josh and I had a list of boy and girl names, but we agreed we wouldn't decide on a name until the baby was born.

My mom sits on the bed next to me and rests her hand on my arm.

"Josh named her Hope, after..." She pauses and looks away from me.

I stare down at Hope, my baby girl, and smile at her.

"Hello, Hope." I hold out my pointer finger, then I hold my breath as Hope reaches up and wraps her small hand around my finger.

The tight squeeze of her grip has me letting out a shuddering breath.

"Hi, baby girl."

When I say this, she smiles and makes a cooing noise.

I let out a harsh exhale. "She's beautiful."

I'm completely awestruck by her monumental accomplishment of smiling. Now I understand why parents are so proud of their babies for babbling, or crawling, or picking their head up—it's incredible.

"She is," my mom says, turning back.

I see that her mascara is smudged and she holds a tissue tightly in her hand. "Josh named her Hope Charlotte. Charlotte was for—"

"His dad," I say.

Before Josh's dad died, he promised him we'd name our baby after him. Charles if he was a boy, and Charlotte if she was a girl. I'm glad he got to keep his promise.

"That's right," my mom says. "And Hope was for you."

Oh Josh.

My mom moves her hand over my arm, rubbing in the same soothing gesture she used to do when I was little and had a fever or a bad cold.

"This little girl was in the NICU for weeks. But she finally got to come home, and she's been growing like a weed ever since." My mom tickles Hope under the chin and Hope happily kicks out her feet. "Do you want to feed her?"

I nod, unable to form the words.

My mom pulls a diaper bag from under the stroller and starts to make a bottle from bottled water and formula.

When it's ready, she says, "She's a gulper, don't tilt it too far up or she'll spit up."

I try to adjust Hope in my arms and she nuzzles at the bottle, making little squeaks and smacking sounds.

Finally she latches on and starts to drink, taking big, noisy swallows. While she drinks, her eyelids drift half-closed and she gets a sleepy, contended look on her face.

While I watch her eyelids droop and her eyelashes flutter, I ask, "Where's Josh?"

My mom pats my arm, "He's on a flight back from LA. He doesn't know you're awake yet." She looks down at her watch. "He should land in about an hour."

There's something lodged in my chest, it feels sharp and painful, and I realize that I'm scared to see him.

My mom studies my face, then she says in a careful voice that I've not heard before, "This has been hard on him."

I try to imagine what it must've been like for him, his baby in the NICU, his fiancée in a coma.

I'm not sure *hard* begins to explore what he went through, but when I try to think about how he must've felt, there's just a blank, black wall of nothing. That feeling of watching myself, observing, comes back. And that Gemma, she shakes her head at me, like she's disappointed.

Hope's head droops to the side and her body relaxes. She's fallen asleep in my arms.

I stare at the thick maroon curtains and the tall gray apartment buildings outside the window. The observer, that other Gemma watching me, notices that my mom and I are sitting shoulder to shoulder on my white sheet-covered hospital bed. We look close but also far apart.

A heaviness descends on the room, my mom looks brittle, like she's afraid to say what she's thinking.

Finally she drops her head and whispers, "I didn't think you were going to wake up."

Her hands tremble in her lap and there's shame in her voice.

"It's okay."

She shakes her head. "Josh never doubted it. He refused to let anyone say otherwise. I should've believed, a good mom wouldn't have given up. But I did, Gemma."

She turns to me and her eyes are dry, although if I wasn't looking at her I'd swear she was crying.

"I came every day, but I said goodbye weeks ago. It's like you died. I didn't..." She closes her eyes, and even though I can't quite feel what she's feeling, I lean into her and rest my head against her shoulder.

"It's okay," I say again.

Although the truth is, I don't think it is okay. I have a horrible feeling that things are going to get much, much worse before they get better. If they ever do.

"When Josh lands he's in for the best news of his life. He's going to be so happy, Gemma. So, so happy."

"What happened to him?" I ask.

I look at the cover of the magazine, still discarded on the floor. I look at his playful smile, the woman kissing him and it makes me hurt. It's less painful to stare out the window, so that's what I do. I watch the sharp rectangular lines of the buildings piercing the sky.

My mom hums under her breath, then says, "He's been flying back and forth between here and LA. He delayed going out for as long as possible, but the production company came after him, demanding he fulfill his contractual obligations, said he had to return the money he was paid if he didn't. I don't know the specifics, but I know it nearly killed him to leave. He comes home for a day or two, then goes back out. He's in bad shape, Gemma. Sometimes, when he came to pick up Hope, he reminded me of how he looked as a little boy, still lost because of his mom leaving. It broke my heart. But now that you're awake, everything's going to be alright."

"Everything's going to be alright," I repeat numbly.

I'm tired. Exhausted.

I clench Hope against my heart and feel the warmth of
her chest, rising up and down in sleep. I stare out the window
and watch the afternoon light leach from the sky.

9

"This is real."

MY FAMILY STAYS FOR ANOTHER HOUR. THE TWINS REGALE ME with tales of their end of school year antics, Dylan cracks jokes, and my dad silently rubs my hand while I hold Hope against my heart.

When my eyelids become heavy and nearly impossible to keep open, my mom shoos everyone out of the room and promises to be back tomorrow.

I kiss Hope and try not to concentrate on how the silence and emptiness of the room matches the silence and emptiness in my chest.

I'm tired. More tired than I've ever been in my life, but every time I start to fall asleep the panic rears up, my eyes fly open, my heart pounds and I'm certain, absolutely certain that if I fall asleep I'll never wake up again.

Ten minutes after my family packed up and filed out of my room, I hear pounding feet running down the hall. Someone calls out an annoyed "Slow down."

There's a crash, a curse word. More pounding feet. I stare at the hall, curious. Then Josh bursts into the room.

God.

God.

He comes to a dead stop at the entrance.

His chest heaves, like he's run miles and his eyes are wild.

There are deep shadows under them, his jaw is unshaven and his shoulders are bent, as if he's been carrying the weight of the world on them.

He's frozen, unmoving as he takes me in, his eyes swallowing me whole. The weight of this moment presses down on me, and time seems to stand still as Josh breathes me in.

I don't know if he's going to come to me.

I don't know what he's thinking or feeling.

His hands tremble, then the rest of him starts to shake, and he takes in a shuddering breath, like he's trying to restrain all the emotion that is avalanching over him.

Then he swallows raggedly as a tear slides down his cheek.

I want...I want to feel him.

I want to feel.

"Josh?" I whisper.

Me whispering his name unlocks whatever force was holding him in place. He tears across the room and falls to his knees at the edge of my hospital bed.

Then, he's touching me. He's touching me everywhere, and breathing my name over and over again like it's a prayer. His hands stroke my arms, my legs, my abdomen, his fingers flutter over me as he prays, "Gemma, Gemma, Gemma."

"I'm here." I reach up and touch his lips. "I'm here."

He stops and the shadows of the deepening evening fall over his face, darkening his eyes.

"You left. You left me," he says, and the sound of his voice painfully cracking causes something to break in my chest, and the force of it is so strong that I'm surprised he doesn't hear it.

I grasp ahold of that balloon string connecting me to myself and try to travel down the string to find the feelings of this moment, to live in this moment and find myself.

"You left," he says again, and his chest shudders as he presses a kiss to my temple, my eyebrows, the arch of my cheeks, my lips.

I can taste the salt of his tears on his lips.

"Don't ever do that again." His fingers grip my arms so hard I think they might leave bruises, but I don't tell him to loosen his hold, because at least I can feel *that*.

"I'm here," I say again, and I realize that I'm trying to reassure myself as much as Josh.

I'm here. I'm awake. This is real. I'm alive.

He's still on his knees, grasping me from the bedside, a raw, desperate look on his face, so I say, "Will you hold me?"

When I ask, he tries to speak, but can't, so instead he presses his lips together, nods his head and climbs up onto the bed, avoiding all the wires, tubes, and devices.

The bed is small, smaller than my twin bed back at my parents' house, but he still manages to squeeze in next to me and pull me onto him, wrapping me in the warmth and the safety of his arms.

All the adjusting has me panting as if I've run a mile, Doctor Matsos said I was deconditioned, that I'd be tired for some time.

So I lie boneless against Josh, rest my head on his chest and listen to the fast, thundering beat of his heart. He's hot, even warmer than usual, and he grips me against him as if he's afraid that if he lets me go I'll slip away.

His gray t-shirt rubs softly against my cheek. It's one of his favorites, he's had it at least ten years and the worn fabric is comforting and familiar. The ink and laundry soap scent of it is an anchor trying to bring me into this reality.

The room light is off, the sun has fallen below the buildings, and the only light comes from the glowing machines and the hallway. We're entombed in silence and each other.

Josh presses a kiss to the top of my head, then his chest rumbles as he asks, "What did the doctors say? Are you okay?"

Even though his voice is flat and calm, I feel his body tense beneath me. I close my eyes and breathe in the scent of him. That panic, that roaring, bubbling panic is starting to erupt.

This is Josh. My Josh. But his voice, his expression, his touch...I feel nothing.

It's like I'm in a dark room and I'm groping around for the feelings I know should be there, but every time I reach out, expecting to find something, my hands only catch air and I come up empty.

I feel nothing for him.

Nothing.

The cold realization settles on me and even the heat of his arms can't warm me. I realize that since I woke up I've been waiting for Josh to get here so that I could feel something.

When I didn't feel with Ian, the doctors, my family, it was okay, because I'd feel something when Josh got here. It would all be okay when Josh got here.

But...it's not.

"Gemma? Did they say anything?"

I nod as the panic smothers me.

He gives a small sigh of relief, and the stubble on his jaw tickles my skin as he presses another kiss to my jaw.

His fingers stroke over my face, gently caressing me. "I've never been so terrified in my life."

"They said I'll recover," I choke out, my voice sounding hollow and strained.

Josh squeezes me and breathes out another prayer of thanks. This should be an intimate moment, a joyous, beautiful moment...and yet...

"You met Hope?" Josh asks.

I nod again, and he smiles, his eyes glowing with love. And there's the Josh I couldn't wait to see, the dad that sang to his baby in the womb and couldn't wait to meet her. The proud Dad that finally got to hold her in his arms. He looks even more in love with our baby than I thought he would.

"She's perfect, isn't she?"

"Yes," I whisper.

"Just like her mom."

My breath is tight in my chest. Something is wrong. Something is horribly, terribly wrong. I woke up, but I didn't, not really.

"What is it?" Josh asks.

The panic is white, hot, a consuming roar.

"I can't feel," I say.

Josh's muscles tense and he says in a strained voice, "What do you mean you can't feel? Should I get help?"

I shake my head, fighting the roaring inside my head. "No. I mean...I can't feel."

"Gemma, what?" He sits up, and his face drains of color.

He's scared now, I know he is, but there's nothing there, nothing I can hold onto. That feeling that drew me to him, that made me want to be his wife, that feeling, it isn't there.

"I can't feel it," I say, the panic devouring me, "I feel nothing. I can't feel..." I take a gulping breath and tell him the awful, terrifying truth of what I've known since I woke up.

What I knew and didn't want to admit. Not to myself, not to anyone.

"I can't feel love..."

He reaches out, touches my hand. "What?"

"Josh...I don't...I can't...it's not there. I don't love you anymore."

10

"You're stronger and more resilient than you ever thought possible."

JOSH BLINKS. THAT'S ALL. ONE, LONG SLOW BLINK.

When he opens his eyes again and I look into the shadows there, it's like he's gathered himself in and pulled himself back, like a piece of string rolled back up and shut away.

I remember what my mom said, how sometimes when Josh came to pick up Hope he reminded her of how lost he looked after his mom left.

This was hard on him, she'd said.

My stomach rolls and even though I haven't eaten any solid food since I woke up, I still feel like I'm going to throw up.

Slowly, he pulls himself away from me. He unravels his hands from mine, takes his warmth away and sits at the edge of my bed. It's only twelve inches at most, but the distance feels insurmountable.

I take in the stiffness of his shoulders and the clenching and unclenching of his hands. My pulse beats in my throat, choking out my breath. I start to descend back into that dark space, the place I couldn't breathe on our wedding day.

I yank my gaze to the window, trying to see the sky, but night has fallen and there's only darkness. I grab for my throat, press against my windpipe, and tell myself, breathe, breathe Gemma, breathe.

"I..." Josh says, and his voice breaks. He clenches his fists and looks away.

The room spins and the edges of my vision bleed red and black. I'm afraid, I'm terrified that I'm going back under. That I woke up only to leave again.

I reach out, blindly grasp for Josh's hand. There's a sharp, gasping desperate noise that sounds nothing like me, but I know has to be me.

Josh looks back to me and I find his hand in the dark. I cling to him, hang on as tightly as I can.

"Gemma?" His voice sounds far away, like he's calling to me over the roaring of the ocean.

He leans closer, peers at my face. Whatever he sees has him jumping up, pulling his hand away and sprinting out the door.

The darkness swallows me and even though I fight to get out, I can't.

"WHAT DO YOU MEAN THIS HAPPENS SOMETIMES?" JOSH ASKS.

His voice is tight and each word is annunciated so precisely that they're like sharp rocks thrown against a glass window. They shatter the stunned silence of my hospital room.

My mom, my dad, and Josh are all here for the little chat with Dr. Matsos. Leah, Hope, and the kids all stayed upstate.

Last night, after my (in hindsight, ill-advised) declaration to Josh, I descended into a full-blown panic attack.

I've never had one before, I didn't realize that panic attack is actually code for all-consuming, crushing, terrifying, onslaught of throat squeezing, body-numbing, heart hammering, you-*know*-you're-gonna-die-any-second-because-the-life-is-being-squeezed-out-of-you joyride to hell.

So.

The doctor on duty last night gave me a dose of something "to calm me" and I spent the night in a dark, dreamless sleep. It was horrible.

Honestly, I'd rather squat in a maelstrom of panic then be shoved back into that deep, dreamless place again.

"It means exactly what I said," Dr. Matsos says in her matter-of-fact way.

I never noticed it before, but Dr. Matsos is pretty. And young. If I had to guess, I'd say she's early thirties. If I saw her on the street I'd never tag her as a doctor. She has wild, unrestrained hair and fire-engine-red lips that clash with the drab green of her hospital scrubs.

Josh clenches his fists and I watch as he pulls in a long, tight breath.

In the twenty-five years that I've known him, I've never, ever seen him look like it's a struggle for him to restrain himself.

Taunt Josh, he smirks.

Bully Josh, he laughs.

Hurt Josh, he shrugs.

When life kicks Josh in the face, he smiles.

His philosophy? If life gives you lemons, laugh.

But now, he's not smiling, he's not laughing, there's no ironic gleam in his eyes or smirk on his face. He doesn't look like the Josh I know.

He drags his hand down his face, pulling at the dark circles under his eyes and the unshaven stubble on his chin, then he shakes his head.

"I don't understand what you're saying," he says stiffly.

He's perched on the edge of my bed, and my mattress shifts when he drops his shoulders and looks down at his clenched hands.

My parents share a look. They understood what Dr. Matsos means. So does Josh, I'm sure, he just doesn't want to admit he understands.

My parents are on the baby blue and orange striped couch, and my dad reaches over to take my mom's hand, comforting her.

Maybe someday I'll need comforting too, but right now, I'm on the same page as Josh, trying to catch up with what Dr. Matsos said.

"This is common?" I ask. "This..."

I grapple for the words, then decide I don't want to say that I don't love anyone, not my family, not my baby, not anyone, out loud again. It seems unnecessarily cruel. To me and to them.

Dr. Matsos' face softens. "After a brain injury, individuals can suffer from anger or aggression, depression or anxiety, or even feel nothing at all. It appears, that's where we're at, Gemma feeling nothing at all."

"Except panic," Josh says. He sits stiffly, leaning away from me.

Ever since Dr. Matsos started talking, he hasn't looked at me once. There's a tight, uncomfortable squeezing in my throat. *Look at me*, I think, *look at me.*

Josh stares straight ahead. Rigid.

Look at me.

He doesn't.

"Correct." Dr. Matsos fidgets with the pager hanging from her scrubs.

She glances at my parents on the couch, at Josh and then at me. "A head injury often affects moods and emotions. It's a wide spectrum that can include severe mood swings, aggression, flat affect, obsessive behavior, egocentric behavior, lack of empathy. To the outside observer this seems like a personality change. Relationships often change with those closest to the injured because they seem like a different person altogether."

Me. She's talking about me.

My mom shifts on the couch and sniffs loudly. I think she's going to start crying, but she surprises me by lifting her chin and smiling at me, as if to say, "We're in this together. I'm here."

The tightness in my throat eases. My mom's here with me, there's that at least.

"Is it permanent?" Josh asks, cutting into the silence.

There's no doubt that he's asking whether or not I'll ever feel again. Whether or not I'll love him.

I look quickly at Dr. Matsos, like her response holds the key to all my future happiness.

She bites her fire-engine-red lips, then says, "I know these changes are frightening to witness. It can feel like the person you knew no longer exists—"

"Is it permanent," Josh interrupts.

The muscles in his back are so tight, and his shoulders are so rigid that I think if I touch him, he'll shatter.

"I don't know," Dr. Matsos says quietly, aware of the tension.

"The brain has a remarkable ability to heal and rewire itself. In a week, a month, a year, ten years...perhaps. But perhaps not."

She shrugs. "In the meantime, Gemma can find effective ways to live a fulfilling life and relearn to connect with others. In fact, many patients have positive results with TBI rehab and cognitive behavioral therapy. They find they're stronger and more resilient than they ever thought possible."

I wait for Josh to smirk at Dr. Matsos's blatantly positive spin on a crappy situation, it's so syrupy it's bordering on kitten poster quote, but he doesn't smirk. Or smile.

Neither do I.

So that's that.

I'm awake, but I'm not the same.

I'm alive, but my life's gone.

I think back to the before, when I was in my wedding dress, walking down the aisle to Josh. My heart so full of love. I picture us dancing in the rain, making love. Josh whispering his vows, promising that our love would last as long as the sky was above.

I wish I could go back in time and take in every moment, savor it again and again, and feel all the feelings, hold them all tight.

I wish that there was a way I could've known that I was in the best days of my life before I left them. I would've savored them more, taken them all in, before they were gone and not even the memories could fill me up.

If there's a time in life where I need my positive outlook and my journal full of "chin up" quotes, this is it.

Dr. Matsos is still talking, answering my dad's question about relationship changes. She's telling a story about a man who had a traumatic brain injury (TBI) and a week later, he up and left his job, his wife and four kids, and moved to Bergen, Norway to carve decorative stilts for a living.

"Stilts, as in those poles you walk on?" my dad asks.

"Shhh. That's not the point." My mom elbows him.

"Then what is the point?"

All of us turn to Dr. Matsos, waiting for the Aesop's Fable-esque point to her story, but honestly, I don't think there is one, so I say, "I think her point is, I likely have a new talent for carving useless objects out of wood."

Josh lets out a surprised, sharp laugh that sounds like it was torn from his chest. He coughs to cover it. Then finally, finally he slowly turns and looks at me.

His messy dark hair falls over his eyes as he tilts his head toward me. Then, he lifts an eyebrow, and there on his face is the smile I was waiting for. The right side of his mouth lifts and his eyes light up.

Are you kidding me right now? he seems to ask.

You bet, I smirk.

I watch him transform back into his old self, wrapping himself up in his life-is-my-playground façade.

And suddenly, I'm thinking about that old nursery rhyme, where Humpty Dumpty falls down and all the king's horses and all the king's men can't put him back together again.

"Josh," I whisper.

He leans close, putting his ear next to my lips.

"What?" he asks in a low, rumbly voice.

"What did Humpty Dumpty say when he fell off the wall?"

Josh pulls back and narrows his eyes like he's trying to decide if I'm suffering some weird delusion.

"What?" he finally asks.

"Buck up, you can fall apart later, old chap, but for now... it's sunny side up."

Josh lets out a sharp, laughing exhale at my twisted humor. "Right. Sunny side up."

Then he moves closer and takes my hand. His callouses scrape against my skin as he squeezes my fingers.

Dr. Matsos is finishing another story, one I've half-ignored about a young woman with a TBI whose husband left her, but then she fell in love with and married a classical pianist after healing through music therapy.

I'm sure it was supposed to be inspiring, but the only bit I can focus on is that the woman's husband left her.

"What's next? What do we do?" I ask.

My voice comes out sharp and strained. I'm tired, and all the talking is starting to scrape at me like a sharp fingernail over an open wound.

Josh glances at me, rubs the back of my hand with his thumb and then looks to Dr. Matsos.

She straightens her white coat and nods. "Right. The first thing I advise patients and their families is to acknowledge the loss. You're changed. You'll never be the same person again, even if you recover, you won't be the same. That person is gone. And that's okay. Accepting this is the first step toward beginning your recovery. Once you accept and acknowledge your new normal, you can move on and start building a new future. Granted, a different future than you previously envisioned, but not necessarily worse."

The air in my lungs feels tight again, and even the cold, dry air blowing from the vent over me can't cool the hot panic licking me. I clench Josh's hand, trying to hold tight to him.

"Gemma will be discharged soon. She'll have physical therapy, TBI rehab, cognitive behavioral therapy, all done as an outpatient..."

Dr. Matsos goes on to describe what I can expect in the next weeks and months. As she talks, I watch Josh. The smile has bled off his face, and although he doesn't look like he's holding back frustration or anger anymore, what I see is even worse. He's scared again.

His face is pale, the lines around his mouth are deep, and

his eyes are haunted as they flick around the room, not landing on anyone or anything, like he's reliving fears from the past or fears of the future.

Ten minutes later, Dr. Matsos leaves, and my mom and dad head to the cafeteria for a cup of coffee.

Josh stays on my bed, clutching my hand. He doesn't speak, and the silence soothes the raw, scraped feeling that had settled on me.

I close my eyes and listen to the hum of the air conditioner and concentrate on the scratchy feel of the cotton blanket, and the artificial smells of disinfectant and silicone.

Josh's thumb circles over the back of my hand, steady and reassuring. I think about all the things I always said I loved about him, that he doesn't judge, that he lets things go, that he has a great sense of humor, that he doesn't take himself too seriously, that he's patient, and kind, and giving, and...

"We'll get out of this," he says.

His voice scratches over me and I can tell he's trying not to cry.

I've only seen him cry twice, the night before his dad's funeral, and last night, when he saw me awake. I don't think he'll cry now.

"How?" I ask.

He studies me and I hold still while he reaches out and tucks a loose strand of hair behind my ear. My heart thumps in my chest like a butterfly trapped in a glass jar.

"You want the truth?" he asks.

I nod.

He rubs the strand of my hair between his fingers then drops his hand to the rumpled bedsheets. I tamp down the hammering of my heart and wait for his answer.

He shakes his head, "The truth is, I don't know. But I have to believe we'll get out of this."

He closes his eyes, his shoulders slump and he lets out a long sigh.

I think he won't say any more, but then he opens his eyes and says, "Because I love you."

My heart, flapping like a butterfly, folds up its wings and dies. I let out a harsh, painful exhale.

"You loved the me that danced in the rain," I say. Then I state the truth, "I'm not her anymore."

Josh is quiet. After a minute of listening to the sounds of people passing in the hallway and watching the sun shine through the window, he kicks off his shoes, climbs onto the bed next to me, drops his head to the pillow and lies down.

He doesn't pull me on top of him, or even touch me, instead he leaves his arm out in invitation.

He lies just like he used to in our bed at home, the exact way he would so that I could curl into him and rest my head on his shoulder. I watch his chest rise and fall as he stares at the ceiling, dry-eyed and waiting for my answer.

Because this is a question, as sure as if he'd spoken it out loud.

Together?

"Okay," I say.

Then I press myself as close to him as possible and lay my head over his heart. I feel the tension melt out of him. He wraps his arms around me and then slowly strokes his hand over my back.

I listen to his breathing and his heartbeat, both steady and slow. After ten minutes of quiet he falls asleep.

Even though I'm exhausted, I keep my eyes open and feel the warmth of him wrapped around me as I stare out the window at the blue light.

11

"This is what happens
when the love dies."

"I HAVE TO GO BACK TO LA," JOSH SAYS WHEN HE WAKES UP.

I realize that I should've expected this. My mom mentioned that he'd been flying back and forth between LA and NYC.

"When?"

His fingers brush through the length of my hair and then down my spine.

"Tonight," he finally says. His eyes are guarded when he leans back and studies my face, waiting for my response.

I blink. I wasn't expecting that. "For how long?"

"A week." His mouth twists, and he looks away from me.

I hear my mom's voice again, *this has been hard on him.*

"You don't want to go?" I ask.

He turns back to me, his eyes confused, as if he's wondering how I could ask that.

Then he seems to come to a conclusion that he doesn't like because he shakes he head and says, "Right. Sorry. No, I don't want to go."

Behind him, on the nightstand is the magazine that Ian

left. The one with Josh on the cover being kissed by another woman. I reach over and pick it up, hand it to him.

"What's this?" he asks.

He flips it over and glances at the cover. When he does, his shoulders stiffen and the magazine crinkles from the strength of his grip.

"I hadn't seen this," he says.

He gives it a cutting glance and then tosses it in the trash next to the nightstand. It clanks loudly as it hits the bottom of the empty bin.

I stare at the bin for a moment and then prop myself up on my elbows and lean against the headboard. Josh sits up and swipes his hand through his messy hair. There's the imprint of a pillow wrinkle on his left cheek.

"Do you want to talk about it?" I ask.

Yesterday, when I saw the cover, I thought that Josh had left me for another woman. Given a few minutes to wake up and come to my senses, I knew that wouldn't happen. I trust him more than I trust a tabloid. I reach out and take his hand.

"It's just garbage. It's not real." He sounds tired, really, really tired.

"You okay?"

He looks away from the trash and the fatigue transforms into a smile, one full of mischief and happiness, ironically, almost identical to the one on the cover of the magazine.

"I'm good, Gem. You know me."

I nod slowly, I do know him.

His smile fades and he closes his eyes.

I think I made a mistake in telling him I couldn't feel anymore. That I didn't love him anymore.

If it's never going away, then I wish I'd kept it a secret wrapped up tight and never shared it with the world. Then Josh, my family, my baby, could've remained happy in the belief that I was back, I was well, I was the same loving, caring Gemma that I'd always been.

I could've pretended for the rest of my life.

People pretend to be what they aren't all the time. Fake it 'til you make it and all that.

If only I hadn't said anything. If only...if only...

Josh opens an eye and peers at me. "You've got a funny look on your face," he says.

I nod. "I realize that I have a bad habit of blurting out inappropriate things. I've got no filter. So, I'm trying really hard to rewind time. Maybe the coma gave me a rewind button superpower."

His shoulders shake with laughter, and he reaches out to stroke my hair. "So random, Gemma. So random."

I grin at him. "Feel free to use that as a plot in your comic."

He pulls me to him and rubs my arms. "If you could rewind time, would you not go through IVF, knowing that you'd end up here?"

I shake my head. "I'd do it all again. If I hadn't had IVF I wouldn't have you, or Hope."

"But you wouldn't be here either," he says, and his voice has a hollow note in it.

"I'm sorry." I lean into his side, and I fit against him just right. "When you get back, I'll have this all figured out. I'll have a plan. Life's always better with a plan."

He looks down at me and lets out a sharp breath that ruffles my hair.

"You know I'm not really a plan kind of guy, I'm more of a go with the flow—"

He lets out an *oof* when I elbow him in the side.

Then he says, "Plan it is."

∽

IT'S THE NEXT AFTERNOON, AND I'M THINKING ABOUT THE FACT that Josh didn't kiss me goodbye.

In fact, he didn't kiss me a single time since I said that I didn't love him anymore. He held me, he cuddled me, he touched my hand and my face, but he never kissed me. I think he must be waiting for...permission.

I try to puzzle it out. When we were just friends, he wouldn't have kissed me. When we were getting closer, he didn't kiss me. He didn't kiss me until he knew that I felt the same about him. So, now that I told him I don't feel the same, he's not...

Right.

No kissing.

No sex.

None of that.

I touch my lips, trace my fingers over the plumpness of my lower lip and the bow in my top lip. They're chapped from the dry, antiseptic-tinted air of the facility, and it stings to run my finger over them. I push hard, dragging my finger down my lip, and think about Josh crushing his mouth against mine in the rain.

"Shit. You still look like hell."

I quickly glance at the entry to my room. It's Ian, carrying a plastic lunch tray full of food. He drops it on the oak coffee table and it clatters loudly. I wince at the noise.

"Get out," I say.

Ian ignores me, grabs the table and tugs it across the floor. The legs screech as they scrape the tile. He stops when the table is positioned in front of the plastic chair next to my bed. Ian drops into the chair and grabs his sandwich.

"I said get out." I glare at him.

He shrugs and takes a bite of his sub. A pickle falls out and plops to the plate.

While he's chewing a big mouthful, he says, "That whole thing about beauty sleep is a crock. Look at you, three months of uninterrupted sleep and you look like zombie-rella. No wonder Josh isn't here. I'd run away too."

I sit up and plant my feet on the ground. A few days awake, some physical therapy, and healthy food and I'm already feeling a little stronger. At least strong enough to look slightly intimidating.

I'm about to give Ian a piece of my mind, when he says, "Sorry about your luck. I was worried about you."

Everything I was about to say disappears, and I take a good look at Ian.

He's in workout clothes again, a ratty gray t-shirt, sweatpants, and a baseball hat. He's still unshaven, and he's devouring his pickle, onion, and cheese sub like he's not had a good meal in days.

I realize that the irritation of him being in my room is completely clouded by curiosity.

"What happened to you?"

Ian pauses with his sandwich halfway to his mouth. He brought another celebrity gossip rag; it's opened on the table by his lunch tray.

He looks at me and quirks an eyebrow. "What do you mean?"

He drops the sub to his plate and opens his celery soda.

I gesture at his clothes, his face, his lunch, the room, everything.

"Ahh," he says.

He pops a sour cream and onion chip into his mouth and crunches loudly.

"The last time you saw me I had the love of millions."

There's an ironic self-aware smile on his mouth. "This is what happens when the love dies."

He goes back to flipping through the pages of his magazine and shoving chips into his mouth. A few crumbs land on his ratty t-shirt. He doesn't wipe them off.

I have to admit, I don't know if I've ever been so disturbed in my life.

I spent seven years half in love with this man. I worshipped him. He was magnetic, powerful, full of conviction and charisma. He could walk into a room and silence it within two seconds with his presence alone. He had salon-styled hair, wore suits that cost thousands, ate with elegant manners at expensive restaurants, and dated models and reality stars.

He was *Ian Fortune*.

This guy, the guy sitting in my room, slurping soda and wearing a t-shirt with holes in the collar, is not the Ian Fortune I knew.

"It can't be that bad," I say.

Ian raises his eyebrows and says sardonically, "I'm the most hated man in America, Gemma. Yesterday, a woman on the street dumped her milkshake on me. Last week, a dog walker threw a sack of dog shit at me. I was evicted from my home. All my private accounts have been hacked and effed with. Last month a nationwide poll came out on the most hated men of all time. I topped the list, right ahead of Saddam Hussein. You may not know this, Gemma, but love is fickle, and once it's gone, you're screwed."

"But...you helped so many people."

Ian looks at me like I have a screw loose, then he scoffs and goes back to eating his sub.

I *know*, I know that Ian is a jerk.

I know that he stole Josh's notebook and used his ideas

for his own gain. I know that he is a cheater, a liar, and a prick. I know that he said horrible things to me as I was miscarrying.

I *know* all this.

Some people might say this is karma and it's exactly what Ian deserves. He deserves a rage mob descending on him, eviction, public shaming, the ruination of his business and more.

But does he really?

I'm not sure. Because even though we're nothing alike, it seems we have one thing in common. We both know what it's like when love dies.

"Why are you here?" I ask.

He ignores me, and keeps reading his magazine, so I lean forward and snap it closed.

"Why are you here?" I ask again.

He sighs. "I told you. The cafeteria smells like Brussel sprouts and dirty socks. Your room *was* quiet."

He says *was* as if he wishes it were quiet again.

"No, I mean, why are you here, at The Whittcombe?"

Ian finally looks at me, and I see a flash of pain before he shutters his eyes with his usual arrogance.

"I volunteer here."

I wrinkle my brow. "I didn't know that."

That's actually really nice. See, he's not all bad.

"I see that soft look on your face. Forget whatever you're thinking," Ian stretches his legs out in front of him and finally flicks the chip crumbs off his t-shirt. "I need approval. It's like a drug for me. This place is full of the brain damaged and senile. It's the only place in New York where people are brainless enough to like me."

I can feel my mouth dropping open in shock. He's... he's...reprehensible.

"There's this woman a few doors down, she thinks I'm her husband. Every time I see her she tells me I'm a handsome devil and wants to dance. Another lady thinks I'm her grandson, she gives me five dollars every time I walk through the door. This old guy, he shares stock tips, his roommate likes to play poker. Taking their money is like taking candy from a baby. Another woman, she gets flowers every week, but she's permanently out of it, so I take them, I used to give them to my dates. What does she care? Plus, if you volunteer here they give you a free meal."

He gestures at his tray. "People too brain damaged to realize they should hate me, and a free meal? What could be better?"

I choke on my words until finally I spit out, "You are the most vile, disgusting person I've ever met."

He waves his hand in a moving on gesture. "Already covered that, Gemma. Remember the koi pond? Or did you lose some of your memory in the coma? Now that would be interesting…"

He gives me a considering look.

I lean forward, pick up the pickle from his tray and throw it. It hits him square in the middle of his forehead, sticks there for a moment and then drops to his lunch tray.

He stares at me for a moment, then says, "I'd like to say that's the first time someone's thrown a pickle at me, but it's not."

"You deserved it."

"Probably."

I think about him using the people here to fill his need for attention and even stealing flowers from a woman in a coma. "You are disturbingly selfish."

He shrugs, completely unrepentant, and goes back to eating his sandwich.

Apparently, Ian thinks the conversation is over, but I can't let it go.

Out of morbid curiosity, I ask, "Have you ever done anything selfless?"

He snorts. "Why would I? Selfless actions are *never* in a man's best interest. My motto, if someone asks you to do something selfless, run."

"You haven't learned a thing," I say. "You haven't changed a bit. This whole slob look you have going, it just matches who you are on the inside. The suits and shiny hair, the charisma, that was the fake you."

"Mhmm," he says. He stands, wipes his hands on his sweatpants, and picks up his tray. "I'll see you next time."

"Don't bother. I still have enough awareness to realize you're vile."

He laughs and strides out the door.

~

THE NEXT FEW DAYS PASS QUICKLY, BROKEN UP BY PHYSICAL therapy, rehab, frequent texts and calls from Josh, and visits from my family and friends.

I see my mom and Hope every afternoon, and today, they surprised me by coming with Hannah, Brook and Carly.

I'm stationed on the couch, my legs curled under me, Hope in my arms while Brook and Hannah argue over whether or not I should be taking a ginseng supplement. Carly flips through the magazine that Ian left behind, and my mom sits on my bed, underlining passages in the romance novel she's reading.

I peer down at Hope. Her gray eyes are sleepy, since she just finished a bottle and I have the feeling she's about to nod off. I poke around in my chest, waiting for that unfurling of unconditional love and bonding, but I don't feel anything, so I stop poking.

"I thought you had bad fashion sense before," Brook says, and I realize that she's talking to me. "But this is worse than anything you ever wore. Forget ginseng. Getting dressed will make you feel better faster than a pill."

I look down at my clinic-issued cafeteria green robe, the blue and gray striped hospital gown, and the brown fuzzy slippers. Maybe she has a point. I reach up and feel my hair, it's a frizzy mess, pulled into a loose ponytail.

My mom sets down her book, "She's right. How can you expect to feel better when you look like this?"

"Feel?" I say. "That's the problem. I don't feel anything at all."

There's an awkward silence as everyone looks everywhere but at each other or me.

"I think ginseng..." Hannah trails off when Brook glares at her.

Carly closes the magazine and stands. She's in a vibrant gold and turquoise tunic dress and high heels, and she looks as out of place in my room as I'd look on a runway. Probably because she's a former model and is one of the most stunningly beautiful people I've ever met. I bet if she were wearing my robe and gown, she'd still look gorgeous.

"I see Josh is in the news," she says in her clipped British accent.

I nod and then look down as Hope makes a big, round-mouthed yawn and squeaks almost like a kitten.

I smile at her and she reaches up and grabs a hank of my hair. She tugs, and it hurts, but I don't pry her fingers open. I'll let her have whatever piece of me that she can hang on to.

"He and that Lisa Freaking Perry," Brook mutters. "She is *not* who I would've cast as Jewell."

I raise my eyebrows and Brook shrugs. "I'm a superfan. Superfans are allowed to moan and complain about casting decisions."

She crosses her arms over her business suit and scowls. Brook uses Josh's comics to unwind from her very long, very stressful days as a criminal defense lawyer.

Hannah clears her throat, "I know you don't want to hear it, but I really think ginseng will help. And acupuncture. And probably some chakra work. While you were in the coma my friend came and did reiki and he said that it really helped you."

I stare at Hannah, dumbfounded. "You brought someone to do reiki on me while I was in a coma?"

She blushes. "Errr. Yes?"

Brook snorts. "Of course he said it helped. Who would disagree with him? The lady in the coma?"

She crosses her arms and shakes her head, but then she gets a happy look on her face and reaches down for her bag. "I forgot. I brought wine. And juice..." She nods at Hannah, who is still pregnant.

She pulls out a sleeve of plastic cups. "We're going to toast Gemma waking up."

Hannah and I both have a cup of pomegranate juice while everyone else has wine.

After the wine starts flowing, the conversation becomes more animated.

Brook stands up like she's arguing a court case and says, "I'm just saying...Lisa Freaking Perry cannot steal Grim, I mean Josh. He's yours."

Carly blinks owlishly. "That's not the point. The point is Gemma told him she doesn't love him anymore. A man doesn't stay with a woman who doesn't love him. A man's ego can't take that sort of blow."

"Your husband stayed with you when he thought you didn't love him," Hannah points out.

"But we were miserable," Carly says.

"He still stayed," Brook argues.

My mom has been quietly drinking wine on the bed, listening to the conversation bloom around her. She clears her throat.

"What is it, Mom?"

She shakes her head and her lips turn down. I didn't notice it before, but she's not wearing makeup. I've not seen her without makeup in years.

"I'm sorry to tell you all this, but after being married thirty years and witnessing more weddings, marriages, and divorces than I can count, I have to tell you all, love fades. Love dies."

I stare at my mom, not quite comprehending where she's going with this. What happened to the mom who set me up with countless blind dates? What happened to the mom whose life goal was to see me happily married? What happened to the queen of Jell-O wedding sculptures?

"What..." Hannah says. Which pretty much sums up what we're all thinking.

My mom frowns. "Gemma fell out of love, and it was out of her control, but it happens to other people every day. Two years in, a couple realizes they don't love each other anymore. Ten years in and two kids later, a couple realizes they're just roommates and not in love. Thirty years in, a couple realizes they haven't felt that spark in decades. It might sneak up on you, or it might hit you like a brick, but a fact of life remains, love dies. Gemma just discovered that fact sooner than most."

I look at my mom more closely. Something's off here. And then I realize what it is.

"Are you and Dad—"

She waves my statement away.

Brook swears and then chugs the rest of the wine in her glass. "This just got heavy."

Hannah stands and rubs her stomach. "If love dies, then what's the point?"

"It doesn't die," Carly says.

My mom shrugs. "Look at the divorce rate. There's your proof that it does."

What happened? What happened to my mom? To her belief in the power of a "good job" and a match made over barbecue wieners and Jell-O molds? What about her plucky theory that our wedding Jell-O sculpture was the metaphor of our marriage: wobbly but unbreakable?

"No really," Hannah says, "if love dies, then why even try?"

I think about it, about why people want love, about why they keep trying to find love, keep hoping for love, about why I'm so terrified that it's gone. I know why.

"Because," I say, "even if it dies, it feels amazing while it lasts."

AFTER MY FRIENDS, MY MOM, AND HOPE ARE GONE, I SIT AND stare out the window. There's something that happened during the visit that's niggling at my mind.

My mom and dad are on the rocks. She confirmed it before she left. Just like Dr. Matsos said, this injury changed more than just me.

Apparently, nearly losing me made my mom rethink her whole life, including her marriage. She and Dad are still together, but they're considering separating.

I think back to the Jell-O sculpture my mom made. Wobbly but unbreakable.

Well, it did break. It spilled all over the floor and made a huge mess. The niggle starts up again, and it feels just like an itch in that place on your back that you can't reach.

The Jell-O sculpture broke, and...

And Josh said, "We'll rebuild it. Easy."

I recall sitting on the floor, covered in Jell-O, Josh grinning at me.

I said, "We can't rebuild this."

The sun comes out from behind a cloud and shines through the window, like the illumination is confirming that I'm on the right track.

Because after I said that it couldn't be rebuilt Josh said, "Then we'll make it again. Everything's better the second time around."

The hair on my arms stands up and my skin tingles. That's it. That's the answer.

Our world may have shattered, all the love I felt may be gone, but that doesn't mean we can't do it again.

We can fall in love a second time.

I didn't believe Josh when he said everything's better the second time around, but maybe he's right.

Josh will fall in love with the changed me.

I'll fall in love with him.

We can recapture our happiness. We can have that life that we envisioned. Marriage, a family, love. We can still have our dreams come true.

We just need to follow the steps that had us falling in love the first time around, and map them out so precisely, following a recipe that worked before, that we can't help but fall in love again.

My body feels electrified, and energy buzzes over me. I

grab a pen from the nightstand next to my bed, pull the magazine to me and start to write out the plan.

It starts with pizza and ice cream and ends with making love on the floor.

This can't fail. I won't let it.

My mom was wrong. Love doesn't die. At least, if it does, that doesn't mean you can't breathe life back into it and experience it a second time around.

12

"Sometimes what's bad for you
is the only thing
that can make you feel alive."

IN A CLINIC OR A HOSPITAL, TIME DOESN'T SEEM TO HAVE MUCH meaning.

Even my window with the view of the morning sky and the evening light can't completely chase away the feeling that time bleeds from one day into another here, blurring the boundary. There's no line of demarcation.

Four days or twenty, five or forty-five, it all feels like one long continuous blur. Time here is a piece of taffy, pulled and pulled and stretched, a long timeline, with nothing to discern one day from another.

The only way I can tell that time has passed is that I'm stronger. I can walk from my room to the cafeteria without help.

At the beginning, a nursing aide had to hold my waist with a support belt in case I fell over. Now I can make it there alone.

I can have a conversation with my whole family in the room without feeling like my skin is being peeled off with a razor blade from all the stimulation.

I can rock Hope when she fusses without her cries shooting violent fireworks off in my brain.

I can talk to Josh on the phone for an hour at a time, and read his texts without getting a headache. I'm getting better.

Ian still comes to my room for lunch. He eats his sandwich and reads glossy gossip magazines. If Josh is featured he leaves the magazine behind, presumably so I can read it.

I stopped looking after the first week featured Josh having lunch at a sidewalk café with Lisa Perry, and the second week showed them walking down a sidewalk together.

Josh said the photos are taken during working lunches with lots of people from the studio, and the tabloid photographers frame the shots so it looks like he and Lisa are alone.

I believe him. I've never had any reason not to.

More importantly, it's been weeks.

That's right, weeks, yes, weeks have passed since I woke.

Josh should've been back, but he was held up in LA. It's not a problem. He'll be back tonight, and even more exciting, today I'm being discharged.

It's barely seven in the morning, and I'm already dressed in real, actual clothes.

My mom brought a fluorescent yellow sheath dress that's truly hideous and black and white checkered shoes. I've never been so happy to wear something so ugly in my entire life. I grin as I brush my hair and put on cherry lip gloss.

The world and my emotions are still muted, like I'm wrapped up in a tight ball of cotton, but even so, I'm glad to be leaving today.

Josh will be back, he'll finally be here in person for me to tell my plan, and we'll be able to move on.

I look up when someone strolls through my room door.

I'm used to all manner of nurses, aides, doctors, and family walking in, and so I smile before I see who it is. When I do, I drop the smile.

"What? Not happy to see me?" Ian asks. He holds out a tall paper cup. "But I brought coffee. I know you love coffee."

I scowl and drop my hairbrush to the bed next to me. "Who'd you steal it from?"

Last week, he brought me a box of cookies. I ate one and then he told me he'd taken it from the "vegetative woman's" room. I spit out the half-chewed cookie and demanded he take it back. He didn't, he just ate the rest of the box in front of me.

"I'm offended," he says. "I bought you a going away present, Gemma. I'll miss your room. Who knows what sort of sad sap they'll bring in after you're gone."

I give him a skeptical look, but the coffee smells delicious. Like bittersweet chocolate, cherries, and cream.

"Fine." I give in, grab the cup and take a sip.

The steaming liquid burns my tongue, so I close my eyes and luxuriate in the stinging feel. It's perfect.

When I open my eyes, Ian sits on the couch next to me and surveys my dress with a critical eye.

"You look like a yellow cab," he says.

He stretches his arms on the couch back and sprawls out, legs wide. "This would be the perfect opportunity for a pick-up line, something like...if you were a Dodge, I'd Ram you."

I shake my head.

He tsks. "No?"

"No."

"Do you believe in love at first sight, or should I drive around the block again?"

I ignore him and take another sip of the delicious coffee. I know he claims he's the most hated man in

America now, but I really can't fathom how he's come to this.

He shifts and scratches his chin. Then perks up.

"How about this one? Hey baby, can I check your fluids with my dipstick?"

I choke and then some of the hot coffee shoots out of my nose.

"Gah!" My eyes water and my nose stings. I wipe at the coffee dribbling down my face and glare at Ian. "Get out!"

He grins at me. "For a woman with no emotions, you certainly get mad enough."

I pause, stunned at what he's insinuating. Do I fell something? Is he purposely being disgusting to rile me up? I do a quick scan. Tight chest, burning nose, stinging eyes, and clenched jaw. That could be anger...except, no.

"I liked you better when you used Josh's quotes rather than speaking your own mind."

He merely shrugs and wipes some of the coffee splatter off of the coffee table.

My shoulders fall. This feels like kicking a dog when it's down, so I reach over and grab his shirt sleeve. Ian stops wiping at the coffee and looks up at me.

"What?"

"Thanks for the coffee. That was really thoughtful."

His stunning, bright white, chin dimple smile makes an appearance, and he almost looks like his old self.

The nurse manager pokes her head into the room, "Gemma, did I happen to leave my coffee in here earlier? I can't seem to find it."

Ian moves, almost imperceptibly to place himself between the nurse manager's line of sight and my cup of coffee on the table.

No.

No freaking way.

"Ummm, what did it look like?" I ask.

"Blue paper cup, white lid. Steaming hot. My husband brought it for me." She shakes her head and the key cards around her neck jingle. "I'm losing my mind. These all-nighters, I'm telling you."

She turns and walks away.

I stare at the blue cup of coffee, with the white lid, and the steam coming out of it. Then I glare at Ian.

He looks just like a little boy who knows he's been caught with his hand in the cookie jar. His eyes are wide and his lips are folded over like he's trying to hold in a laugh. We listen as the nurse manager's footsteps fade down the hall.

Then Ian snorts, he doubles over and holds his waist while he laughs, wheezing and gasping for air. When he sits back up his eyes have tears in them.

"I hate you," I say.

He smirks. "Please. Try to be original. The whole world hates me. Wouldn't it be more fun to love me? Don't be a follower, Gemma."

"Her husband brought her this coffee," I hiss. "You stole it."

"Boys were rewarded in Sparta for stealing. It was seen as a virtue. Only the best could steal and not get caught."

I shake my head. "Too bad you always get caught."

"Mhmm," he says. He crosses a leg over his knee and settles back into the lumpy couch.

Ugh.

I stare at the coffee. It was good. Really, really good. And it'd be a shame to let it go to waste. I grab it and take another sip. Ian chuckles.

"Waste not, want not," I mutter.

He laughs even harder.

Evil, evil man.

"So, how's Saint Josh taking everything? Has he declared his undying love for you? Is everything sparkles and sunshine in the eternal bliss of your love?"

I narrow my eyes on Ian. "We're not going to talk about Josh. I know you hate him."

He takes a bite of his ham and egg sandwich and chews noisily.

"I don't hate him." I see a bit of yellow egg and pink ham, since he talks with his mouth full. "How could I hate such a nice guy?"

"He punched you," I remind Ian.

Ian smiles, like he's reliving a particularly pleasant memory.

"I don't trust you," I say.

He nods, like this should be obvious.

"I heard through the grapevine that you told Josh you don't love him," Ian says.

I drop the cup of coffee to the table and a bit of the brown liquid spills out of the lid. The coffee runs over the side and onto the table.

"You heard wrong."

Ian lifts an eyebrow, his disbelief clear, and I feel my cheeks heating.

"Sadly for you, your neighbor can hear your conversations through the vent, and she's a terrible gossip. Motorcycle accident, lost her filter." He waves his hand in the air and calls, "Morning, Linda. I'll be by in a few."

All these weeks that Ian's been coming by, leaving magazines featuring Josh, he's *known*.

Ian studies my expression, one eyebrow lifted.

"It's none of your business." I cross my arms over my chest. "You can go."

He takes another bite of his sandwich and says, "I know you, Gemma. You're all gooey affirmations and positive thinking. I bet you already have a plan to get your life back. You think you can fall right back in love with Josh and that everything will be the same as it always was."

There's a lump in my throat that's preventing me from responding. He's saying all this like I'm stupid to believe it.

Ian looks at my face and nods. "That's what I thought."

I dig my fingers into the bright yellow fabric of my dress.

"What does it matter to you?" I finally manage to get out.

Ian sets down his sandwich and wipes his hands, crumbs falling to the floor. He takes a moment to consider his answer.

Then he says, "I told you before. I'm broken. You're broken. Our jagged edges make a good fit."

"I'm not broken," I say.

But my shoulders hunch forward a little, because isn't that what I've been worried about? That I've broken so much this time that I'm not fixable?

"Mhmm," he says.

"I'm not."

Ian crumples up the wrapper from his sandwich and throws it across the room. It lands in the trash.

"Gemma. I said this before, I'm going to say it again. Josh has always had the same problem. He's not a doer. He has no initiative."

"That's not true. He's a worldwide phenomenon. People love him."

Ian snorts. "Yeah. That'll work out."

I think that hit a little too close to home. Ian knows what happens when you're no longer in fashion.

He sighs and brushes back his hair. "Look. When the going gets tough, Josh bails. He takes the path of least resistance, which is why he never came after me. Which is why it took him years to ask you on a date."

I go to say something but Ian interrupts me. "Which is why he's been in LA for weeks instead of here with you. The path of least resistance. He's not a fighter."

I turn away from Ian, not wanting him to see that his last statement hit a place that felt similar to a painful truth.

"If you don't fight for what you love, you lose it."

"I thought it was already lost," I shoot back.

A slow, bitter smile spreads over his face. "Exactly."

I stand up, grab the cup of coffee, take it across the room and drop it in the trash can. When I turn back, the smile has left Ian's face.

"I don't need your advice. You don't know Josh. You don't know me. Thanks for the company, but you should go. Josh will be here soon to take me home. I don't want you here when he comes."

He stares at me a moment, and I have the strangest thought that I've hurt his feelings.

"I'm just trying to help," he says. He nods at the hallway. "I've been around long enough to know that Josh isn't going to stick around."

I shake my head in denial.

Ian holds up his hand. "I'll be here when he's gone."

"What for?"

Ian walks toward the door, and I don't think he hears me, until at the last minute he turns around and says, "Because I'm bad for you. And sometimes, Gemma, what's bad for you is the only thing that can make you feel alive."

I stare at the empty doorway for a full minute after his bombshell. Then, I kick the trashcan. The coffee sloshes into the bottom of the plastic trash bag.

13

"The only thing focusing on the past does is prevent you from living today."

I'M HOME.

Josh closes the door behind us, the click of the lock loud in the quiet gray light of the entry.

Home is the loft that Josh renovated last year. It's large, sprawling, brick-walled, wood-floored, and light-filled. We're on the first floor.

The building is from the 1800s and has been at one time or another a brewery, a pickle factory, a furniture store, a florist, a playhouse, and the headquarters for the beautification of the waterfront.

Now it's a home.

My shoulders relax and the tension I carried on the trip here melts away. The smooth white walls and high ceilings, the tall light-filled windows streaming in afternoon sun, the uncluttered, spartan furnishings, it's all so quiet, so unobtrusive that I finally can relax.

I didn't realize how much I'd been shielded in the clinic until our car ride home. The noise of the city, the long blares of honking horns, the hissing of buses, the rumbling of the subway, the shrieking and booming of construction and all the colors, flashing lights, all the frenetic movement.

The city was a heaving, chaotic mess that felt like a dentist's drill whirring into my skull. I kept my eyes closed for almost the entire car ride home, trying to shut it all out.

Josh stayed quiet for the drive too. We were in the backseat of a taxi, the air conditioning blowing against my closed eyelids, the smell of evergreen air freshener almost overpowering the scent of cracked vinyl and grease.

He rested his hand over mine, so I concentrated on the weight of his hand and let everything else fade away.

Now we're home and I look it all over, grateful for the light gray furniture, the brown leather couch, the wood floors, the soundproof windows. This place always reminded me of a grove in the middle of Central Park, a peaceful spot, untouched by the city. Now, even more so.

"You alright?" Josh asks.

He's watching me with a careful expression, like he doesn't know what to expect next. The entry is tight and small, filled with his worry.

"I'm okay. I was just thinking how glad I am that you decorated with only white and gray."

He gives me a surprised smile, then nods at the living room. "You should sit. I'll make you something to eat."

I've learned that whenever Josh wants to show someone he loves them or that he's worried about them he makes them food. He did it for his dad, and while I was pregnant he did it for me.

But the thought of food makes me queasy. I move into the living room.

Josh follows, but instead of agreeing to food, I say, "We need to talk."

The sound of Josh's footsteps stop and I turn around to

see him standing completely still, his face draining of color. He swallows and I watch his Adam's apple bob.

"Alright," he says.

I sit down on the leather couch, and Josh sits at the other end. He leans back against the cushions. To any outsider he'd seem relaxed, his legs out, a small smile on his lips, but I know him, and he's anything but relaxed.

Behind the smile, his jaw clenches, and behind the sprawled legs and lounging posture, his body is as tight as a wire.

That's alright. I'm not relaxed either. There's a huge elephant in the living room, and we have to address it. The sooner the better.

"We didn't get married," I say.

"No."

"I don't feel what I used to." There's no point in denying it or tiptoeing around it.

"I know," he says, and this time, he looks away from me, down the hall toward the bedrooms.

There's the bedroom we shared, with its king-size bed covered in a fluffy white down comforter and a soft gray cashmere throw. There's the guest bedroom where my parents stay when they come down occasionally for a Broadway show. And then there's the nursery.

Hope will be here soon. My mom's bringing her down tonight.

Josh's hands clench and he turns back to me. "I'm sorry, Gemma."

He moves closer, until his knees touch mine. The brush of his legs on mine sends a sensation through me and I look up quickly at his face. There are shadows under his eyes, and his hair is messy from how often he's run his hands through it.

"What do you have to be sorry for?" I ask, confused.

"For not being able to prevent this. For not being there for you. For being in LA when I wish to God I could've been here." His jaw clenches again and he's full of swirling emotion, his eyes dark.

I reach out and put my hand on his leg. I can feel the heat of him through his jeans. "The only thing focusing on the past does is prevent you from living today."

He's silent for a moment, then he scoffs, "You can't quote me back to me."

"I can."

He nods, then says carefully, "Maybe I'm focusing on the past because I'm afraid of the future."

Everything that makes Josh himself fades, and somehow he seems diminished when he says, "If you're going to leave me, Gemma, tell me now. If you don't want to be with me, if you can't see staying with someone you don't love, don't drag me along. Just tell me. I can't say I won't do my best to convince you otherwise, but I need to know."

The silence of the apartment, soothing before, is now uncomfortable and heavy. I stare at Josh, stunned that while I was trying to think of a way to tell him my plan to fall back in love, he thought I was trying to think of a way to tell him I was leaving.

Josh's shoulders drop and he lets out a long sigh. "Before you answer, I'd like to say, I love you enough to carry the both of us. I love you and Hope enough for all three of us. You can take as long as you need. Fifty years even. My love has never been conditional on you loving me back."

My breath feels tight in my chest. Ian was wrong. Josh isn't leaving, he isn't going anywhere.

But that reality is almost worse than him leaving because what he's saying is that he'll stay in a relationship where he isn't loved. Where he doesn't expect love.

I can't do that to him. I won't. He deserves better. He deserves more.

What would he live on if he stayed with me? The memories of romance? The memories of love? They'd be sucked dry, like marrow from a bone, within a year, maybe two, and then what?

You can't live on memories alone. You have to have a present and a future too.

I reach out and hesitantly touch my fingers to his face, dragging them down the roughness of his stubble. His eyes flutter closed at my touch and I feel his sharp exhale on my fingertips.

"I have a plan," I say.

His eyes open and they spark with amusement. "Gemma, I just told you I'll love you to the end of eternity and you reply, 'I have a plan'?" His lips twist into a smile and he shakes his head.

"What do you want me to say? That you deserve better than this?" I ask.

"No. Definitely not the reply I want."

"Then what?"

He doesn't answer for a moment, until he says, "I want you to feel something again. Whether that's you realizing you love me or loathe me, I want you to be able to answer me when I say I love you. For example, I say, 'I love you, Gemma, I love you to the end of the earth' and then you say, 'Go jump off the edge then you ass.'"

I snort. "I wouldn't."

He shrugs. "I'd take that over silence. The opposite of love isn't hate, it's apathy."

Oh.

Ouch.

I don't want to be apathetic. I don't want to be numb.

I just need help learning to feel again.

"You've always liked my plans in the past," I point out.

All the worry and the frustration and fear that was rolling off him before fades into his laughing expression.

"Alright. I'm game. What kind of plan?"

I lick my lips, and his eyes catch on my mouth. He wants to kiss me, I can always tell when Josh is thinking about kissing. His eyes become hot and dark, like the city on a sweltering summer night, consumed by the bright flashing lights of Times Square.

My lips tingle and I lean closer, drawn to him.

He focuses on me, and I get the feeling that if I tell him I want to make love, right here, right now, we'll be on the floor in a millisecond. My mouth goes dry and my heart pounds in my ears.

Would having sex bring everything back?

I picture it in detail. Josh dropping me to the rug, holding me down, yanking up my dress, tugging my underwear over my hip bones and down my legs. He'd kiss my clit, because he can never resist tonguing me, he'd stroke me and tease me, until I begged, until my hands couldn't stop pulling him to me, begging him to enter me, and then he'd grab both my hands, spread my legs and make love to me until I was crying out his name.

And then, at the end of this amazing, orgasm-crushing sex-on-the-rug scene, he'd whisper in my ear, 'I love you,' and in this imagining, I lie there, physically floating on a cloud of bliss, but still, inevitably, numb. In this stupid sex fantasy, I don't say I love you back.

I blink and Josh is still there, staring at my mouth.

"My plan." I clear my throat and Josh's eyes flick to mine. He nods.

"I have it all figured out. Dr. Matsos and my therapists

said my brain will relearn emotional connection. It'll all come back. Time will help. But so will training."

That's my theory at least.

I open my eyes wide to express the importance of what I'm saying, "It's just like when you learn an instrument. Remember when I started playing the trumpet in fifth grade?"

Josh cringes. "Cats dying sounded prettier."

He's not wrong. "Exactly. I practiced an hour every day. There wasn't any difference for the first month or two, then suddenly, there was. I was a little bit better."

"A little less awful," he agrees. "I think your dad stopped wearing ear plugs after four months."

I grin, good old Dad, he never said anything until years later. Everybody knew but me. "And then, after two years, I was almost decent."

"Then you quit," Josh says.

"Not the point," I say. "The point is, I was training, and it took a while to learn this skill, because learning a new skill takes time and practice."

"So, you want to play me like a trumpet?" he says, a joking light in his eyes.

I elbow him. "Gutter. Meet Josh."

He smiles and I see that he's happier, more relaxed, and I'm glad for it. "You see where I'm going?"

He wraps his arm around me and pulls me close. His fingers stroke down my shoulder and play with the strap of my tank top.

"You're not leaving."

"I'm not leaving," I agree. "I'm going to relearn our love."

His fingers pause for a moment, then start up again, rubbing a circle over the sensitive place where my shoulder meets my neck.

"How are you going to do that?"

I turn to him and lift my chin. "I fell in love once before. It was easy."

He smiles at that. "Easy, huh?"

"Well, maybe not *easy*, exactly. But now we have a blueprint for the successful way to elicit the emotion of love. All we have to do is train. Practice."

"Practice being in love?" Josh asks.

I can't quite pin down his expression, but it reminds me of when we went out to dinner and he ordered steak and instead the waiter brought him tofu steak. Vegan steak, all the name, none of the meat.

Is practice love like that? All the name, none of the meat?

Nah.

"It's going to work," I say. "Here's what we'll do, romantic dinners, illicit rendezvous in the park."

"Rendezvous?" he says incredulously, his eyebrows going high.

I frown. "I don't know if I can find someone to bash a painting over your head."

"What?" he laughs.

"We'll go to another party, maybe Carly will have one, or maybe we can do a burlesque show."

He coughs and his cheeks flush pink. I pat him on the back and continue, "Don't worry, you just have to be you. I'll have a practice session for us every day and then soon...it'll work."

Josh leans back. His black hair falls over his left eye, and he brushes it aside. When I catch his expression, it's skeptical but amused, which to me means he's covering up his real feelings.

"What do you think?" I ask.

I bite my tongue and concentrate on the sting of my teeth clamping down on the tip of my tongue.

"Let me see if I have this right. You want to have daily practice sessions to re-fall in love? Using our previous encounters as your guide?"

I stop biting my tongue. It feels hot and raw. "That about sums it up."

He shakes his head. "Sorry. No."

A hot dizziness fills me. "No?"

The dizziness sweeps over me and I look around the cool, uncluttered room, the sleek-lined leather couch, the white gauze curtains, and try to find something to concentrate on. There's a fat rectangle of sunlight spilling on the hardwood floor, a dull-edged puddle of ochre-colored warmth. I focus on it.

Then I say, "I don't know what else to do." My voice breaks, but I can't look at him.

Josh puts his hand on my arm and squeezes gently. "I don't want to relive the same story. I'm not that Josh and you're not that Gemma. You can't..." He stops.

I force my eyes from the safe rectangle of light back to Josh. I'm surprised when I see that he's smiling at me.

"Hey," he says.

"Hi." I smile back.

His eyes crinkle. "You can't reanimate past love like some corpse bride, it'll always result in a zombie apocalypse with blood, gore, and brains being eaten."

I snort, but say, "I beg to differ."

He shakes his head. "I have hundreds of novels, movies, and comics to support me. Reanimation is a horror not a romance."

I blow out a breath. "Fine. What would you do then?"

He shrugs. "I'd trust myself. I'd trust that a new, stronger love would grow."

"And if it doesn't?"

Josh's stare challenges me, as if he's angry that I'd even suggest that, as if he's daring me to even consider that everything won't work out.

I shift uncomfortably. Annoyingly, Ian's voice pops into my mind, *"Josh always takes the road of least resistance."*

Is refusing to have a plan the road of least resistance? Leaving our future happiness, our marriage, our family to the *chance* that love will grow?

Finally, Josh's gaze softens. "You really want to do this?"

I nod. There's a lump in my throat.

"Alright," he agrees.

The lump in my throat loosens. That must be relief.

"But I want the sessions to be original. No going back through the old motions. If we're going to practice love, then let's at least make it interesting," he says. He's staring at my mouth again.

"No sex," I blurt out. "No kissing."

He blinks. Surprise flits across his face. Apparently he wasn't thinking about sex. But now...now he is.

He gives me a delighted grin. "But isn't that part of our previous encounters? Isn't that an illicit rendezvous?"

I shake my head. I don't want him to know that I'm terrified that when we kiss, when we make love, I'll feel nothing. The thought leaves me in a cold sweat.

"I've changed my mind. No sex. No kissing. Not until..."

His nods and his mouth softens. "I understand."

Now it looks like he's laughing at himself. "This part's the same. Unrequited love is like an old t-shirt, almost too easy to put back on."

"Feeling sorry for yourself?" I ask, because if I don't tease him, that shadow will bleed through his eyes and I don't want to see that.

He flashes a grin and the shadow recedes. "Never. I like old t-shirts."

"This'll work." I reach out and grab his hand.

"Question."

"Yeah?"

"Do you still like Jell-O?" He's watching me with more concern than a question like this should warrant, which means he must've seen my food tray when he came to pick me up at the clinic.

"No," I whisper.

"Why not?"

"It just doesn't taste good anymore. I don't want it. It's gross. It's...tastes change." I shrug.

My lifelong love affair with Jell-O ended the minute I woke up. I suppose it had to end sometime.

Josh stares across the room, and I don't quite understand it, but the fact that I don't like Jell-O anymore has him looking more shaken than almost anything else I've said since waking up.

"You okay?"

He swallows, then slowly nods. "Sure."

But when he looks at me, the shadows in his eyes are back.

14

"As long as the sky is above,
we love you."

I BRUSH MY FINGERS OVER HOPE'S BROW AND SHE SIGHS IN HER sleep. She's home. I'm home.

My mom brought her two hours ago, along with her favorite pacifier connected to a silky fox and her diaper bag.

When I was in the coma, my mom watched Hope while Josh was in LA, and then when Josh flew back he picked Hope up and they stayed here.

So, Hope has two houses that are chock full of every possible baby-related item, two strollers, two car seats, two cribs, two baby swings, two nurseries, two wardrobes full of onesies, diapers, and blankets. Two everything. But only one home.

"Welcome home, baby," I whisper.

I sit in the rocker next to her crib and watch the rise and fall of her chest, I watch how her forehead wrinkles while she sleeps, and I watch her fingers open and close. It's nearly nine o'clock, the little moon-shaped lamp next to her bed glows yellow and plays a soothing lullaby.

The last time I saw the nursery it was painted a solid

buttercup yellow. Now, there's barely a trace of yellow in the room. Instead, all four walls of the room are painted to look like a meadow.

There's emerald green grass near the carpet, each blade painted individually, they tilt and bend, and looking at them you can almost feel the breeze moving over them, and smell their green, grassy scent.

If you look carefully you can spot a ladybug in the grass, an ant here and there, a tiny white moth, perched on a single blade. Interspersed in the tall grass, there are flowers. The lacey white of Queen Anne's lace, the happy bright blue and white of daisy-like asters, and the only yellow in the room, the sharp pop of dandelions. The flowers and grass blend into the sky, a gradient of blues ranging from the saturated blue of a clear autumn sky to the blue gray of...well, my eyes.

Then amidst the wispy, barely-there clouds, Josh painted a quote in the sky. *As long as the sky is above, we love you.*

When we brought Hope in earlier, and I saw the room for the first time, Josh stopped at the doorway, as if he was waiting for my reaction. I spun around in a slow circle, taking it all in.

I couldn't find the words. It reminded me of something, a memory at the edge of my mind that I couldn't quite grasp.

"When did you do this?" I whispered.

He cleared his throat and shifted, "While she was in the NICU. When I couldn't sleep."

I thought about how many hours this must have taken, and how many hours of not being able to sleep that was.

Then his phone rang, Dylan was outside. So I stayed with Hope, while Josh went to see what my brother was doing in the city.

That was a half hour ago. Josh let Dylan in and I've heard the low rumble of their voices ever since.

I reach between the white wood slats of Hope's crib and slip my pointer finger into the small, delicate curve of her curled hand. Her fingers flutter and then her hand falls open. I pull my hand back and rest it in my lap. I don't want to wake her, it took nearly two hours of rocking and feeding and coaxing to get her to sleep.

Josh says that she usually wakes up in the middle of the night for another bottle, but until then, she should stay asleep.

My eyes drift to the wall again, there's a gnarled walnut tree in the distance on the far wall. And suddenly, I know why this mural is familiar. Josh painted the park we used to picnic in when we were kids. We'd go as a family, and after eating, we'd all lie in the grass and hold hands, spotting animals in the clouds.

Now that I look at the clouds more closely, I can see that some of them are shaped like animals. A rabbit, a turtle, a fox.

I think Josh must have hesitated at the door, because he was waiting for me to recognize it. I smile. It's perfect. It's more than perfect.

I stand, the rocking chair creaking as I do, and I head toward the kitchen where I can hear Dylan and Josh talking.

I'm so caught up in telling Josh about my realization that I'm almost to the kitchen before I realize that Dylan is talking about me. He's not particularly quiet, he never is, but I don't think I'm meant to hear this.

"She's not herself," Dylan says. "You can't B.S. me, Josh. You can't stand there and tell me that things are fine. That's bullshit."

Dylan sounds more upset than I've heard him since I accidentally melted his G.I. Joe in the microwave when he was ten. Okay, I know *accidentally*, *melted*, and *microwave* don't go together, but the point is, I haven't heard him this upset in more than twenty years.

"Leave it alone," Josh says, and his voice is so quiet I can barely hear him.

I realize that I've stopped walking. I'm at the edge of the hallway, and I press my back to the cool plaster wall. I should go around the corner, I should let them know I'm here. Nothing good ever comes from listening in when you aren't meant to hear.

I'm about to push off the wall and walk around the corner when I hear someone smack the countertop. I jump.

"I won't leave it," Dylan says.

My heart pounds, and I push my hands to the wall. Okay, I'm not going around the corner. Instead I should go back and sit with Hope. But I don't. I wait to hear what Dylan has to say.

"She's my sister. I love her. I want her to be happy, but I don't want her to be happy at your expense."

I blink, stunned. I've never heard Dylan talk like this. Usually he's joking around, watching football, or trying to get Mom to make him some pot roast or pancakes.

There's a short silence, probably Dylan waiting for Josh to say something, but he doesn't.

"I'm sure you've seen it yourself," Dylan continues, "but in case you've missed it, she's not the same person. The kids are all excited to visit her, and she looks at them like she's never seen them before. The other day Colin asked her to help tie his shoes, you know what happened?"

I know. I didn't know that Dylan did. I feel a flush come to my cheeks.

"She couldn't remember," Dylan says. "Gemma couldn't remember how to tie a shoe."

That's not exactly fair. I couldn't remember *at that exact moment*. It came back to me.

"When we all got there when she woke up, everybody was crying. Was she? No, not a single tear. She just stared at the wall, for a good ten minutes. *She just stared at the wall.* Do you remember how much Gemma used to laugh, and cry, and jump around like a frickin' firecracker? Because I do. That's not her anymore. She's not a firecracker, she's all...she's gone. She's absent. The other day, Mom and I were there when she wanted to call you. She put her phone up to her ear, and held it there for a good thirty seconds. Then she turned to Mom and said, 'It's not working.' Then Mom said, 'You have to press call.' Gemma forgot that between picking up the phone and holding it to your ear you actually have to hit the person's name to call them. Do you see what I'm getting at?"

I hold my breath and wait for Josh's answer.

"No," he says. "Get to the point."

He sounds angry, more than angry, he sounds pissed. Although I'm not sure whether or not he's pissed at Dylan or the situation we're in.

"She doesn't love you," Dylan says. "Jeez. Calm down, man. I'm not saying anything you haven't heard. Jeez."

Dylan mutters something and I hear the scraping of barstools against the tile floor.

"I've been your best friend for twenty-five years. If I can't say this, then we aren't best friends. Sister or not, I have to say this. The Gemma you love, she isn't coming back. You say you're fine, but I was your friend after your mom left, I saw what your punk-ass kid self went through. I saw what you went through when your dad died. And I saw you when Gemma went down. And I see you now. You can fool yourself, and the rest of the frickin' world, but you can't fool me. You'll stick with her for the next fifty years, because that's the kind of guy you are. But you'll be miserable. And she'll be miserable too. Because she can't love you anymore and she knows it. You need to let it go. Let her go. Then you can both move on. We'll all stay friends. You know you'll always be family. But don't...don't ruin your life for this...this..."

I strain my ears, trying to hear what else Dylan says, but he's done talking.

Do you know, if I were my old self, the one Dylan is mourning for, I'd be so angry right now. I'd tell Dylan it wasn't his place to step in, that this isn't some made-for-TV drama where the big brother-slash-best friend gets to dictate people's lives. And then Dylan would make some snarky comment back and laugh at me.

But I'm not the old me and I'm not angry. Because a big part of me knows that everything he said is the truth. I'm not the same. I do have trouble remembering how to do some things. It'll come back to me, but it'll take time.

He's also right that I don't laugh as much, or cry, and it's hard to be around the kids, and I do lose track of time. All those things are true. But even more, he's right about Josh.

Josh will stay with me because he loves me, and because he said he would. And he'll do it even if he's miserable.

So, for Dylan to tell him that it's okay to leave me, I appreciate him for that. He's a terrible big brother. But also, the best big brother I could ever have. He's looking out for Josh. How could I not love him for that?

The silence from the kitchen has stretched into the uncomfortable, awkward territory. I hear a stool scrape again, discordant in the quiet.

"I'm going to say this one time," Josh says, voice precise, slicing coldly through the air. "Stay out of my life. Stay out of my relationship. We're *fine*. Everything is *fine*."

The word *fine* is sharp and hurting and sounds like it

should be a different four-letter word. I press my hand to my chest and push against the throbbing ache there.

"Don't ever talk about Gemma like that again," Josh says. "I beat your ass in the seventh grade, and I'll do it again if you ever insinuate she's in any way less—"

"Fine. Whatever. It's your life." Dylan's breathing is heavy, he's pissed. I hear him pick up his coat and car keys, then, "Don't expect my sympathy when all this goes to hell."

I listen as Dylan stomps out of the kitchen and slams the front door.

My heart pounds and I push away from the wall, expecting Josh to come around the corner any minute. I imagine he'll want to check on me and Hope.

But after a minute of silence, he still hasn't left the kitchen. Slowly, I walk around the corner, my bare feet not making any noise on the hardwood.

Josh's back is to me. He's hunched over the kitchen table, the one we picked out together on a trip to IKEA. We ran around the store, falling into all the chairs and fake eating at all the showroom tables. We picked this one, because he said it was perfect for resting your elbows on. I'd said you should never put your elbows on a table, and he'd laughed. So we got it.

Right now, both of his elbows are on the table.

My breath comes in short, hard, painful bursts, because Josh is holding his head in his hands, his back is bowed, and his shoulders are shaking.

He's sobbing.

He's not making a noise. Not a sound. But his whole body is curved inward, shaking with the strength of his tears. I've brought him to this. My laughing Josh, sobbing without a sound.

I stand fifteen feet away, unable to cross the short distance. I'm the reason he's like this.

He asked for heaven and I gave him heartbreak.

Slowly, quietly, I back out of the kitchen, then on soundless feet I tiptoe to the back of the dark hallway. Then I bend forward, wrap my arms around my stomach and try to pull myself back together, zip myself up, and keep all that panic, the swirling, unrelenting panic inside.

Josh.

He's...

What is he doing?

I'll give this a month.

I swear I'll love him again.

I'll do anything to make him smile again. His real smile.

I'll do anything so that he doesn't have to cry soundless tears in the kitchen.

I swear.

And I'll do it in a month.

If I can't make it happen in that time, then I'll let him go.

I swear.

I stand straight, pinch my cheeks, take a deep breath, and march loudly down the hall, purposely knocking against the wall and making as much noise as possible.

When I'm almost to the kitchen, I've knocked over a side table, kicked a ceramic pot, bumped a painting on the wall, and exclaimed "Oh my goodness" so loudly that Josh couldn't fail to hear me coming.

And I'm right, because when I round the corner, he's filling up the kettle with water from the faucet.

"Hey," I say.

He looks up and gives me a quirky, eye-crinkling smile. If I hadn't seen him sobbing two minutes ago, I'd never believe that anything was wrong.

Sunny side up, right?

"Hey you. Want some tea?" he asks.

I walk into the kitchen, step behind him and wrap my arms around his waist. He stiffens and sets the kettle on the counter.

"What's this?"

I rest my head against his back. "Just missed you."

The muscles in his back relax, and he stands still letting me rest against him.

"It's only been an hour," he says, laughter in his voice.

My heart thumps.

He reaches up and puts his hands over mine, pressing them into his warmth.

"I have some work to do tonight, want to stay up with me?" he asks, sounding hesitant.

In the past, when Josh worked at night, he'd take a sketchpad and draw on the couch, while I cuddled up next to him and read a book. Lately, reading hurts my head, but I can listen to audiobooks. Or I can just sit next to him and dream.

"That sounds really nice," I say.

So we end up on the couch, under a fuzzy blanket, me with a cup of honey chamomile tea, Josh with English breakfast.

I take a sip of the herby, sweet tea. The sound of Josh's pencil flicking over paper is comforting and familiar.

Which reminds me. "I realized what you painted. In the nursery."

Josh looks up from his paper and smiles, "Oh yeah?"

I grin back. "Do you think we could take Hope for a picnic sometime?"

"Definitely."

We stare into each other's eyes for a moment, his turning the hopeful color of freshly turned soil, warm and rich and welcome. And suddenly I'm thinking of a future with him, one full of picnics and arguments over whether a cloud looks like a rabbit or a motorcycle.

"What's that smile for?" he asks.

"We should go on a picnic tomorrow."

He looks at my lips and I know he's thinking of kissing again. But when he looks back up his eyes are clear of any hint of kissing.

"Alright."

I set my tea on the coffee table and lie on the couch, my feet resting on his lap.

I fall asleep to the smell of graphite and eraser and the sound of pencil scratching over paper.

15

"Saying something is meant to be
is taking the easy way out."

I WAKE UP WHEN THE FIRST PUDDLE OF LIGHT SPLASHES through the living room windows.

I'm still on the couch, but I have a soft pillow under my head and a light gray cashmere throw tucked up to my chin.

I rub my cheek against the soft fabric. Josh must've brought the pillow and blanket for me sometime last night.

I smile and blink at the filtered morning light. The apartment is quiet.

I don't know when Josh finally went to bed, and I don't remember hearing Hope last night. I'm sure she woke up, both my mom and Josh said she frequently wakes during the night, but I was completely out.

It was the first night in weeks that I haven't been woken by nurses checking my vitals, the phlegmy coughs of the man across the hall, or the ever-present half-light, half-dark twilight of hospital nights. To say I slept hard is an understatement.

I stretch and wriggle my toes. My limbs are heavy and I

feel as content as a cat sprawled in a window seat, sunlight spilling over its fur. Last night, all the worries I had, the fear over Josh's hurt, it's all soothed by the tranquility of the early morning.

It's a new day, and I'm suddenly reminded that every single day I have the opportunity to make my life what I want. Today is the first day of the rest of my life.

I grin and hop off the couch.

I gave myself thirty days to experience love, to fall in love with Josh again. But I won't even need that long. If I stay positive, if I tell myself that I'm capable of love, that I am loving, then it'll happen in a snap.

I know exactly what I'm going to start with. My stomach growls as I walk into the kitchen.

I'm going to make Josh chocolate chip pancakes, bacon, and coffee. We'll sit at the kitchen table as a family, a stack of perfect, fluffy golden pancakes between us, and Josh'll run his foot up and down my leg as we scarf down a delicious breakfast. Perfect.

The clock on the stove says quarter to six. Josh is usually up by six thirty so this is perfect.

I slide a tray of bacon into the oven and then pull down a bowl and start mixing up the batter for the pancakes. Flour, baking powder, salt, milk, eggs, butter. I whip it together, the whisk slapping the side of the metal bowl and making a metallic whooshing sound.

The griddle is hot and ready and I drizzle two perfectly round pancakes into the pan and then sprinkle a handful of chocolate chips into each.

"Perfect," I say, grinning at the empty kitchen.

Now for coffee.

The coffee maker sits on the counter opposite the stove

and before I turn my back on the pancakes, I check to make sure they're not cooking too fast. Nope. All good.

I head over and take a moment to appreciate the coffee lover's dream in front of me.

The coffee maker is new. I haven't used it before. It's one of those countertop, stainless steel espresso and coffee combo machines that are always pictured in home and style magazines.

Usually, there's a wife wearing a white oxford and pearls, the husband is rugged but smart, and there's a golden retriever curled at their feet. Their kitchen is pristine, with sparkly white marble countertops, tile floors, and flat-fronted birch cabinets, and they are both sipping perfect, tiny shots of steaming espresso.

Also, they all look like they just had fabulous sex. Well, not the golden retriever. The couple. The golden retriever probably just watched.

Pervy dog.

I snort.

See, this is why I don't have a dog. And also why I went into social media marketing and not espresso-cum-coffee maker marketing. Cum as in with or and, not cum as in, the ruggedly handsome man made the white oxford lady cum while the dog watched.

I blink at the coffee machine and try to reel in my thoughts.

Where was I?

Ah.

Coffee.

I grab a bag of beans and pour them into the burr grinder. Then once the beans are ground, I poke around the machine and try to figure out where, how, and what.

It takes about five seconds for me to realize using this thing is going to be about as simple as installing a solar array onto the International Space Station. While in space. With zero gravity.

I sigh and blow my bangs out of my eyes.

Maybe there's a manual.

I check the cupboards nearby. The drawers. I don't see anything.

The junk drawer has about twenty pens, a load of rubber bands, Post-it notes, and a stack of takeout menus, but no space age coffee machine manual.

No wonder the couple in the advertisement always look so smugly sexed, they read the manual.

It's just like when you have sex the first time. Leading up to it, you think it's going to be like that delicious cappuccino you drank at Stumptown from the barista that won the world's best barista competition, but really it's like cowboy coffee. Beans boiled in the bottom of a cast iron and then strained out through a sweaty bandana.

Huh.

Except, well, the first time I had sex was with Josh, and while it wasn't Stumptown, it wasn't cowboy coffee either.

Hmmm.

It was more...

I bite my lip as I remember the frantic unbuttoning of his jeans, the hard concrete of the floor, the whispered words, and his breath, hot against my ear.

Okay, the first time wasn't terrible.

Maybe the manual is in the pantry. I head to the door and step inside. The automatic light flips on and I look over the shelves as the door swings shut.

On the shelves are canned goods, an entire case of lime sparkling water, pasta, flour and sugar, spices, and an entire wall of baby bottles, formula, and the cutest bright yellow pureed baby food maker.

I pull it down. It's like a food processor, but cuter. The blender has a smiley face on it, and there are these sweet little food trays, and brightly colored containers with lids, and there's a recipe book and a matching spatula and oh my gosh, I've never seen anything so adorable in my life.

I could make baby food!

I flip through the recipes, and visions dance through my head of feeding Hope banana, sweet potato, pea, peach, pear, and butternut squash puree. It's like a rainbow of purees all waiting to be explored.

I pull down the blender, the containers, the spatula, and grab both recipe books, and elbow my way out of the pantry.

Then I stop.

The kitchen is full of smoke.

Crap!

The pancakes. The bacon. I forgot. I completely forgot I was making breakfast.

A high shrieking beep pierces the silence, loud and horrible. It hurts, a knife stabbing my brain. What do I do? What do I do?

I stand in the middle of the smoky kitchen, the alarm shrieks overhead, and I can't think...I can't think, I don't...

The pancakes on top of the griddle burst into flame.

I drop everything in my arms, the baby food maker, the containers, the spatula all crash to the floor. I hear screaming now, it's Hope, her angry, shrill wails even sharper than the alarm.

My eyes burn and I cough. Then I run to the sink and grab the spray faucet. I shove the faucet to high and yank the nozzle up and around and spray a high pressure blast of ice cold water at the stove. Right as I do, Josh sprints into the kitchen.

He's naked, because yeah, Josh sleeps naked.

I can't avert the spray in time, it smacks him full frontal, catching him by surprise. One second, he looks frantic, the next he's being sprayed with a blast of icy water.

He yelps and jumps out of the way. He shouts something that I can't make out over the alarm and the baby shrieking.

"It's on fire," I yell, and aim the faucet at the stove.

I can't help it, the blast catches him again and he gives me a look like, *are you kidding me?!*

My spray is completely ineffectual against the chocolate char-fueled flame on the stove.

Josh grabs a large lid from the pot rack, slams it down on the fire. The fire winks out in a second flat.

Then he yanks a potholder from the counter and flings open the oven. A nasty billow of black smoke rolls out. He throws the tray of blackened bacon into the sink.

I stand with the nozzle in my hand, cold water dribbling over my fingers.

Josh lunges to the windows, opens all of them, and then climbs on a chair and disables the fire alarm.

All of this is done in less than fifteen seconds.

My brain is only just catching up. I'm still standing in the center of the kitchen, holding the spray faucet, letting the residual water flow drip to the floor, watching naked Josh take care of business.

The smoke floats around us, snaking toward the windows and out of the apartment.

Josh jumps off the chair and turns to me. "You okay?"

I take in his wet, water-streaked chest. The flat muscles of his abdomen, how his broad shoulders taper in an upside down triangle shape to his narrow hips. He has a dark line of hair that runs from his belly button down to his shaft. My eyes catch on it, and my fingers completely loosen from the nozzle, the water trickle stops.

I blink.

"Gemma, you okay?" he asks again.

I yank my eyes up, back to his face. He's sleep rumpled, his hair sticks straight up, there's an ink smudge on his cheek, and he's watching me like he knows that I just got lost ogling his assets.

"Okay." I say, which apparently is all the verbiage I'm capable of.

He puts up a finger. "Hold that thought."

He runs out of the room, hopping over the baby food blender and containers spread across the floor, slipping a bit when he hits a puddle of water. I run a hand down my face and close my eyes.

The smoke in my throat makes me cough, which turns into a half-sob.

Dylan was right. I'm not me anymore.

I completely forgot that I was making pancakes and bacon.

First, the coffee distracted me, then finding the manual distracted me, then I was distracted by the baby food. As soon as I turned my back on the pancakes, they ceased to exist for me.

Literally, as soon as they were out of sight, I forgot them. It's just like when I didn't remember that I needed to dial a phone to make a call.

Dylan's right.

I'm not me anymore.

Tight, coiled panic snakes around my chest and squeezes. The acrid smoke bites at my lungs and my legs shake. No, no, no, no, no.

No, no, no.

I shake my head.

Pull it together, Gemma.

Pull it together.

My ears flood with a roaring noise like the loud thundering of rush hour traffic through the Lincoln Tunnel. Nonstop roaring.

I whimper and wrap my arms around my stomach, the faucet nozzle still in my hand.

Pull it together. Pull it together. Pull it together.

I'm me. I'm me. I'm still me.

It'll be okay. Everything will be okay.

Today is a new day. This is a new moment. This is the first minute of the rest of my life. It's okay.

I pull in a shuddering breath. Thankfully the steamroller of panic has receded and my heart slows its frantic pace.

Only a light haze of smoke remains, and it almost looks normal, like the smog of the west side highway during morning traffic, instead of a thick, black, smoky emergency.

I look up when Josh walks back into the kitchen. He has Hope in his arms, she's in a sleep onesie, and I realize now that it was quieter in here, because he got her from her crib and she'd stopped crying. He's bouncing her in his arms and patting her back.

He also managed to throw on a pair of low slung jeans. No shirt though.

He grins at me over Hope's shoulder. "Now that was some wake up."

His bottom lip curls into a playful smile and he winks at me.

I can't believe it. He is so...so...a rush of warmth spreads through me.

"I was making pancakes." My eyes burn and I blink away the liquid there.

It's the smoke. I'm not crying about this.

He studies me and shifts Hope in his arms. She's squirming, trying to turn around and get a look at me. She waves her arms and makes a gurgly noise.

"Hey baby," I say.

I realize that I'm still holding the nozzle so I walk back to the sink and put the hose back in its holder.

Josh walks behind me and puts his hand on my back. His fingers spread over my low back and I lean into him.

"I like pancakes," he says.

I nod. Then I can't hold it in anymore. "I turned my back for one second and I forgot. I completely forgot I was cooking anything."

I look up at him, fear pushing me, "I...what if I'm always like this...what if I never..."

I can't say any more, because what I mean is, what if I never love you again.

Instead I say, "What if all this happened before we got married because we're not actually meant to be?"

He reaches up and brushes my messy morning hair away from my face. When he does I let out a ragged sigh.

"I don't think there's such a thing as meant to be." He lifts a shoulder in a shrug, and Hope reaches up and tugs on his ear. He smiles.

"You don't?"

He shakes his head. "No. Saying something is meant to be is taking the easy way out. Because when things go wrong, you can say it wasn't meant to be after all. It's so you can stop trying and not feel guilty. That's what my mom did."

He so rarely mentions his mom that I lean toward him. I

know she left Josh and his dad, but I don't know much more. Josh doesn't talk about her.

He wrinkles his brow, then seems to shut the door on that topic.

He unconsciously pats Hopes back and says, "Everyone can say it's meant to be when things are good. Being in a relationship is easy when there's plenty of money, or everyone's healthy, or everybody has a job. But when somebody gets sick, or you go broke, or someone's in trouble, that's when you know whether your relationship is built on sand, or something stronger."

He steps away and reaches up into the cupboard, pulling out a bottle. I watch the muscles in his back as he stretches to reach the jar of formula. He has a strong back. He turns around and quirks an eyebrow at me.

"There's no meant to be," he says. "You either stick with it or you don't."

I look around the mess of the kitchen. "What if sticking with it catches the whole thing on fire?"

He gives me a slow smile. "I like playing with fire."

I think for a moment about grabbing the hose and spraying him with another blast of cold water. The look in his eyes is enough to make a virgin's cotton underwear combust.

But then he shuts that look away and says, "I'll clean up if you want to give Hope her bottle?"

I nod and hold out my arms. "Come here, baby girl."

I'm struck suddenly with the fact that Josh has been taking care of Hope for months now. She has a fresh diaper on, a cute onesie, she's clean and happy. He holds her like he's held her that way forever.

I watch him make a bottle with quick efficiency. I clutch her against me and press a quick, hard kiss to her head.

Josh looks back at me and grins.

Flustered, I drop to a chair at the kitchen table and start bouncing Hope on my knee, singing patty cake to her. When I trace the B on her stomach she lets out a happy squeal that makes my heart feel like it's going to burst.

Once Hope has finished her bottle, Josh has thrown out the ruined griddle, mopped up the water from the floor, and scrubbed the broiling pan clean of bacon char. I pop Hope into her bouncy seat and she starts to hop up and down and grab at the toys.

It's only six fifteen in the morning.

"So…" Josh says.

We stand and watch as Hope tries to chew on a plastic flower attached to the seat.

"She's got a tooth coming." Josh motions at her gumming the flower petals.

I nod, but I can't think of anything to say to that.

"Do you still want pancakes?" Josh asks.

My stomach chooses that moment to let out a long, hungry growl.

Josh laughs, "I'll take that as a yes."

He starts to turn to the stove but I put a hand on his arm to stop him. He pauses and looks at me, his eyebrow lifted, a slight smile on his face.

He seems happy, but I can't help but remember him in this same kitchen last night. Sobbing because I'm not the same Gemma he loved.

"I'm scared."

He doesn't say anything, he just waits for me to continue.

I curl my fingers into his arm. "I can't even make pancakes."

He stays quiet, watching me, but I don't say anything more.

So finally he nods and says, "It's more fun making them together anyway."

The way he says it, offhanded and casual, creates a little fissure that lets a trickle of light into that dark space inside me. I look up at him, eyes wide and hopeful.

He tilts his chin to the stove. "Come on."

We stand in front of the stove. Josh holds his hand over mine as we drop perfect dollops of batter onto the hot skillet.

He holds his hand on mine as we toss chocolate chips into the bubbling batter. He holds his hand over mine as we flip the pancakes to reveal their perfectly golden surfaces.

He holds my hand as we take the spatula and together we flip beautifully cooked chocolate chip pancakes onto a white ceramic plate.

I don't turn my back on the stove, I don't concentrate on anything but the feel of his hand engulfing mine, his calluses brushing over the back of my hand, the firmness of his grip as he clasps my hand over the spatula, the length of his fingers as we toss chocolate chips.

"More?"

I swallow and nod. I want him to keep touching me, I want the feel of his hand on mine.

I may not be able to do two, three, four things at once anymore, but I can concentrate on one thing with everything that I have.

He holds my hand as we dip a measuring cup into the batter. I fill it to the top.

"You like 'em big," he says and I can hear the laughter in his voice.

"Always have."

I don't have to look up to know that he's smiling.

The batter sizzles as he guides my hand, tilting the

measuring cup so the batter pours in a long stream onto the skillet.

When I drop the cup back into the bowl, Josh grabs a handful of chocolate chips, then presses them one by one into my hand. The warmth of the stove, and of my hands, melts the chocolate so that even after I've dropped them into the batter, my palm is still covered in melted chocolate.

Josh smiles down at me, lifts my hand, and then, with his eyes catching mine, he brings my hand to his mouth. My breath feels short and tight as he watches me watching him suck the chocolate from my skin.

His tongue is hot and his lips clamp down, sucking and nipping, and with his final hard suck on my palm, there's an answering clench in my abdomen. I suck in breath. He knows. In the back of his eyes, there's a hunger that's responding to what he sees on my face.

Slowly, he lowers my hand from his mouth, pressing a final kiss in the center, before he picks up the spatula, and we flip the pancake together.

The syrupy golden color is lovely, the smell is heavenly, chocolate and butter and crisp batter, and the sound of sizzling pancake is the sound that I imagine is happening inside me right now. A sparkling, sizzling awareness that I thought was gone.

But it's not.

Josh and I hold the spatula together and take the final pancake and slide it onto the plate.

"Hungry?" he asks.

I look at him quickly. His voice was low and sounded so much like it did when we made love that I wondered if he was insinuating something else. But he's not looking at me, he's looking at the pancakes.

I nod and pull my hand from his.

"Starving," I say. "Thank you. Thanks for making them, for helping me...thank you."

He takes his gaze from the plate of pancakes up to me, surprise in his eyes. "Of course."

"What were you thinking about?"

He smiles. "About how much I could use another cold shower."

I blush. So he was feeling exactly what I was.

"We don't have to wait."

He shakes his head. "No. You were right. I want you to be comfortable. I'll wait."

My shoulders drop. He's right. I was right. I can't make love to him until I know. It would be horrible to make love and feel *nothing*.

Except, there's hope. Because that wasn't nothing I felt when he was licking my hand. That definitely wasn't nothing.

We sit at the table. No bacon, but Josh does manage to make us two cups of espresso from the space age coffee maker. He's shirtless, rumpled, and incredibly sexy as he works the machine.

I try not to laugh as he's making it, but I do say, "Have you ever thought about getting a golden retriever?"

He shakes his head, "No. Why?"

I shrug. "No reason."

"So random," he says.

Then he puts the coffee between us and we sit and devour the stack of golden pancakes.

Just like in my early morning imaginings he runs his bare foot up and down my calf. Stroking me as he eats pancake after pancake.

I grin at him, then laugh when Hope starts to bounce up and down enthusiastically, flashing the lights and playing the music buttons on her bouncer.

"Still up for a picnic tonight?" I ask.

"Sounds good. I'll pick up some food on my way home."

"Perfect."

Two hours later, Josh heads to his work studio, a rented space with great light, huge drawing tables, white boards, computers with all the graphic programs he needs, and massive monitors.

My mom arrives, more upbeat then I've seen her in a while, ready to babysit Hope. And I head out to catch a taxi for my outpatient therapy appointment at The Whittcombe.

16

"I'll never take a hit for you again."

THE WAITING ROOM FOR OUTPATIENT THERAPY IS REALLY JUST A sitting area with blue plastic chairs spaced in a U-shape around a check-in desk.

It's open to the rest of the clinic, on the same floor that I stayed on, just down from the cafeteria. There's a door behind the check-in desk that leads to the therapy rooms. There are half a dozen physical therapy rooms with massage tables and therapeutic ultrasound machines and machines that deliver low-level electric stimulation.

Then there's cognitive therapy rooms with comfy couches, fake house plants and oil paintings that look like pastel-colored Rorschach pictures.

Finally, there's a big gym area covered in those mats you somersault on in gym class in elementary school, mirrors, and fancy gadgets to help people with mobility.

I've been in almost all the rooms, and done enough talking and exercising to last a lifetime. I know it's only been a few weeks since I woke up, but it feels like forever.

I'm on a schedule now, a couple days a week I'll come

back for a few hours of therapy with all the specialists. If I try hard enough, maybe soon I'll be able to start working again. Before the coma, my business *was* thriving. Now, it's dead on the vine. Or maybe, if I try hard enough, I'll be a great mom. Or I'll be a great wife.

Or maybe trying hard has nothing at all to do with the outcome of my life.

I can try as hard as I want and it won't change the fact that I'm here and not there, where I used to be.

I bite my lip and glare at the uninterrupted pea green of the wallpaper behind the check-in desk. When the wallpaper starts to blur, I turn away and glance toward the hall, wishing that they'd call me back. Then I wrinkle my forehead, because I think that's Ian walking down the hall.

No, I don't think. It is.

He has a huge bouquet of flowers in his hands. He's actually in jeans and a tight black t-shirt today, instead of the dirty sweatpants and ratty t-shirts he's been wearing lately. His hair is combed and he almost, almost has a spark of charisma in his walk.

I lean forward in the hard plastic folding chair and watch as he strolls closer. There's a coffee table full of magazines and a row of chairs separating us, but he's still only about fifteen feet away.

Which means I have a perfect view of the gorgeous flowers he's holding. There are a dozen white roses, frilly-edged deep purple carnations, lavender-colored lilies, baby's breath, and deep green eucalyptus all gathered into a purple and white cacophony of color. It's beautiful.

Ian slows when he sees me, then he looks at the bouquet, back at me, and winks.

My breath catches in my throat.

He's stealing the bouquet!

These are the flowers he was talking about. These are the flowers that belong to the woman he says doesn't know any better because she's in a coma.

He's *stealing* them.

Rage.

Holy, hot tamale, that's rage I feel.

I jump up and run after him, shoving through the empty folding chairs. They clatter apart and I stumble after him.

"Ian," I shout.

He's already farther down the hall, heading in the direction of the cafeteria.

"Ian. I swear, turn around this minute. Drop those flowers or there will be hell to pay!"

It's like that moment in the movies, when the out-of-towner enters the bar, the record player scratches, the music stops, and everyone turns to stare.

The white-haired man doing the crossword in the waiting room gasps. The patient walking arm in arm with a woman that looks like her daughter stops and stares. A nurse down the hall swings toward me, her mouth dropping open. The tech at the out-patient check-in desk drops her phone and snorts.

A furious heat spreads across my cheeks.

Ian grins at me. It's a rabid smile, one you'd expect on a frothy-mouthed feral dog that's just caught sight of a particularly tempting prey that he wants to take apart bite by bite. I step back, away from him, realize what I'm doing and stop. I put my hands on my hips and glare.

I'm not intimated by his feral, I'm-a-rabid-jerk, I-steal-flowers-from-comatose-patients smile.

"Put those flowers back where you found them," I say. Loudly.

We have an audience. I don't care.

I point at him and then thrust my thumb back in the direction from where he came.

"Put them back."

At my words his eyes darken and then he laughs. It's a beautiful laugh, just exactly the sort of laugh you'd expect from a horrible man that masquerades as a beautiful man. It's deep and rich and runs all over your skin and plucks up all the goosebumps on you like someone strumming the strings on a guitar.

"Goodness," the old woman says. "I'll take the flowers."

"I'll take the man," her maybe-daughter says.

I turn and shake my head at them. "That's Ian Fortune, you don't want him or his flowers."

"Who is Ian Fortune?" the older woman asks.

Her daughter whispers something in her ear.

The older woman gasps and says, "Oh my," then they turn and wander the other way.

"Do you always have to ruin my fun?" Ian asks.

I jump, startled. I didn't realize he'd made his way to my side.

I wrinkle my nose. The flowers smell amazing.

I glare at him. "I'm surprised you didn't ask that in the Hamptons when we walked in on your...whatever that was."

It was Valentine's Day, he'd brought me to his cottage in the Hamptons, but when we'd opened the door there'd already been another woman there. Naked.

His eyes light up and his rabid smile becomes more wolfish and playful. "Is this bantering, Gemma? Are we bantering?"

"No," I say, wanting to put the kibosh on anything that he enjoys. "This is me telling you to put the flowers back where you found them."

I have no idea how it's possible they let such a degenerate run around here without supervision.

"How did you even pass the volunteer screening?"

He frowns and looks up at the ceiling, like he's actively considering my question.

Then he looks back at me, smiles and says, "I'm charming."

I shake my head. "How long have you been volunteering here again?"

"Hmm. Give or take twenty years."

I look at him in shock. "Twenty years?"

He lifts an eyebrow. "Yes?"

I can't even fathom this. He's been pilfering flowers, stealing coffee, fooling people with brain injuries, and using unsuspecting patients to stroke his ego since he was *twelve*.

"What's wrong?" he asks.

He studies my face, tilting his head to take in my expression. "You look like someone just crapped on your morning meditation journal."

Ugh.

"Nothing's wrong," I say. "I'm just trying to recalibrate the past twenty years. I thought you didn't become this"—I wave my hands—"until adulthood. It freaks me out that twelve-year-old Ian was also a degenerate."

He chuckles. "Gemma, I'm more of a degenerate than you can ever imagine. It's part of my charm."

I wince. "Ugh. Yuck. I just puked in my mouth."

"I could find you a coffee to wash it out with."

A laugh escapes me. I clamp down my mouth and hope that Ian thought it was a cough and not me enjoying his idiocy.

The appearance of his chin dimple and his toothy white grin tells me he definitely realizes that he made me laugh.

This conversation needs to end.

"Take the flowers back," I say. I start to walk back toward the waiting area.

"Only if you walk with me."

I turn and frown at him. "I have an appointment."

He glances at the clock. "It's ten 'til, I bet your appointment isn't until eleven."

He's not wrong.

"I won't take them back unless you come with me." He shrugs. "I have no conscience. You have to be my Jiminy Cricket."

I put my hands on my hips. "That's blackmail."

He nods happily. "See. You're already doing your job as my conscience. I had no idea I was blackmailing you."

He winks and I imagine wrapping my hands around his throat and squeezing. Just for a second.

"Good. Job done," I say through gritted teeth. "Now you can stop blackmailing me and return the flowers. Like a good, decent human being."

He shakes his head. "Didn't you watch *Pinocchio*? He never took Jiminy Cricket's advice. Sorry."

Ian turns and starts walking away, back toward the cafeteria.

Unbelievable.

I don't want to walk with him or talk with him. He's infuriating. He makes me feel so...so...

My eyes widen.

He makes me feel.

Holy crap.

He makes me feel *a lot*.

I look at the clock over the check-in desk. I have eight minutes until my appointment.

It's decided then.

I hurry after Ian. Trust me, I don't miss the irony in this.

"Wait," I call. "Wait up."

My breath is a bit short when I catch him, even though it was only a twenty-foot jog. I tug on his t-shirt. "Slow down."

He looks down at me and I see surprised pleasure in his eyes that he quickly hides behind self-derision. "Jiminy! You didn't give up on me after all. Hoping to turn me good?"

I poke him in his bicep. It's harder than I thought so I think my finger probably hurts more than his arm, but I say, "Turn around and march back the way you came."

"I have a secret," he whispers loudly. So loudly that all the people in the cafeteria can hear him.

"What?"

"I walked past the waiting room six times before you looked up. Her room is this way." He nods at the direction he was walking.

I blink at him, trying to catch up with what he's saying. Did he...? Did he just admit that he walked back and forth in front of the waiting room to...

"Give it a second. It'll come to you," he says.

I growl at him.

He walked back and forth in front of the waiting room to taunt me.

"You wanted me to catch you," I say. Shocked, I ask, "How'd you even know I'd be here?" Eww. "Are you stalking me?"

"Settle down, Jiminy. I saw you on my first pass, then I decided, what the hell, what else am I going to do? Help Mr. Mason to the bathroom? Watch Mrs. Peters try to remember her son? Yeah. Pass on that. You're much more fun."

I sigh. "Whatever. Let's go."

I march down the hall, and Ian follows next to me, a happy spring in his step.

"How is it possible they've kept you on for twenty years?" It really does boggle the mind.

I also wonder why he never mentioned volunteering here in all the years I worked for him or during the time we dated. He was never shy about giving himself accolades. And this, from an outside, objective perspective, is a really nice thing to do.

He slows down and says in a slow, patient voice, "I told you, I'm charming."

I snort and then he grins, the full wattage of all that Ian Fortune charm bursting off him.

I blink. Sort of blinded by it. He hasn't smiled like that since his fall from grace.

But then he flips it off, like a light switch, and I'm left looking at the world-weary, scruffy, self-denigrating version of Ian.

"Hmmm," I say. "I guess."

He isn't bothered by my less than enthusiastic response.

"Here's the room." He gestures at a wooden door that's open to the hall.

I step inside and Ian follows. The room is almost identical to the room that I stayed in, except this one is more lived in.

There are clothes hanging in the wardrobe, a pair of blue slippers next to the bed, a photo album sitting on the nightstand. On the ugly striped couch that is identical to the one in my old room, there's a fuzzy fleece blanket with a Siamese cat print. The television is turned on and muted. It's playing a detective show.

Whoever stays in this room has been here for a long time. It feels lived in.

"I thought you said she was in a coma."

He looks around the room and shrugs. "I said she was too out of it to know the difference."

I narrow my eyes. I don't think that's what he said, but I can't actually remember.

I point at the coffee table. "Put them back then."

He sets them down and quirks an eyebrow at me. "How's that?"

I tap my foot, feeling antsy. "I want your word that you won't steal her flowers again."

He looks at my foot and then laughingly back at my face. "What'll you give me in exchange?"

"Blackmail," I say slowly. "Blackmail is bad."

He laughs, and the richness of it plucks at my goosebumps.

"I don't do selfless. You're ruining my free flower parade. What do I get in exchange?"

I sigh and try to think of something he'll like. "Coffee?"

He snorts. "I can find my own coffee."

"No you won't," I warn.

He holds up his hand. "Calm down."

If there's one thing guaranteed to infuriate a woman, it's a man telling her to calm down.

"How about this," I hiss. "I'll promise not to rip your balls off and make you eat them, and you'll promise not to steal patients' flowers."

Holy crap.

Ian blinks at me. Stares for a moment. I shocked him.

I've shocked me.

Then Ian murmurs, "I didn't know we were starting the dirty talk so soon. Foreplay this early in the relationship Gemma? Aren't you with another man? Saint Josh?"

I grit my teeth. Then pull in a breath. I'm angry. Really, really angry. But I can't be upset about it because I'm *feeling*. And the feeling is all red and sharp and hot and pokey and its jaggedness feels amazing.

"We're not in a relationship."

Ian's eyebrows go up. "You and Josh broke up? That was faster than I thought."

I scowl. "No! You and me. We aren't in a relationship. Josh and I are engaged."

"Mhmm," he says, and he smiles at me like a patronizing jerk.

A fresh wave of anger boils over me and I savor it like a piping hot cup of coffee burning my throat.

"You look flushed, Gemma. How's it feel? Have you been this hot and bothered with Josh too?"

I clench my fists. I'm feeling. If I can feel panic, and now anger, and this morning I felt, well, flutters, then I can feel other things. I can feel love.

"You haven't felt with him, have you?" Ian's gloating. "You only feel with me."

He has an annoying self-satisfied expression on his face.

"Leave the poor lady a note," I say, moving the conversation away from us.

"What?" He can't keep up, apparently.

I point to the notepad and pen on her nightstand. "Leave her note. Tell her sorry for stealing her flowers all this time."

Ian sighs, so I cross my arms over my chest.

"If you don't, I'll tell the nurse manager."

He shakes his head, like I've ruined our game, but he walks to the nightstand and grabs the pen and paper. I watch as he bends down and writes a short note.

It says, *Sorry about the flowers, please forgive me, Ian.* He signs it with a flourish and leaves the note by the vase.

"How's that?"

I purse my lips, trying to think about how he might wrangle out of this. "Don't come back and throw it out."

He snorts and then starts walking toward the door. "Your appointment is in two minutes."

I hurry after him. As we walk down the hall he says, "I'll wait for you. I'll walk you out."

I stop walking. No way. "It's three hours. I'm here for three hours."

He shrugs. "I literally have no life, Gemma. The second I walk out these doors I get pelted by dog shit and milkshakes. The other day, the pigeon lady in Central Park threw a pile of birdseed on me and I got attacked by two hundred ravenous birds." He pulls up his shirt. I see a bit of smooth skin and then red claw marks all down his torso. "Those beasts have talons. Pigeons are psychotic. I'll wait. I literally have nothing better to do."

He drops his shirt and I look back up at his face. Now that I notice it, he has light red scratches on his face and his neck too.

Wow.

I keep forgetting that this irritating, annoying Ian is also the most loathed man in the city and that he hasn't found a way to climb back up after falling down the ladder of success. Probably because he hit every rung on the way down, knocked out all his teeth, got a concussion and then landed in a pile of crap. I grimace.

"You could move to another country," I suggest.

He looks at me like I'm crazy. "I'm not leaving the city."

I frown. "Why not? You don't have family here. You're miserable. What's keeping you?"

He wags his eyebrows at me. "Maybe you are."

Yeah. Right. I roll my eyes.

"No. You're right. It's not you." He shrugs. Then he snaps his fingers. "It's probably the pizza. No wait, I hate pizza."

I shake my head and walk back toward the waiting room. Who hates pizza?

"I'll wait," he calls.

I wave my hand at him, hoping that he doesn't.

But, three hours later, there he is, sitting in the waiting room, reading a *Reader's Digest* from 1999.

When the door closes behind me, he looks up and smiles.

"Remember Y2K?" He waves the magazine at me.

I glare at him. "Why are you still here?"

He puts down the magazine and holds out a cup to me. "I got you coffee."

"I don't want it."

It's probably stolen. In fact, that's someone else's name written on the side. Lucia, I think. Ridiculous.

"Your loss," he says.

I shrug. I just want to process what my therapist said. We talked about my returning emotions, anger so far. We talked about Josh. Hope. We talked about love.

I practiced cognitive exercises. I did sequencing tasks. Then in physical therapy I practiced mobility and worked on stamina. There's more. Three hours more. But really, I just want to be quiet and let it all soak in before I get back home.

I don't want to talk to Ian.

I walk past him and toward the exit. He jumps up and follows me, like a stray puppy hoping for a bone, or a wolf, stalking an injured deer. Take your pick.

"Where are we going?"

"I'm going home," I say. "I don't know where you're going."

When we get to the exit he steps in front of me and holds open the door. I squint at him, trying to decipher his ulterior motive. He scoffs, like he knows exactly what I'm thinking.

"We should do this more often," he says.

"No. We shouldn't."

He smiles, like I just agreed to a second date.

"I make you feel alive, Gemma."

I ignore him and walk down the block toward the busy cross street. I'll be able to hail a cab from there.

Ian keeps pace with me. The street is busy-ish. It's summer and school is out, so kids are out on scooters heading to the playground down the block, nannies are out pushing strollers, and a few businesspeople walk by.

There are also two women half a block away.

When they saw Ian and me they both did a double take. I slow my pace. Because now they're pointing at Ian and whispering to each other.

One has short spiky black hair and the other has a nose ring and long brown hair. Neither of them look happy. In fact, they glower at us.

I think...I think I might get what Ian is saying about being the most hated man in the world. I sort of thought he was exaggerating about getting pelted with dog crap every time he stepped outside, but now I'm not so sure.

Those two women look really, really angry.

Maybe I'm being paranoid, but I think they're about to throw something our way.

"Umm Ian..."

"You can deny it all you want, Gemma. But I can tell, you want—"

Okay, yeah. Those two women are definitely up to no good.

"Ian," I interrupt.

"What?"

"That!"

I point at the two women hurrying toward us. They have a grocery bag, and one of them has pulled a container out of it.

"What this time?" He sighs. "I like this shirt."

I stare between him and the women. He's completely resigned to his fate.

"You might want to step behind me," he says.

"What? Are you kidding? We should run."

"Doesn't work."

I can't believe this. The women are only two sidewalk lengths away from us. They've pulled the plastic container open. It's a roast. A big slab of gravy-covered meat.

"Last chance, Gemma. You might want to step back. That really is a nice outfit you have on. In case I didn't mention it."

Holy crap.

With a shout, the spiky-haired woman launches the roast at Ian. He stands there, eyebrow lifted, as it smacks him square in the chest.

"That's a rump roast. You ass," the woman with the short spiky hair snarls.

The roast falls to the concrete with a squelching thud, gravy splattering around it in a starburst pattern.

"Disgusting woman hater," the brown-haired one snarls. She launches a large Styrofoam container at Ian. Mashed potatoes splatter over his t-shirt.

I didn't move fast enough. Okay, correction, I didn't move at all. I'm still standing next to Ian. I guess, I just didn't believe that two normal-looking women would actually throw food at a stranger in the street.

But they did. And now I'm also covered in mashed potatoes and gravy.

It's unbelievable.

The spiky-haired woman points at me. "You're a traitor to women." Then she pulls another item out of her shopping bag.

"Frickin' hell," says Ian.

Yeah, that about sums it up.

Still, I don't step back soon enough. My reflexes are not what they used to be.

The woman tilts back her elbow and flings the whip-cream-covered chocolate silk pie. It arches through the air, coming right at me. Ian swears. And then, at the last second, he shoves me behind him and takes the pie right in the chest.

The whip cream and chocolate explode, goop rains around us, and then the tin falls to the sidewalk, hitting with a metallic clank.

I stare at it, stunned.

Then I stare at Ian's back.

Even more stunned.

The women run past us.

Everyone else walking on the sidewalk ignores us or crosses the street to avoid us. This is New York after all.

I peek around Ian and look at the mess of food on the ground. Slowly, he turns around. I look at his meat, gravy, mashed potato, pie covered shirt and then I look up at his face.

He has whip cream and chocolate splatters all over his jaw and a big dollop on his nose.

I hold my breath, trying not to laugh. I really, really shouldn't laugh at him. It's awful. Strangers attack him in the street with poo and pies and pigeons.

But...but...

I can't help it. My eyes water and my lungs burn. All my breath bursts out of me and I laugh and laugh.

"What," he asks, "may I ask, is so funny?"

It must be really hard for him to keep that serious, censorious expression when he's covered in someone's dinner.

I wipe at my eyes. I'm practically crying I'm laughing so hard. "You—"

He lifts an eyebrow.

"—you finally did something selfless," I laugh. "And you were right. It really, really wasn't in your best interest."

I descend into laughter at the outraged look in his eyes.

"Next time, I won't step in front of you. I'll never take a hit for you again," he says. "I was momentarily confused by your Jiminy Cricket conscience badgering."

I snort and wipe at my eyes.

A cab drives past and Ian throws his arm in the air. The taxi slows and the driver rolls down his window.

"You can't come in here," the driver says.

"It's not for me," Ian says in a cold voice. He opens the back door to the cab and gestures for me to climb in. "See you next time."

I smile at him. I would've told him that he won't see me next time, because there's no reason to see each other again, but he took a pie for me, so I think that'd be in poor taste.

"Thank you."

He nods, and after I slide into the backseat of the cab he shuts the door.

I tell the driver my address, and as we drive off, I smile. I'm still smiling when I get back home.

17

*"Everything I'm doing,
I'm doing to find my way
back to you."*

MY MOM IS DOWN ON THE FLOOR IN THE LIVING ROOM, PLAYING with Hope for tummy time. She's rolled out a colorful mat with bright primary colors and toys that dangle above Hope's head.

It's the sweetest picture, and I stop for a moment to take in the cuteness.

After a minute I close the front door and my mom looks up. "There you are. How was it?"

"Good. What are you guys up to?" I walk into the living room and scoop Hope up. I press a kiss to her head and breathe in her sweet baby scent.

"Hi baby." I hold her close and she grabs for my hair, wraps a lock in her fist and tugs.

"She just woke up from her nap. She had a bottle and now we're having fun."

I shift Hope in my arms and carefully unwind my hair from her hands. "Did you have a good day with Grandma?"

Hope gives me a gummy smile and I grin back. She's so perfect. I drop to the mat and set her on the floor, then I proceed to blow raspberries on her belly and her neck and fake nibble at her fingers and toes. Her eyes squinch together and she squeals and laughs.

My breath catches. I pull my mouth away from her chubby foot.

"Did you hear that?"

My mom nods.

"Is that the first time she's laughed?"

She's squealed, she's gurgled, she's smiled, but I've never heard a full belly laugh.

My mom nods again.

Oh my word. Hope's happy. Hope laughed. I may have missed her first cry, her first smile, her first sleep, nursing her, rocking her, but she gave me her first laugh. A well of gratitude opens up inside me and I'm filled with so much thankfulness.

"My baby's happy," I whisper.

She doesn't know what's happened in our lives, she doesn't know what's gone wrong, she's just happy. She's loved. My lips wobble as I smile at her. She looks so much like Josh, black hair, dimples, full bottom lip. I'm so grateful for them both. It wells up inside me, and I blow another raspberry on Hope's foot, my heart bursting at the sound of her laugh.

"You used to laugh like that," my mom says, a wistful note in her voice.

"Yeah?" I look over at her.

She's sitting on the leather couch that I slept on last night. I didn't notice it this morning, but my mom looks classy. She's in a blue cotton dress, a silk scarf, her hair's braided. But her shoulders are slumped.

"You doing okay?" I ask.

My mom's forehead wrinkles as she studies me.

"Are you happy, Gemma?" she asks, deflecting my question.

A flame of panic sprouts in my chest. Stupid, annoying panic. I want to say I am happy, but it's not true, and I've never been able to lie to my mom.

"I'm not sad," I say.

My mom takes this exactly as you'd expect.

She purses her lips and says, "Well, how can you expect to be happy wearing a shirt covered in...what is that?"

"Mashed potatoes." I poke at the streaks of crusty white gunge on my shirt.

She takes this in stride, like she'd expect nothing else from me. "I put a new dress on your bed. When Josh gets home, you and I are going shopping."

Oh no. Not another dress. My mom's ability to turn me into a pumpkin, a construction cone and other horrendous visions is unsurpassable.

"Well..." I hedge. "We were actually going on a family picnic tonight..."

My mom shakes her head and folds her hands in her lap. "Nope. I called Josh. He understood. You and I are going shopping."

Argh. "I don't really need any new clothes."

"It's not for clothing," my mom says.

Then she blushes. My mom is pale, so in the rare cases when she does blush, her face turns as red as a cherry tomato. Unfortunately, there is only one thing that makes my mom blush.

Sex.

When I was a teenager and sex scenes would come on in movies, my mom would turn bright, technicolor red. If a friend came by the house and made a crude joke, she'd go red.

When Dylan was in his early twenties and my mom found a pack of condoms in his laundry, she turned the shade of cherry Jell-O.

The examples are endless, but the point is, she only goes red when sex is involved.

So. What the heck.

"What are we shopping for?"

Her eyes flit around the room, avoiding my gaze completely.

"Mom."

Her face lights up like the bright red Christmas lights on the Rockefeller tree.

"Mom. What are you planning?"

Abruptly, she stands and paces across the room. When she whirls back, she has a bit of her embarrassment under control.

"Your father and I have drifted apart."

My chest squeezes. I don't like hearing that. Even when you're in your thirties you don't want to contemplate your parents separating.

"I read a book," she says.

"Okay..." I have no idea what a book has to do with any of this.

"It recommended sex every day."

I cough. Gag a bit. Cough some more.

When I think I can talk again I say, "What?"

I look down at Hope, wondering if I should cover her ears. This feels like a conversation I should be covering her ears for. Even though, yeah, I know, she can't understand what my mom's talking about. But still.

My mom adjusts the scarf around her neck and straightens her shoulders.

"During your coma, I reevaluated my life. I thought you

were gone. That hit me upside the head hard. I realized I don't have anything in common with your father except our children and the parties we throw."

"Mom..."

She shakes her head and shushes me. "I want to feel valued."

Jeez.

Jeez.

"Can't you just tell Dad that?"

She tugs on the scarf at her neck and says, "The book recommended sex every day. Sex releases endorphins, dopamine, oxytocin, and in turn these lead to increased intimacy and bonding. Even if the sex lasts only thirty seconds, the sex book says—"

"Let's not talk about the sex book."

My mom frowns at me, "Please. I was born in the sixties. Talking about sex is in my social DNA."

Who is this woman, and what did she do with my mom?

"We're going to a lingerie shop," she says.

I frown at her. That's not what I was expecting her to say. I was imagining an adult toy shop or something super kinky. But then I realize exactly what a lingerie shop means. Gross.

"No way. I do not want to help you pick out lingerie for your sexathon. Gross, Mom."

I won't go to a sexy lingerie shop with my mom.

Then, shocked, I ask, "Did you tell this to Josh?"

"Of course not!" She frowns at me. "I told him we needed some mother-daughter bonding time."

I rub my hand over my face, scrubbing at my eyes. I give my mom a good thirty seconds to change her mind, but when I look back at her she's still stubbornly frowning at me. But beneath that stubborn look, I catch a glimpse of something else.

"You're really scared? You really think you and Dad are..."

Hope kicks out her feet and starts to fuss.

When she puts her fist in her mouth, my mom tsks, "Bottle time."

I follow my mom to the kitchen, Hope in my arms.

My mom pulls out the formula and a clean bottle.

"Have your feelings for Josh started to come back?" she asks.

She carefully measures the formula, waiting for my answer.

"It's fine," I say.

Then I flinch, because that's the exact thing Josh said to Dylan. We're *fine*.

My mom dumps the formula in the bottle. "It sounds like you need some dopamine too."

I'm quiet. I don't mention my ban on sex and kissing or my fear that when Josh and I are intimate I'll feel nothing. After all, maybe she's right. Maybe all I need is a rush of hormones to feel in love. But that's a depressing thought. Because if the feeling of love is only a chemical reaction to an external stimulus, then...well, then love was never meant to last.

But I don't, *can't* believe that.

"You really need my help?" I ask my mom.

She screws the bottle together and hands it to me. "No. But I'd like some support. I've never bought any lingerie." Her cheeks turn red again.

I raise my eyebrows. "You've *never* bought lingerie. In thirty years of marriage you've *never* bought lingerie?" I find that insight into her marriage somewhat hard to believe and entirely depressing.

She shrugs. "I never saw the point. Now I do."

I close my eyes. Then, "Okay. Fine. I'll help."

I'M IN THE BEDROOM. SURE ENOUGH, MY MOM HAS LAID OUT A new avocado green and hot pink striped dress.

It's small, but for once, I think it'll fit. I weigh nearly thirty pounds less than I did before getting pregnant, all my curves are gone and my figure is more like my sister's and mom's now. Stick thin. Being in a coma and having only IV nutrients for three months really did a number on my figure.

Oh well.

I look at myself in the large mirror on top of the chest of drawers. It's funny. I look different than I used to. I guess I could chalk it up to the weight loss, but it's more than that.

If I had passed this version of me a year ago on the sidewalk, I don't think I would've recognized myself. I may have thought, huh, that woman looks a little like my sister. But I wouldn't have been like, "Holy crap, that's me!"

I guess it has to do with the expression on my face, or the look in my eyes.

If I had to put my finger on it I'd say they look...worn. Like an acid-washed pair of jeans, run too many times through the washing machine.

I frown at myself, then stick out my tongue.

Josh walks into the bedroom and appears in the mirror behind me.

He gives me a lopsided smile. "Hey, Gem."

I pull my tongue back in my mouth. "Eeee...hi."

His hair is windblown and his cheeks are red. He's a little sweaty; he looks like he ran home. His smile kicks up a notch when he sees my embarrassment.

He stands next to me in front of the mirror and puts his

hand to my low back. His fingers spread out and I want to stretch into his hand, like a frisky cat.

"Was that tongue for me?" he asks.

Then he notices the crunchy mashed potato stains on my shirt. "Why do you have—"he waves his hands at my chest —"jizz on you."

I snort and then I shove at him. "It's mashed potatoes."

He lifts an eyebrow, then grins at me. Then he pulls his t-shirt over his head. The action was so unexpected that my mouth goes completely dry.

His skin is smooth, his muscles are defined, and he has a few freckles. One on his left rib, another near his belly button, and a third on his upper chest. I remember exactly how each one of them feels under my mouth. In fact, I think I dreamed about those freckles while he was in LA.

He drops his shirt to the floor and then unbuttons his pants and pushes them down his legs.

I know I saw him naked this morning, but watching him undress feels like a punch to the gut. My breath is coming out all short and tight.

Josh steps out of his pants and kicks them and his shirt toward the hamper in the closet.

Holy crap. Holy, moly crap.

"So what happened?" He's digging through the closet, pulling out a clean pair of jeans and a t-shirt.

He has no idea the effect he's having on me right now. He's completely and totally unaware that I can't take my eyes off the wide muscles of his back and his thick shoulders.

"What?" I ask, blinking out of the daze that all his naked skin has pulled me into.

"Why do you have mashed potatoes on you? Did you feed Hope some for lunch?"

He pulls the clean jeans on and yanks the t-shirt over

his head. The shirt has a silhouette of King Ghidorah, one of Josh's favorite kaiju. You'd think that a grown man wearing a fictional monster t-shirt would distract from his hotness, but no, no it does not. It just makes him *endearingly* hot.

Now that Josh is covered up again, my mental faculties are returning. I unbutton the front of my potato-covered shirt and toss it into the hamper. I have a skimpy camisole on that Josh takes a second to admire.

"It's actually a ridiculous story," I say.

He smiles and leans back against the bed, like he's taking up position to watch me undress. Did he know I was watching him undress? Is this tit for tat?

"Yeah?" he asks, and his eyelids droop down. In my mind I can hear him growling, *"Floor or bed, Gemma, you decide."*

I grab the avocado-green dress off the bedspread and step back quickly. "Yeah. Really stupid, ridiculous. I was on the sidewalk with Ian and these two women came up to us and they just randomly took this gravy-covered roast out of their grocery bag and threw it at him. And then they pulled out mashed potatoes, and they got everywhere, I mean more on him than me, but then they pulled out a chocolate pie and...and..."

I stop babbling, stutter for a second, because Josh isn't looking all relaxed and sexy anymore. He's standing now and his mouth is turned down.

"Ian who?"

"What?" I can't tell if he's confused or upset.

"You said you were on the sidewalk with Ian. Ian who?"

I have trouble swallowing the sudden lump in my throat.

"Ian Fortune?" I don't know why it comes out as a question, so I say, "Ian Fortune."

Josh looks me over to see if I'm okay, then decides I must

be, because he says, "Weird that you ran into him on the sidewalk."

When I don't respond, he says, "Must've been hard seeing him after so long. Sorry I wasn't there, Gem."

I shake my head and clutch the dress to my chest. "Well, it wasn't exactly like that."

Josh gives me a funny look.

Oh. This feels awkward. I should've mentioned Ian before. I realize that now.

"It wasn't the first time I've seen him. Ian was there when I woke up."

Josh is silent for a moment. But it's the loud kind of silence. I shift uncomfortably.

"What does that mean?"

I dig my toe into the rug. "He volunteers at The Whittcombe. He's there nearly every day. I've been seeing him around for weeks now."

At the look on Josh's face I say, "It's not a big deal."

"What do you mean it's not a big deal?" His mouth turns down in a hard line.

I shrug. "He'd come and eat lunch with me. Hang around and bother me. Bring me coffee."

At the mention of Ian bringing me coffee, Josh's face darkens. "Gemma. I didn't think I needed to tell you this, but Ian Fortune is not a nice guy."

I lick my dry lips. "I know. He's mentioned that."

Josh scoffs. "He manipulates and uses people."

I nod. "He mentioned that too."

"He isn't good for you."

"Yeah. He said the same thing."

Josh throws his hands in the air. "Then why are you..."

He looks around the room, searching for the words. He can't find them. Instead he shakes his head.

"I don't think you should see him. He's not good for you. I don't know what he wants but I guarantee it isn't for your benefit."

A hot flush burns my cheeks. He's treating me like I don't know my own mind, like I can't decide for myself whether or not someone is good for me. Josh doesn't know. He can't feel what's inside me. He doesn't understand what all this is like.

"That's not for you to decide," I say quietly. "It's not your decision."

Josh sucks in a sharp breath, like he hadn't considered that I might disagree with him.

"You'll keep seeing him?" he asks, incredulous.

"Probably. If he's there."

Josh runs a hand through his hair. He has no words.

"Why does it matter?"

He looks at me like I've lost my mind. "Why does it matter? Do I need to remind you about the Hamptons? Or how he treated you the day you miscarried?"

I flinch.

Josh sighs. "Sorry. Just. Just don't. Don't go there."

I clench my jaw. "I have to."

He stares at me, like he's not sure he knows me anymore. "Why, Gemma?"

I reach down inside, to that little spark that's still glowing from earlier today.

"Because he makes me feel," I say. My voice carries all the awe that comes with that. "Really, really feel."

Josh steps back, like he's been punched.

When I see the expression on his face I realize how that sounded, how he must've taken it. "I don't mean—"

He shakes his head, holds up a hand. "It's fine."

It's not fine.

None of this is fine.

"Your mom said she's taking you shopping tonight?" he asks, his voice completely neutral.

He's trying to pull up his I-don't-have-a-care-in-the-world smile. He can't quite manage it.

I step forward and press my hand to Josh's chest. He winces but then stands completely still.

"Do you trust me?"

He looks down at my hand pressing against his heart.

"I did," he says. Then he corrects himself. "I do."

I wait for him to lift his eyes to mine and then say, "Trust me. Everything I'm doing, I'm doing to find my way back to you."

He closes his eyes, like he can't look at me anymore.

"Just don't get lost on the way," he whispers.

I drop my hand, like I've been burned. When I step back, Josh slips out of the room, leaving me alone.

18

"There's one thing about the night
that you forgot.
We dream at night."

MY MOM AND I SPENT TWO HOURS AT A LINGERIE BOUTIQUE ON the Lower East Side, and by the time we finished shopping I was both starving and ready to get back to Josh.

It wasn't as awkward as I thought it'd be helping my mom find nighties, thongs, and lacey bras.

My mom and I even had a good laugh at the mannequins ironically posed in overtly sexual positions around the shop. At least, I hope they were ironically posed that way.

We're back now. I hold up my hand to wave goodbye as my mom pulls out of her parking spot and heads home. Her brake lights glow red at the stop sign and then she turns, disappearing into the steady stream of traffic.

I breathe in the humid evening air filled with exhaust and the smell of hot brownstone and concrete. Car horns honk a few blocks away. They're such a constant soundtrack that I only notice them when I concentrate on the noise.

I shift the bags in my arms. I have a discreet bag filled with tissue paper from the lingerie shop. I couldn't help joining in my mom's enthusiasm for all things lacey and see-through. I also have a plastic takeout bag that's so full of food, the handles are leaving red indents in the skin of my wrists.

I don't feel great about the way that Josh and I left things tonight. Honestly, I don't feel great about how things have been since I woke up.

Tonight, I'm going to start fixing them.

I hitch up the bags and hurry into the apartment. The soothing colors and the quiet greet me. I shut the front door and block out all the horns, traffic and noises of the city.

Josh is on the couch in the living room, a sketchpad in his lap. He has a pencil behind his ear and an art pen in his hand.

When I close the door behind me, he stiffens, but keeps drawing for a few seconds before looking up.

"Hey," he says, smiling hesitantly. That hesitant smile, it feels like the Grand Canyon opening up between us.

He carefully sets the drawing pad on the couch next to him and stands. "You have fun?"

"Yeah. A lot of fun."

"Good." He puts his hands behind his back and nods, waiting for me to say more.

I look around the living room. It's clean, all the baby stuff is put away and I don't see Hope.

"Did you put Hope to bed?"

"About thirty minutes ago," he says in a stilted, awkward way that he's never had with me. Jeez. Jeez.

"What are you up to?" I ask, hoping to break the itchy, uncomfortable tightness arching between us.

He looks back to the sketchpad, and his expression lightens a bit and his shoulders relax.

"I'm working on a new concept. I'm swamped during the day working on the spinoff of Grim with the studio, busy as all get out. But the whole thing is creativity by committee. It's frustrating and stifling and frankly working that way is as fun as running a cheese grater over your balls."

I snort and his eyes crinkle. I see the irreverent Josh peek out at me.

"Don't tell them I said that."

There's a flutter low in my belly at the grin on his face.

"I won't." I smile back and make the my-lips-are-sealed gesture.

He grunts in appreciation then searches my face before continuing. "I've learned a lot these last few months. But the biggest thing I've learned is that I make comics, not television. This is the last time I'll be doing anything like this."

"You really don't like it?"

"Cheese grater, Gem," he says slowly.

And I laugh.

We're both surprised by the sound. He looks at me for a moment and then we both start to speak at the same time.

"So what're you drawing—"

"What do you have in the bags?"

We both stop. He clears his throat. I shuffle my feet. This feels like a first date. That first date we never had.

At that thought I step forward and say, "I still wanted that picnic. I brought food."

I hold up the plastic bag, the handles still digging into my forearm. "We could pop a blanket on the floor..."

His eyes soften. "That sounds perfect."

"Yeah?"

His eyes drift to my mouth.

"Yeah," he says, and then I remember how much Josh likes being on the floor with me.

The discreet lingerie bag feels heavy and hot in my hands.

"I'm starving," Josh says.

He takes the plastic bag full of food and heads back into the living room. I drop the bag of lingerie next to the door and follow him. In the living room I spread the fuzzy couch throw blanket onto the plush area rug. I drop to my knees and when Josh sprawls out next to me, I grab the takeout bag and start pulling out containers full of food.

"What'd you get?"

I tap the lid of each container. "Spring rolls, edamame, tom kha gai."

Josh groans when I mention his favorite soup and I continue tapping each lid. "Green papaya salad, lemongrass chicken, tofu skin wrapped with bok choy, mango bubble tea, and drum roll please…"

I drum my fingers on the containers top, making a snare drum noise. "A four pack of chocolate pudding cups."

Josh laughs. I knew he would. I always crack him up when I grab delicious dinners and then top them off with ninety-nine-cents dessert snack packs of pudding or Jell-O from convenience stores.

He's still laughing when he leans forward to kiss me. It's automatic. A natural reaction to what we've done a thousand times. I make a joke, he laughs and presses a kiss over my mouth. It's something we've done so often it's almost a muscle memory. It's natural.

What isn't natural is that he stops six inches from my mouth, and I see the exact moment that he realizes what he's doing. He blinks and then makes like he wasn't going to kiss me and instead reaches forward to grab the container of soup.

"You did good," he says.

He grabs a spoon from the bag, peels the lid off the

container and starts to eat like it's his job. The smell of coconut, lemongrass, and chicken drifts up from the soup.

My heart knocks around in my chest, like a can kicked down an alley, clattering about noisily. I'm the one who doesn't want kissing.

I lick my lips, tasting the flavor of coconut in the air. I reach for the box of spring rolls and take a big bite. At the crunch of the roll, Josh looks up and smiles.

"Question," he says.

"Yeah?" I take another bite.

"You said you feel with Ian."

I stop chewing. He turns to the containers, opening the lids, peeking at the contents. When he finds the chicken he pulls the whole container in front of him.

I swallow my bite of spring roll, but it sticks in my throat. I drink a bit of tea to clear it away. Josh watches me while slowly chewing a piece of chicken.

"I do," I say.

Then I shake my head. "It's not a good feeling. He makes me feel anger, rage, frustration. But it's a feeling."

Josh takes a second to process what I'm saying then he pushes the green papaya salad toward me. He knows that's my favorite.

He waits for me to scoop some up, then says, "That's all it is?"

I nod. "That's all."

He's quiet while he eats a few more slices of chicken, then pulls open the bok choy.

It's comfortable sitting cross-legged on the blanket, scooping up spicy bits of food. We're not in a park, staring up at the sky, but we're still together on our little island of blanket, eating a good meal.

I nibble on a handful of salted edamame while I watch

Josh go back to the soup and savor the flavor. I can tell he's thinking things over. When the soup is gone he puts the empty carton back in the bag.

"When you woke up," he starts.

I nod and he continues, "You said you couldn't feel. That you didn't feel like you loved me anymore."

"Right," I whisper.

His eyes search mine. "But now you say you feel anger. Is there anything else?"

I push the food away from me. "You're asking if I'm starting to feel love again?"

"Yeah," he says, voice thick.

I think about the past few weeks and try to find a way to describe it. "It's hard to say."

He frowns and I continue, "Imagine it's the middle of the night and the sky is completely covered in clouds, so there's no stars and no moon. And you're in the middle of nowhere, so there aren't any city lights either."

"Alright," he says. "Pitch dark."

I nod. "I remember what it was like to live in the daylight. You were like the sun." I smile at him and he focuses on me, giving me all his attention. "Now though, it's all dark. Sometimes, the clouds move, and I catch a little light from a star. That's a bit of happiness, or a flash of anger. When I hold Hope, there's a star, poking through the clouds. When you're near me, I feel the echo of day, like I know the morning's coming. Sometime. But you know, the sun, it's all the way on the other side of the world. I can't reach it."

Josh pushes his hair back from his forehead and lets out a long breath.

Then he says, "I guess the sun will just have to come to you."

Then he pushes the containers aside, clears a space on

the blanket and gently pulls me in between his legs. He leans his back against the leather couch and I lean against his warmth. After a minute, I rest my head on his chest.

We both look up at the ceiling, and I imagine it's the sky, with clouds floating overhead.

"What was it like while I was in the coma?"

He tenses, then he puts his arms around me and pulls me even closer.

He rubs his hands over my arms. "It was hell, Gemma."

I wait for him to say more.

"I didn't know if you were gone or if you were coming back. I didn't know what you wanted. I couldn't talk to you and ask. Hope was in the NICU, your mom was a wreck. Hell, I was a wreck. At the start, every time one of Hope's doctors or nurses asked what I wanted to do, my first thought was, what would Gemma do. It scared me, not knowing. Then, a few weeks in, I stopped wondering what you'd do, and that scared me even more. When I had to go out to LA to work on the set, a thousand times a day, I'd think, I can't wait to tell Gemma about this, then I'd remember…"

"You couldn't."

His breath tickles my ear as he slowly blows out a long sigh. "Right. So those thoughts stopped coming too. It was hell. I felt so guilty being in California while you and Hope were here. My body was there, but the rest of me was with you. Then Hope got out of the hospital, and I brought her home. I'd like you to think it was easy."

"It wasn't?"

He shakes his head, "No." That one word carries a whole lot of weight.

"When we came home, and you weren't here, I didn't take it well." He shrugs and I think about him in the kitchen, his shoulders bowed, sobbing quietly.

"But then, Hope had to be changed, fed, put to bed. There was too much for me to learn. To do. I didn't have time to think. Yet every time she did something new, smiled, made a noise, kicked her feet, grabbed my finger, I'd think, I wish Gemma were here."

He pauses, and his voice breaks when he says, "I needed you...every day..."

His heart thunders against my chest. "I never thought you'd leave me."

I didn't mean to. I didn't want to.

His hands still on my arms. "And you still haven't come back. You woke up, but you're not back yet."

"I'm sorry." Then I admit my greatest fear. "I may never get back."

His hand drifts up to my hair and smooths it back from my face. "I know you said that you don't want sex. You don't want kissing. But I'd like to touch you."

I turn my head and tilt my chin to look at him. I think about dopamine, and oxytocin, and all the chemical rush that people supposedly experience when they're intimate. And I bet you don't need sex to experience them either. I have to tell Josh my fears. It's not fair not to.

"I'm scared that when we kiss or have sex, that I still won't feel anything."

His eyes sharpen on my face, catching onto the implication that eventually we will have sex, and that right now, I do want to touch.

"Then we'll just have to lead into it," he says. "Build up to it."

I search his eyes.

"Trust me?" he asks, repeating what I asked earlier today.

I'm scared, but...

"I do. Always."

The reserve vanishes from his face and the cocky, Gemma's-my-playground smile pops into existence.

"Lie down," he commands. He moves out from behind me and makes room on the blanket for me to sprawl out.

I let my limbs fall loose and my hair spread in a halo around me. Josh leans over me, his muscles taut, his eyes hungry. I blink up at him. The overhead light shines around him, blinding me.

"Tell me what feels good."

I lick my dry lips. "Okay."

He tugs at one of my shoes and I stiffen at the implication. "Trust me?"

I relax back into the blanket. "Yes."

He takes off my other shoe, tossing both of them onto the rug. Now my feet and legs are bare, I'm only wearing the short striped dress that has climbed so far up my legs that my underwear is almost visible.

"If it's too much, tell me to stop."

I nod, "Okay."

"Close your eyes," he says. I look at him, and when I do, his lips curve into a smile, "Close your eyes, Gemma."

I do.

"Keep them closed."

"I will."

I hear him pull his phone out of his pocket and then music starts to quietly play over the living room speakers.

"It's Liszt. Liebestraum," he says, and somehow with my eyes closed his voice is richer and deeper.

"It means Love Dream." His fingers grasp my ankle and I let out a gasp.

His hand is hot and the callouses on his fingers scrape over my skin. "I was thinking, when you were describing the dark, that there's one thing about the night that you forgot."

His thumb slips up my inner ankle and a spark of light shoots up my calf, higher.

"What?" I ask, wanting him to continue.

"We dream at night. We dream, Gemma."

Bright pinpricks of light filter through my eyelids as he moves over me, casting shadows of stars onto my closed eyelids.

The piano music starts to pick up and as it does, he slips his hand up my calf, drawing up and up and up until his fingers swipe the sensitive skin underneath my knee.

I gasp as his fingers play over me, and when his hands slip higher, reaching my thighs, I let out a ragged noise that is covered by the crescendo of the music.

All of my senses are concentrating on where Josh is going to touch me next.

His hands curl around my hips, trail to my inner thigh and up, where an answering throb pulls deep inside me.

The longing in the piano music, the soulful way his fingers brush over my thighs, up to my hip bones, how he teases the edge of my dress, it all pulses in the darkness.

And I wonder, is this a dream? Where my body thrums in time to the music, where I'm pulled taut from the dragging tension of Josh's fingers over my skin? Where my body feels so much that I can barely remain still on the floor, but where my emotions still remain hidden in the periphery?

My dress rustles as he brushes the edge of the fabric and slowly, slowly inches it up, over my hip bones, over my abdomen, leaving my skin to pucker in the cool air.

His fingers circle over my hip bones, slide under the lace of my thong, and then his hands roughly, tightly grasp my hips.

I sink down into the dark well of longing that's growing between my legs, underneath the heavy pressure of his hands pinning me down. It's dark there too, in the swallowing, hungry need.

Josh's breath sounds harsh and jagged over the music as he slowly drifts higher, fingers kissing my stomach, my ribs, the underside of my breasts.

Then he reaches up and brushes his hand over the dip at the base of my neck.

My eyelashes flutter at the contact but I keep my eyes closed, even when he leans down, presses his lips to my ear and starts to whisper.

"If you can't feel my love, I want you to feel this. Me touching you." His thumb presses into my collarbone and then up my neck and along my jaw.

"Can you feel this?" He takes his fingers and presses them gently into my lips, a kiss.

"Yes," I whisper.

He groans at my yes. His fingers pause on my mouth, pulling down on my lower lip and touching the wetness there.

Then he starts to move again. His hands fall over my cheeks, my closed eyelids, my jawline, his hands greedily stroke me, matching the mounting pace of the piano. I can barely drink in the sensations.

He pulls his fingers through my hair, grasps it in his hand, then gently tugs. I arch my neck, lifting to him, and he presses his fingers to my throat, another kiss that isn't a kiss.

Can you feel this? He seems to ask.

"Yes," I say.

He tugs again, pulls my neck back further. I hold my breath, concentrating on the ache that's growing.

"It's a dream," he says, and his fingers tease my bare skin, each touch a star in the darkness. "And in dreams, we can feel whatever we want. We can be whatever we want. We can do whatever we want."

His hands work back down my ribcage, licking at the underside of my breasts, stroking my abdomen. My breath comes in short, heavy, bursts.

"We can imagine any future we want," I whisper.

In this future, I imagine Josh and me, married, in love.

"What are you dreaming?" His voice is rough and it scratches over me, so that I instinctively arch up, to get closer to him.

"I'm always dreaming of you," he says, answering for me.

His hands cup my thighs, stroke the sensitive place at the edge of my panty line.

I clench my thighs and a hot, needy, desperate feeling floods over me. A stifled sob escapes my lips.

I'm feeling. The physical sensations, every single one of them, rush over me, overwhelming my senses. I want nothing more than to have Josh pull down my thong, press himself over me, and slide into me.

"What's your dream?" he asks again.

His fingers press into my thighs, trailing not-kisses down my legs, leaving marks of possession on me.

My eyes are closed, the music is mounting, Josh's touch has carried me through the darkness, but I'm still grasping thin air, trying to find...me.

I want him. I want him desperately. I ache for him. I'm wet, needy, throbbing.

But...

I open my eyes. He's staring at my mouth. Fixated on it. His cheeks are flushed, his eyes are dark and hungry.

When he sees that I've opened my eyes, his flare and his fingers tighten on my hips. He looks like a man who is about to make love for hours. And hours.

Floor or bed, Gemma?

I stare into the depth of his eyes, get lost in the darkness of them.

But...

I'm still grasping in the dark, the feeling of love, of us, slipping like water through my closed fingers, until I'm holding nothing.

"Why are you crying?" he asks.

I blink, and feel the hot burn of them. "I didn't know I was."

He nods, like this makes perfect sense, and then reaches up and wipes the moisture away from my cheeks.

"I love you," he says. My throat tightens and he smiles. "Don't worry, Gemma. It'll come back."

"I want to love you," I say. "I desperately want to love you. In my dreams, I do."

He stares down at me for a moment, an expression on his face that leaves my chest feeling bruised. Then he carefully pulls my dress back down until it hits my thighs, covering me up.

"Do you want to see what I've been working on?" he asks, nodding to his drawing pad on the couch.

"I'd like that very much," I say. Then, "Thank you for letting me."

The right side of his mouth kicks up into a half-smile. "Of course. Who else would I show?"

We climb onto the leather couch, I cuddle into Josh's side, and he takes me through the pages of sketches and world-building he's working on. A new comic. A new hero. A new adventure.

"Does this mean you're leaving Grim and Jewel behind?"

He reaches up and taps my nose. "They have their happily ever after."

"Do they?"

He knows what I'm asking. "They do."

I believe him. One hundred percent. His confidence could carry the world on his back, like Atlas shouldering the globe. It's nearing eleven and my eyes droop. I try unsuccessfully to cover a yawn.

"Tired?"

"Mhmm." I remember that instead of falling asleep on the couch, we'll probably sleep in bed together. A warm flush travels through me.

There's a buzz and I look quickly at the door. It sounds again, an insistent, impatient ringing. It's the doorbell. "That's weird."

Josh frowns at me, then crosses to the door and hits the video intercom. "Hello?"

I walk up behind Josh, wondering who the heck shows up unannounced at eleven at night. The video screen comes on.

It's a beautiful woman, short black hair, impatient brown eyes, sharp jaw, wide lips. She glares at the video camera. I recognize her, I don't know who she is, but for some reason I recognize her.

"Lisa?" Josh says. He sounds as confused as I feel.

A cold sweat breaks out on the back of my neck.

Lisa leans closer and says, clear as day, "Josh, you ass, why aren't you answering your phone? I'm pregnant. Let me in. We have to talk."

Suddenly, I realize why she looks familiar. She's Lisa Perry. The woman from the magazine covers. The actress the magazines claimed was dating Josh.

There's a rushing, deafening sound in my ears. And although I know Josh is talking, I can't hear a word he's saying, I can't hear anything but the noise of my world falling apart again.

19

"Everything that feels bad is good."

I'VE EXPERIENCED THIS EXACT FEELING BEFORE. Unfortunately, we're well acquainted.

The roiling volcano of panic that had been dormant starts to rumble, threatening to overwhelm me.

It rushes up, engulfing me. Which is when self-preservation takes over. My thoughts stop, my body goes numb, my feelings turn off, and I step outside of myself. Everything seals off. Even my hearing. I go back to observing myself from far away. There I am, standing next to Josh while he buzzes Lisa into the apartment.

Two minutes ago Josh was practically making love to me on the floor, promising undying love, and now, he's inviting his pregnant lover (is she his lover?) into our home. Where our baby sleeps not fifty feet away.

I'm outside of my body, completely disconnected.

Josh turns to me, he's upset. He rubs his hand through his hair and shakes his head, agitated. I can't hear him, but I can read his lips, "Sorry, Gemma. Sorry."

My head moves up and down, like a puppet on a string, nodding yes.

"It's okay," I think I say.

I'm cold now, shivering, sweaty cold. The me outside of me, watching all this unfold, is urging me to walk away, to leave, to grab Hope and go. But the me that's stuck inside the numbness can't move from the spot my feet are stuck to.

Josh opens the door and the woman flings herself into his arms. I stand still and watch her close her eyes and give a happy, delighted smile.

Then, like the world is in slow motion I watch her open her eyes and see me standing behind Josh. Her mouth makes a perfect, surprised O. She unwraps her arms from Josh and steps awkwardly back.

Then she blushes. Her Snow White pale cheeks turn petal pink, and I can see why she's a much-loved movie star. She's really, really beautiful.

She says something to me, her mouth is moving, and I know she's talking, but I can't hear a word she says.

I nod.

Josh says something to me. He looks really upset. He's studying my face like he's trying to decipher every single emotion that I'm feeling and everything that I'm thinking. If I could I'd tell him what I'm feeling. Nothing. I feel nothing. I'm thinking about nothing.

I'm like a victim after a car crash. My emotions and my brain have shut down in self-preservation.

Lisa looks between Josh and me. It's clear she didn't realize I was here, maybe she didn't even know that I existed. It's also clear she really wants to talk to Josh and she wishes I weren't around.

Josh says something else. I see his lips moving, but I can't make sense of the words. The panic is threatening to overwhelm the numbness and the only thing I can think of is escape. I need to get away. Both Josh and Lisa are looking at me, waiting for a response. I don't know what they're asking me.

My lips are numb and heavy. I push out through them, "I'm going to go check on Hope."

Josh wrinkles his forehead, like this isn't any answer he expected. He reaches out and touches my hand. I look down and he pulls away. When I look back up I smile at him. It's my brilliant, happy smile, one that even numb Gemma can give.

Josh frowns, but I can't stay a second longer. I leave Josh and Lisa at the front door and hurry down the dark hall to the nursery.

Hope is asleep. Her baby mouth is open, and there's a touch of drool falling onto the crib sheet. I drop down next to her crib, lie on my side, and then pull my legs up to my chest, wrapping my arms around my knees.

Slowly, as I stare at the wall of the nursery, the one Josh painted of our meadow and our clouds, I come back into myself. The wall of numbness recedes and I can think again, I can feel my body again.

I poke at the swirl of sensation inside me. There's low-level panic. Okay. There's anger. That's new. So far, I'd only felt that with Ian. There's overwhelming sadness. That's new too.

Maybe Ian was right, everything that feels bad is good. Maybe I need pain to jumpstart my heart.

Tonight, Josh told me a bit of how hard it was when I was in the coma. *It was hell*, he'd said. I don't know that hell even touches the edge of what it was. I brush away the wetness on my cheek.

Here's the thing. If being with Lisa helped him get through the hell of it all, then...

If she was the one bright bit of sunlight in the hell that was his life, then...

If he broke, then...

Josh is good. Josh has always been good. But even good people make mistakes.

He asked me if I trust him.

I trust him enough to explain.

I lift my hand to the crib mattress and reach in until I feel Hope's hand. I close my eyes and listen to the sound of her breathing.

After an hour of waiting for Josh to come and him not coming, I drift off to sleep.

~

I WAKE UP AT SIX, MY BACK STIFF AND MY LEFT ARM HALF-ASLEEP and full of pins and needles.

Sometime in the night, Josh came in and put a blanket over me. I've been home for two nights, and haven't slept in our bed for either of them. I stand and arch backwards, rubbing my sacrum. I glance at Hope. She's asleep.

It looks like Josh came in and took care of her too. She has on a new onesie, and from what I can tell, a fresh diaper. There's an empty bottle by the crib.

I tiptoe down the hall toward our bedroom, then push open the door. I stop at the entry. Josh is sprawled out across the mattress, the blankets are kicked on the floor, and the white sheet is tangled around him.

He's completely out, his breathing is rhythmic and heavy and he looks exhausted. His black hair is a wild mess and there are blue smudges under his eyes.

I wonder how long Lisa stayed and what time he got to bed.

I squeeze the edge of the door. It's hard to take my eyes away from him. He's facing my side of the bed, like he expects that I'll be there, sleeping with him. His hands are curled into my pillow, as if even when he's asleep he wants me there.

Oh Josh. What the heck are we doing?

I sigh and then tiptoe into the bedroom, careful not to wake him. We need to talk, but I'd rather do it tonight, not in the morning, when we're both exhausted and my mom is due to arrive in half an hour.

I'm heading over to The Whittcombe again for my half-day of therapy.

I grab a pair of jeans and a silk camisole from the closet. I forgo underwear and bra, my drawer squeaks and I don't want to wake Josh.

I grab a quick shower, slip into my clothes, and put my hair in a messy bun. I'd forget about the makeup, but the bags under my eyes are enough to make babies cry, so I spend a few minutes trying to make myself look a little less *Night of the Living Dead* and more "just need some coffee."

A few minutes 'til seven my mom pulls up. I open the door so she doesn't have to knock or ring the buzzer and wake Josh.

"I'm going to head out to therapy early," I tell her in a quiet voice. "Josh is still sleeping."

"Ahh. The lingerie did its job," she says, her eyes sparkling. She doesn't notice the unopened bag of lingerie still sitting on the floor next to the front door.

"You look exhausted," she tsks at my messy bun and tries to smooth out my flyaway bangs.

"I am," I say truthfully.

I lean in and peck her cheek. She's pretty amazing. She agreed to come on days that I have therapy so that Josh can have some uninterrupted worktime since he's at the final crunch point of his contract. She's pretty much a life saver. We could hire a nanny or a helper, but I'd take Grandma over a nanny any day.

"Thanks for watching Hope. I know it's a long drive."

She waves that away, like driving two plus hours is no big deal. "You won't need me at all in a bit. Then what'll I do?"

I think about the fact that Josh may have another baby soon. He may decide to be with Lisa. Which means...I'll be moving back home? We'll have shared custody of Hope? I shut down the door on those thoughts. I'm not going to consider any of it until I talk to Josh. Instead I steer the conversation to the familiar comfort of family quirks.

"What'll you do? You'll baby Dylan of course."

She scoffs. "That boy."

"He's a man-child," I say, rolling my eyes.

I hear Hope let out a little mewl, her just waking up cry. My mom does too.

She waves her hands toward the front door. "Go on now. I'm here for my granddaughter time."

I close the door behind me and hurry out into the morning light. Ten minutes into my taxi ride to The Whittcombe my phone chimes with a new text. I shift on the black vinyl seat of the cab, and it squeaks as I root around in my purse for my phone.

The taxi driver has a large cup of coffee in his cup holder and the smell of hazelnut creamer and his cologne fills the car. But as I dig around in my purse, a deep hobo bag, the smell of baby wipes and pacifier puffs up to me. I fish out my phone and look at the glowing screen.

It's Josh. I read the first few words: *Morning. You should've woken me up. Sorry about last night, I...*

I shove my phone face down onto the cracked vinyl seat. The coolness of the phone case presses into my hand.

I stare out the window at the people walking to work, the dog walkers leading dogs to the park, the kids weaving their scooters around slower pedestrians.

I stare at the brown brick buildings with uniform windows, the perfectly spaced fire hydrants, and the newsstands, fruit stands, and coffee stands. The phone warms under my hand, a heated reminder that Josh is on the other side of the phone, waiting for my response.

He's probably in the kitchen, making a cup of coffee, checking his phone screen, waiting for my reply text to pop up. I picture him in ripped jeans, a Kumonga t-shirt, barefoot, getting ready to head to his studio, waiting for my reply.

I grip the hard edges of the phone until my fingers hurt.

I'm not having this conversation over text. *I'm not.*

I'll see him tonight. Without looking at the display, I power off my phone and shove it back into my purse. I take an eraser and wipe away the image of Josh, barefoot and messy haired, from the blackboard in my mind.

20

"This may not be the life you want,
but it's the one you've got.
Live it."

I SPEND NEARLY TWO HOURS SITTING AT AN OUTDOOR CAFÉ table, sipping a French press coffee and picking at a dinner plate-sized buckwheat crepe filled with gruyere, tomatoes, and basil.

I'm at a little creperie a few blocks away from The Whittcombe. I'm not hungry, my stomach feels like it's been twisted around and turned inside out, but I'm forcing myself to eat—at least a little.

The morning commute exhaust hangs in the air and as the day heats up I know it's going to be a hot one. I already have a sheen of sweat at my hairline, and an occasional drop of sweat slips between my breasts. My silk tank is sticky against my skin.

People hustle by, not sparing a glance for me or the little metal tables and chairs shoved against the brick café wall. A steady stream of taxis and buses chug by. A construction crew noisily sets up scaffolding a few buildings down.

I rest my chin in my hand and watch, taking care not to think. To just watch and let the world flow by.

It takes almost the whole two hours, but finally I realize that something's different. I'm not overwhelmed by all the input. I don't need to close my eyes, I don't feel itchy or dizzy, or like my brain is being scraped from all the sights and the sounds. I'm not so sensitive to all the sensory input.

I can sit in it and be okay.

I sit up straight and look around, taking in the frenetic bustle of New York in the morning.

I'm getting better.

I'm feeling, I'm taking in sights and sounds, I'm getting better.

My hands shake as I grab my coffee cup and take a long swallow.

Then I open my purse and reach for my phone to call Josh. He's going to be so happy.

Then in a flash I remember that Josh had sex with Lisa Perry while I was in a coma. That Josh and I probably aren't Josh and I anymore. I drop my phone back into the depths of my purse.

And then I delete the thought that Josh and I aren't Josh and I anymore.

I don't know how we're going to get out of this, but if I doubt that he loves me, if I doubt us, then I may as well end things now.

I flag down the waiter and then head toward The Whittcombe.

There's still an hour until my first appointment, but I don't mind sitting in the cool air-conditioned waiting room. I'll read a twenty-year-old *Reader's Digest* and zone out to the elevator music they have on repeat.

When I push open the double glass front doors, I immediately realize that my plan to zone out isn't going to happen. Even in the lobby, where I show my ID at the security desk, I can hear a band warming up, playing little snatches of jazz music.

"What's going on?" I ask.

The woman at the security desk, her nametag says Marina, shrugs. "It's birthday day. They do it every year. Cake. Pizza. Music. Whatever."

"Whose birthday is it?" It seems like a big deal.

She frowns. "No one's."

I have no idea what that means. "Then why..."

"The activity coordinator thought it'd be a great idea to celebrate every patient's birthday on the same day. So, it's happy birthday everyone. Staff, patients, family. Everybody is special today." She wiggles her fingers in the air and gives a sarcastic, "Yay."

Okaaay. "Happy Birthday then."

She blinks at me, and I think she's trying to figure out whether or not I'm joking.

Then I guess she decides that she doesn't care whether I am or not because she says, "Happy flipping birthday."

I give her a wide smile and she grunts.

And that's the extent of Marina's interest in me or what's happening inside. She hands me back my ID, and I finish signing in. She puts a time stamp next to my name, and I walk on through the entry, heading toward the waiting room. As I do, the music gets louder.

Honestly, I'm amazed. It's only nine in the morning, and there's already red balloons and floral-themed birthday cards taped to each patient door. Far down the hall, near the cafeteria, there's a metal tray with a massive sheet cake.

I'm curious about the band warming up. They're probably in the community room just past the cafeteria, but as I near the waiting room, I stop walking.

Ian Fortune is sprawled out in a chair at the edge of the

waiting room, his long legs spread out into the hall, a tripping hazard to everyone that passes.

He's in jeans, a form-fitting black t-shirt, and his hair is slicked back. He looks better than the last time I saw him when he was covered in potatoes and pie.

In fact, he looks better every time I see him, like he's slowly putting himself back together.

He's reading a magazine. My eyes snag on the headline, "Who's the Father?"

It's above a picture of Lisa Perry, stressed out with a hand on her slightly (okay miniscule-y) rounded belly. Under Lisa there's photos of three men—one of them Josh.

I make a strangled, gagging sort of noise. When I do, Ian looks up. He sees me, and a slow, teasing smile spreads over his face.

"Gemma. What a surprise. Happy birthday. We should celebrate," he says, his voice laden with innuendo.

But then he takes in my expression, which I'm guessing is pretty awful, because his smile falters and his teasing, I'm-a-sexy-bad-boy look falls apart at the edges.

I glance back at the cover of the magazine he's reading, yup, the cover's still the same, and I go cold.

Surprisingly, Ian quickly puts the magazine face down on the chair next to him, almost as if he's sorry that I saw it. Then he stands smoothly, with that built-in grace I remember he used to have, and takes my arm.

"Walk with me, birthday girl."

"It's not my birthday."

He squeezes my arm, "Au contraire. It's everyone's birthday today."

I remember that he's been volunteering here for years, so to distract myself I ask, "Do you always come for this?"

"Every year."

He leads me down the hall at a slow, sedate pace, toward the cafeteria.

"Why?"

He looks down at me, quickly passes his eyes over my face, cataloguing my expression—I think to see how I'm holding up—then says, "This is the only day in the entire year when people wish me happy birthday. Why wouldn't I come?"

I'm so stunned that I stop walking. "Is that true?"

His flashes me a grin and his famous chin dimple makes an appearance. "Would I lie to you?"

"Yes." I don't even have to think about that one.

He laughs, a full belly laugh, and it vibrates through him and spills onto me. "Maybe I want to eat cake that hasn't been thrown at me?"

I start walking again, and because he's holding onto my arm, he starts again too.

"You don't have to lie to distract me," I say. The backs of my eyes itch and I fight the urge to rub at them.

Ian glances at me from the side of his eyes. I forget sometimes how tall he is. And how perceptive.

"So, Saint Josh fell from his pedestal."

His words make me angry. "I never said he was a saint. And it's none of your business."

I try to pull out of Ian's grip, but he shakes his head. "Gemma. Easy. I only mean that even though I said he would fall, I'm sorry that I was right."

My anger dissipates, like a popped balloon. I change the topic.

"When is your birthday? Really?"

I'm surprised I don't actually know this. In seven years of worshiping Ian, I never looked up his birthday.

He shrugs. "I don't celebrate it."

"Why not?"

I love birthdays. My family always has huge celebrations, all of us crammed around the dinner table, paper plates, party hats, and a big messy cake stacked full of candles.

"I'd rather talk about you." He guides me toward the cafeteria and I let him.

We come to a stop before the sheet cake. It's a good three feet wide, covered in white bakery frosting, sprinkles, colorful fondant balloons, rosettes, and Happy Birthday scripted in bright red frosting across the top. It looks like a rainbow unicorn exploded and this cake is what was left behind.

"So Josh is going to be a father. Again," Ian says.

"That's not talking about me." I turn away from the cake and keep walking down the hall. Ian hurries to catch up.

"What are you going to do?"

His questions are like a hot poker, digging into my side. "What do you care?"

For once, Ian seems surprised. "Why wouldn't I care?"

"Because you don't care about anyone but yourself," I say slowly.

Ian isn't shy about sharing this fact. It shouldn't come as a surprise.

The openness in his expression shuts down. "Right. I don't. Too true."

A small sliver of regret pulses through me. "I'm sorry."

He reaches over and taps me on my nose. "This is why I've always liked you. I'm the worst sort of person, yet you're still sorry when you think you've hurt me. I'd rip Josh apart if I hadn't already done worse to you. But me tearing into him would be hypocritical and that's one thing I'm not. Asshole, yes. Hypocrite, no."

He flashes a bright smile at me and taps my nose again.

"Stop tapping my nose."

He grunts and steers me forward again. And I let him, because right now, being led around by arrogant, annoying Ian is better than thinking about Josh.

We make it past the cafeteria and I see that I was right. The band has set up on a portable platform in the large community room. All the chairs have been pushed to the side of the room, and streamers and balloons hang from the ceiling.

At the edge of the room is a big table stacked with a pile of about a hundred presents, bowls of chips, and two liters of soda.

"Look at all those presents," I say.

They're book-sized rectangles all wrapped in beautiful gold and pink floral wrapping paper.

"It's my book," Ian says. "All autographed."

I frown at him, "You're kidding."

He nudges me toward the table. "Open one."

"I'm not opening one! That's...stealing."

He rolls his eyes. "Open one."

"Fine."

Just like every other person on the planet, I can't resist a beautifully wrapped gift, with crisply folded edges, small squares of tape, and frilly ribbons. I have a pulse of delight as I tear the paper back, and I reveal exactly what Ian said I would.

It's his book, *Live Your Best Life*. It's from two years ago, back when he was still loved.

He's in a navy blue suit, one of my favorites, and has his confident guru smile firmly in place. His look says, I've found nirvana, if you listen to what I say, you'll find it too.

I glance up at him. He doesn't have that look anymore. He hasn't had it for a long time.

"Read the autograph," he says impatiently.

I flip open the cover and read his scrawled writing out loud, "Happy birthday. This may not be the life you want, but it's the one you've got—" I cut off and look up at him, shocked.

He scowls and waves his hand. "Read on."

This isn't a Josh quote. This can only be an Ian quote, earned from life experience.

I look back down at the book. "This may not be the life you want, but it's the one you've got. Live it. Ian."

I close the cover and crumple the wrapping paper in my hand.

"It sort of feels like you wrote that for me," I say, letting a bit of honesty shine through.

He levels his gaze on me, and I think he's going to tell me, that yes, he did write it for me, but instead he holds out his hand and says, "Will you dance, birthday girl?"

His hand is open, his expression self-mocking, and I ask, "Did you come here this morning because you saw that article and you were worried about me?"

He shakes his head. "I would've come today no matter what."

"Because it's everyone's birthday?"

He stares at me, his hand still hanging there. "Sure, Gemma. We'll go with that."

Holy crap.

I set the book and the wrapping paper on the table. The band is small, there's a keyboard, a trumpet, a bass, a guitar, and drums, and some more instruments set to the side. They've started playing a song, and I quickly place it. I love Cole Porter, it's "Love for Sale."

Ian's lips twist. He's always appreciated these little cosmic jokes.

I walk back to him and set my hand in his. When I do, his

eyes glint and he leads me to the middle of the room. He presses one hand to my lower back and leaves his other grasping mine, loosely though, like I can let go anytime I want.

I put my free hand on his shoulder. When I do he smiles at me. A happy smile.

"This doesn't mean anything," I say.

"Happy birthday," he says.

I huff, but then I remember what he said about this being the only day that anyone ever says happy birthday to him, so I say, "You too, Ian. Happy birthday."

It feels ridiculous saying it, but his smile grows bigger.

"I can't believe you donated all those books. Trying to buy love?" I ask, referencing the song we're dancing to.

He lifts his eyebrows and shifts me around in a slow circle. "I've been addicted to other people's approval my whole life."

I stumble a bit and he steadies me. "What do you mean?"

He smirks at me. "Just that. Getting other people's approval was what I lived for. I've always needed people to like me."

What? I shake my head. "No. That's not you."

No one with Ian's amount of self-confidence could need other people's approval.

"You realize I do have a modicum of self-awareness? I assure you, it's me."

He dips me a bit and then spins me again. We're the only ones in the room dancing to the warming up band. If they care that we're here, they haven't said anything. If they recognize Ian...they haven't thrown anything.

When we settle back into a slow rocking rhythm, he says, "It was as easy as breathing having millions of people I've never met love me. It's the hardest thing I've ever been through to have millions of people I've never met hate me. Death threats, threats of violence, thousands of hate messages on social media. Think about it, people I've never met send me death threats, tell me I deserve to die, that my mother should've aborted me, that I'm everything wrong in the world. What sort of world encourages this?"

"I don't know." I squeeze his hand.

He nods. "I don't know either. On social media, on the news, they crucify people without trial. They are judge, jury, and executioner. I was hounded. And there was nothing I could say, or do, to make them approve of me. It doesn't matter if everything they said about me was true or not. The mob was on a witch hunt..."

He stops, seeming embarrassed that he's said as much as he has and admitted what he's felt.

So I finish for him, "The mob was on a witch hunt and they were going to find a witch."

He gives me a surprised look.

I shrug. "Everyone knows, if a mob grabs the torches and goes on a witch hunt, they're going to find someone to tie up and throw in the lake. Float, you're a witch. Sink, you're not a witch, but you're still dead. The mob always finds a witch."

He lets out a short huff of air.

"Just so you know, I never asked anyone to light torches on my behalf," I say.

"I know." His voice is low and deep and there's a ghost of a smile on his lips.

He stares into my eyes and I suddenly have the feeling that he wants to kiss me. His eyes move down to my mouth, and I *know* he wants to kiss me. I clear my throat and look away, breaking the moment.

I think we both realize at the same time that we've stopped dancing. The band is still playing "Love for Sale," so

Ian starts moving again, guiding me into the steps of our slow dance. My heart beats harder in my chest, and my low back, where Ian's hand presses into me, burns hot.

"I know," he says again. "It's taken a bit, but I think this whole thing has been good for me."

"Yeah?" I ask. Then I frown. "I'd really like to say that about what's happened to me too."

He laughs and the tension I was still holding onto clears.

"That's because you're Gemma, and you always want to put a positive spin on life."

I glare at him and he laughs again. The band segues into another song, "I Get a Kick Out of You," but I don't try to pull away or stop dancing.

"I do not," I say. Then, "Fine. I do."

He winks at me.

I smile at him, and I think it's a goofy smile, one that matches the jazzy music and the ridiculousness of a table full of book presents, a cake for everyone, and a universal birthday party where Ian Fortune is dancing with me in an empty room.

"I'm still a bad guy," he warns.

"I know," I say with a smile.

He gives me a skeptical look. "I stole Saint Josh's journal."

"Yup."

"I told you to get your shit together when you were miscarrying."

"Mhmm." Then I pinch him. "How'd you know I was miscarrying?"

He lowers his eyebrows. "I figured it out. There weren't many reasons you would've said 'I'm bleeding' and freaked out like that during a live conference you worked months on. I connected the dots."

"Hmmm."

He licks his lips and stares down at me. "You can keep hating me."

I nod. "I do."

"I'm not selfless."

"Your pie-covered shirt said otherwise," I remind him.

He lifts an eyebrow and then looks over my shoulder at the pile of wrapped books.

He jerks his chin in their direction. "I donated the books for a tax deduction."

I half cough, half laugh.

"And because my publisher cut my contract for breaking the morals clause. I have about five hundred books I need to offload. Didn't feel like throwing them away. Then I figured, well I can always foist them off on those poor saps at The Whittcombe—"

I kick him in the shin and he cuts off with an *oof*.

"Why are you trying to convince me that you're horrible? I already know you are."

He lets out a long-suffering sigh. "Gemma, can't you just have fun and not question my motives?"

I can't hold back my snort. "No. No I can't."

He stops dancing, and I hold still in his arms as he looks down at me.

"I want you to like me," he finally says. "This is my backwards way of going about it."

My throat goes dry and I swallow, trying to break out of the spell of his words. "I thought you said this whole thing was good for you? That you learned to stop seeking approval? Stop needing people to like you?"

"I never said that."

I think back. He's right. He didn't.

And I suddenly remember what he said one of the first times I saw him after waking up. He gestured at himself, at his scruffy appearance, and said, "This is what happens when the love dies."

He'd looked horrible, like an addict forcibly removed from his fix. Or like someone who was hated by the whole world, when he spent his life trying to earn everyone's love.

I take a step back, out of his arms.

"I'm going to be late for my appointment."

Ian looks like he's going to argue, it's still fifteen minutes until it starts and he knows it, but then he gives a sharp nod.

"Don't forget your book. It's a gift."

"Okay. Thanks." I grab the book from the table and shove it in my purse.

As I'm hurrying from the room, he jogs after me and gently touches my arm. I stop but don't turn.

"I'll save a piece of cake for you. When you're done, swing back down. I'll be here. You deserve some fun."

A hundred responses flick through my mind. Why? What do you want? Why do you care? What are you doing?

But all I say is, "Maybe."

The band stops playing. There's a long measured beat of silence around us.

As I walk out of the room, Ian calls after me, "Don't forget, Gemma, sometimes what feels bad is actually good. This is your life. Live it."

I hurry down the hall, practically running away from him.

21

*"Even birds with
broken wings can sing."*

I DON'T KNOW WHETHER OR NOT JOSH TEXTS OR CALLS DURING my physical therapy.

I also don't know whether he texts or calls during any of my other appointments.

I'm tempted about five hundred and sixty times to turn on my phone and look, but I can't. Every time I think about what he might say, jaws of panic threaten to open up and swallow me.

My appointments are finished for the day. It's early afternoon and I could catch a cab and head home, but instead, I walk down the hallway toward the cafeteria. The physical therapist cleared me, today was my last day. I'm fit. Physically healthy.

I still have more cognitive therapy, but that's coming along too. My therapist, a large, bearded, gentle-voiced man from Eastern Europe, told me I'm making fast progress.

When I'm on the couch in his office, I feel like I'm okay and that I can handle anything. It's only after I leave I realize how unprepared I am to face my life.

I didn't mention Josh, or Lisa, or Ian, or anything else about my personal life. I just talked about sensory stimulation, and the returning emotions, and panic and the odd feeling of being disconnected from myself. He reassured, in his gentle, rumbly voice that all of these things were "normal" and that I was healing.

I wondered (again, for the hundredth time) if I would heal back to the way I was or if at some point in time I'd stop healing and end somewhere between who I used to be and who I am now.

I walk past the cafeteria. It smells like pizza. Melted cheese, pepperoni, spicy sausage, green peppers and onions.

The halls are crowded, lots of families are here visiting, there are little kids, teens, and parents, most of them carry presents or flowers. Staff members walk out of the cafeteria with paper plates full of steaming hot pizza and cans of celery soda.

I remember that celery soda is one of Ian's favorites, and there's a funny feeling in my stomach that tells me he donated the drinks too. Which means, maybe he also donated the pizza? And the cake?

No. That's probably taking this "Ian is nice" line of thinking too far.

The band plays in the community room. They've stuck with jazz hits and right now they're playing "Every Time We Say Goodbye." A small crowd mills at the entry to the room. I stop a few feet away.

I could turn around, head home. Talk to Josh.

My first marriage ended, shortly after it began, when I found Jeremy buck naked, having sex with another woman. Ten years later, Jeremy and the other woman are married, have a minivan full of kids, and it's clear that I was the interloper.

Now, my second almost-marriage looks like it might end just like the first.

Lisa Perry is having a baby.

Josh is...the father?

I sit with that thought. When I found Jeremy with his pants down, he adopted the strategy deny, deny, deny. He took gaslighting to the Olympic sport level. Thinking back on our relationship, Jeremy never said he loved me like Josh has. He never showed me he loved me like Josh has.

I wonder what will happen to us?

I wonder if everything Josh has said since I woke up has been a lie. Or maybe last night was the lie. I don't know.

What I wish more than anything is that I could show Josh how much I love him. Still. Always. I wish I could feel that high, that rush again. So far I've only found one route that leads back to depth of feeling.

So, instead of heading home, I walk into the community room. Certain I'll find Ian inside.

I FIND IAN EASILY. HE'S IN THE CENTER OF THE ROOM, DANCING with a woman in her early sixties.

Ian doesn't notice me or realize that he has an audience. In fact, except for the three other couples dancing, nearly everyone in the room is watching him.

Yes, he's that good looking.

I lean against the wall and take in the scene. He's head and shoulders taller than the woman. She's about five foot four, petite, with long curly gray hair. She's wearing a long green skirt and a cream-colored floaty top. She looks like a garden fairy.

Her eyes are unfocused and here's what causes me to

push off the wall and stand up straight. Her smile—she's practically worshipping Ian.

I'm struck by her expression, because I haven't seen that look on anyone around Ian in more than a year.

No wonder he said he likes coming here. Like he said, the long-term residents have no idea that he's hated by the whole world. I get it now. He needs approval, and the people here, they like him. More than like him.

If I didn't know better, I'd say this woman adores, no, *loves* Ian. She reaches up and puts her hand to his cheek. Instead of smirking at her, like I expect, he gives her a soft, gentle smile and puts his hand over hers.

Suddenly, I feel like I'm spying on an intimate moment. Like this is something that I shouldn't be witnessing. Neither of them seems aware that anyone else is in the room.

The woman stands on her tiptoes and says something. Ian's eyes flash, and there's the mocking self-awareness I've come to know. His mouth twists, he closes his eyes, and he turns his head away from her. It's just for a moment, but I get the feeling that he's hurt. But then the moment is gone, he opens his eyes, expression clear. And he looks over her head, right at me.

My breath catches.

His brown eyes open wide. He's both surprised and delighted to see me.

You came, they seem to say.

I shrug. *I wanted cake*, I nod at the thirty-six-inch-long sheet cake next to the presents.

He flashes his white-toothed grin. Then he leans down and says something to the woman.

She nods and pats his cheek. Then I'm watching Ian walk across the room, my mouth dry and my nerves tingling.

"You came for the cake?" he asks, stopping a foot away.

"Who was that?" I ask, nodding at the woman he danced with.

He doesn't look where I'm gesturing. "Why?"

I narrow my eyes. "Because. I don't think it's right for you to come here and use these people to stroke your ego."

He lifts his eyebrows. "Isn't that the point?"

I cross my arms over my chest. "I get it. They don't know you're the devil. But it's not right for you to mislead people like that. That woman"—I gesture her way again—"she looked like she..." I don't want to say love. "She looked like she was infatuated with you."

His jaw tightens. "So what."

"So what?" I growl, "You make me so angry."

He does. There's a hot ember of anger in my chest. Just because Ian is an approval addict doesn't mean he has to use and manipulate unsuspecting people to get his fix.

He grins at my expression. "Good. Let's have cake."

He strides to the long rectangular sheet cake and picks up the spatula, scooping a large square piece with two-inch-thick vanilla frosting and a big red fondant balloon. He grabs a fork, sticks it in the cake, and hands me the plate.

I shake my head.

He sighs. "Come on, Gemma. Don't be this way. It's your birthday party."

He waves the cake in front of my face, "Mmmm. Sugar. Frosting. Chocolate. Mmmmm. You know you want it."

"Who was she?" I ask.

Ian looks at me like he's disappointed in my response. He grabs the fork and takes a bite of the cake.

With his mouth full, he says, "The flowers lady."

My mouth drops open. "The lady you steal flowers from? That lady?"

He lifts a shoulder in a half shrug and takes another bite. "This is really good cake. You should try some."

He scoops up another bite and holds the fork out to me. I'm not going to be distracted by cake.

"You steal from her and she still looks at you like that?"

"She thinks I'm her husband," he says, then he shoves the bite of cake in his mouth. "Fondant. Gross." He cringes, but still swallows.

"And you let her?"

He stares at me for a moment, the cake forgotten. If I didn't know better I'd think he was angry.

"Jeez, Gemma. I don't *let* her. It's not like I encourage her. I can't *stop* her. What do you want from me?"

"Maybe you should tell her that you aren't her husband? Try starting with the truth."

He shakes his head, exasperated. "There you go again. Trying to Jiminy Cricket my life."

I purse my lips, fighting the urge to tell him to follow my advice.

"Hey, Slick!" An older man in a newsboy hat limps up and slaps Ian on the back. "Come on, we've got a card game going."

This must be the stock tip guy Ian told me about. The one he beats at cards and wins tons of money from.

I scowl at Ian. He shoves his plate of cake into my hands. I take it, because otherwise it would fall to the floor.

"Don't leave. I'll be back after I take all their money."

The man lets out a loud phlegmy laugh and limps after Ian to sit at a small circular table in the corner of the room.

I look down at the cake. It's chocolate with a mile-high layer of white frosting, crystallized from the mass amount of sugar. It sparkles like snow in the sunshine.

I should go. I set the cake down on the table. I'm not going to eat it. I'm not going to give Ian the satisfaction.

I look toward him and see that he's watching me, a knowing smile flickers over his face. He turns back to the table and the cards being dealt.

I hoist my purse on my shoulder.

"You know my Peter?"

I stiffen, then slowly turn toward the woman next to me. It's the shorter, gray-haired lady that was dancing with Ian. My stomach twists into a knot. I don't want to be a part of this deception.

"Who?" I ask, deciding that pretending ignorance is the best course of action.

The lady's brown eyes go soft and she gestures at the card table.

"My Peter. He threw this birthday party for me."

My knotted stomach drops. That's really, really going too far. I glare at the table, sending mental daggers at Ian. He looks up, like he can feel them. When he sees who I'm talking to, he half-stands, a worried expression on his face. I sigh and gesture for him to stay sitting. I'm not going to out him.

He sits back down, but I can tell that he doesn't want to.

"Sorry, I don't know Peter," I say.

The woman gives a noncommittal hum. I look more closely at her. Her eyes are even more unfocused up close, like only a little part of her is in this world.

"We've been married twelve years."

Gross. Ian has been volunteering here for about twenty years. I wonder how long he's been faking this lady out, and I wonder what her real husband thinks about it. Or if she even has a real husband? Or has he been her "husband" for twelve years?

Ian keeps looking over at us, his expression troubled.

He isn't paying any attention to the card game. In fact, by the happy chortles of the men with him, I'd guess he's losing.

"We have a boy. He looks just like his dad. So handsome. I wish he were here, you could meet him. He's the sweetest boy you'll ever meet. Loves his mama."

She looks at me, waiting for me to comment. "I have a daughter," I say.

The woman gives me a happy smile, just like the one she gave Ian.

"Then you understand. Is your husband as wonderful as my Peter?"

I feel the blood drain from my face and my skin goes cold and clammy. I can't do this. I can't.

"I'm sorry. I have to go."

I turn and push toward the door, weaving through the crowd. The jazz music fades once I'm in the hall and my breath comes a little easier.

What the heck?

What the heck?

I don't care how hard Ian had it with the social media mob. He's sick. It's sick to use people. It's sick to make them think you're someone you're not.

It's wrong.

There's no excuse.

Anger bubbles through me, frothing around the edges and I gather it up. I push forward, eyes on the ground, stewing over Ian, when I collide with another person.

I let out an oomph. Then look up. It's the nurse manager who "misplaced" her coffee.

"Gemma, hi!" She says with a wide smile. "I didn't know you were here today. How are you?"

I flush, look back into the community room and then

back to the nurse. I have to tell her. I can't let this go on. "I'm great."

"That's wonderful," she says. I notice there's a blue cup of coffee in her hand. Probably from her husband.

"I wanted to ask…" I say, but then I trail off because I'm not sure how to say this.

"Hmmm?"

I point back toward the party, at the gray-haired woman. "Why do you let Ian Fortune pretend he's her husband?"

My throat feels tight, like I shouldn't be betraying him like this. Except, he's awful, and what he's doing is wrong.

The nurse manager looks at the woman, then back at me, her brows drawn.

"What do you mean?"

Frustration froths inside me, "I mean, it's wrong. Isn't it against the rules for a volunteer to lie to patients? To claim a relationship that doesn't exist?"

The nurse manager looks at me as if I've lost my mind. So much so that I begin to wonder if I have.

Her knuckles turn white on her cup, then she finally says, "It *is* against the rules for a volunteer to do such. However, Ian isn't a volunteer." She frowns at me, then pats my arm. "Your concern is admirable, but misplaced."

My mind sort of stops working, and I can't connect the dots that are there to connect. The nurse manager clicks her tongue, then says, "Nice seeing you, Gemma." She weaves into the community room, presumably in search of cake.

Ian isn't a volunteer?

He said he was a volunteer.

He said he's volunteered here for almost twenty years.

I blink at the lights in the hallway. The balloons. The people.

He's not a patient.

He's not a volunteer.

He's...

I turn back to the community room. Look at the woman with the curly gray hair swaying to the music.

My legs move forward, carrying me back to her. She's still at the edge of the cake and present table. Ian is still playing cards. Badly.

He looks up and smirks at me.

He threw this birthday party for me.

He looks just like his dad.

Loves his mama.

Holy crap.

"Excuse me," I tap the woman on her arm.

She turns to me, and I realize that she doesn't remember me. There's not even a spark of recognition there. "Sorry. I was just wondering, you said you have a son?"

Her eyes light up, and there's a happy warm glow in their brown depths. "Yes. Do you know him?"

I swallow, my mouth is so dry. I almost don't want to ask. "Maybe. I might know him. What's his name?"

Her eyes crinkle up. "Ian. He's the sweetest boy. He looks just like his dad."

My eyes fly to Ian's face.

He's her son.

This is his mom.

He's...what?

Ian shoves his chair back and stands. His cards spill across the table. The men with him shout out protests.

I turn from the room and flee down the hall.

"Gemma!" he shouts.

I shake my head.

No.

Nope.

All this time he's been pretending to be a horrible, detestable, unredeemable jerk, and it's all been a lie. He's been visiting his mom. For *twenty* years.

"Gemma!"

I jog down the hall toward the front doors. I hate this. Why would he lie to me? What was the point?

I hurry past the security desk, waving to Marina.

Then I shove the front doors open and push onto the street. The heat hits me, a humid, steaming washcloth-over-the-mouth kind of hot. And immediately my shirt sticks to my skin and little drops of sweat line my brow.

I blink into the bright sunshine. There aren't any taxis on the street. No worries. I turn to the right and start walking, head down.

I hear the doors bang shut behind me.

"Gemma, wait!"

Ian grabs my arm and pulls me around to face him. I can't fathom why, but his expression is almost desperate.

"Let me go!" I snap, shaking my arm.

He drops my arm and steps back, wiping the expression from his face.

"What?" I say. And when he doesn't say anything, all that anger snaps. "She's your mother!"

He flinches, and that flinch is double confirmation.

"Why didn't you tell me? How hard is it to tell the truth?"

Ian's face loses color. People on the sidewalk stream around us, smoothly moving past our confrontation, a jagged rock in the stream of pedestrians.

"Why do you want me to think the worst of you?" I ask, my voice shaking. "You weren't stealing flowers from her. Who would steal flowers from their mom? You were bringing them!"

His jaw clenches. Another confirmation.

"And this party, you help throw it, don't you?"

"No," he says.

"Yes. And the card games, I think you lose them. You don't steal their money. You play with them because you're nice."

"Don't make me into a good guy, Gemma. I'm not."

I shove my finger into his chest. "Why are you hiding?"

"I'm not," he snarls.

"I can't imagine how hard it is on you—for your own mom to forget who you are. For her to think that you're your father. I can't imagine."

"Stop it." He glares down at me, anger swirls around him, but pain too.

"You always said we were both broken and that's why we fit. I didn't realize this is what you meant."

"Stop it, Gemma." He clutches my arms and his fingers dig into my bare skin. "Stop it."

"No. I won't stop. You stop. Your mom said you were a sweet boy. What happened?"

"Drop it. It's not your business."

"You made it my business. You kept coming to my room. Bringing me stolen coffee. Lying about your mom. Telling me that I needed you, that I need to experience what's bad for me. You keep making me feel. And I want to know why. Why are you doing this? Am I some sort of project? You can't fix your mom, so you'll fix me? Listen to me, Ian. I'm not your redemption. I'm not your salvation. I'm not some bird with a broken wing that you're going to help fly again. Guess what? I don't need to fly, because even birds with broken wings can sing. How's that for positive affirmations? I don't need you. I thought I did, but I don't. We don't fit. You're wrong."

"Shut up, Gemma," he growls. His fingers dig into my arms. He steps closer, looming over me.

"Or what? You'll lie to me some more? You'll make up another story about how bad you are?"

His eyes flare with an unnamable emotion. And my heart pounds in my chest. There's an awful realization swirling around inside me, spurred by the look on his face.

"Ian?"

"What?" he glares at me, eyes hooded.

"Do you..." I whisper, try again. "Do you...love me?"

His stony expression doesn't change. The air crackles between us, an almost visible tension. The river of people flowing past us, the traffic, the noise disappears.

He nods, the sharp line of his jaw dipping. "I *want* to love you. Badly. Is that enough?" His lips twist into his familiar self-mocking smile.

The noise of traffic floods my ears and the world comes back into focus. The sentence has an awful familiarity. I think that's almost the exact same thing that I said to Josh last night.

Not, I love you, but I *want* to love you.

Ian looks over my shoulder, and his body radiates sudden tension. His eyes snap to mine and there's something there that I can't put my finger on.

It's like we're standing at the edge of a cliff, and he's about to grab my hand and jump off the edge.

"What is it?" I ask, afraid of his answer.

"You'll thank me for this later."

"What does that—" mean, I'm going to say, but he cuts me off. He bends down, his mouth crashing into mine, a storm descending over me.

The first time Ian and I kissed, we were outside my apartment. It was winter, the air was biting cold, his lips were cold, and I felt nothing.

This time...

Feelings crash around me. The world spins. I'm like that globe on the teacher's desk in elementary school. I used to stand there during break time and spin it and spin it, flicking my hand across its surface until it was spinning so fast that the continents and oceans were one muddy blue-brown blur. I loved to set that globe spinning, wildly blurring on its metal stand.

That's me now.

The sidewalk is the desk. Ian is the metal stand holding me up. I grab his shoulders, dig my hands into him, certain I'm about to fall over. He bites my lips and I gasp.

Anger, rage, confusion, irritation, dizziness, more confusion. When I gasp he slips his tongue into my mouth and licks my lips, circles my tongue with his own. His mouth is hot. Liquid fire. I think I've stopped breathing.

My word.

There's so much feeling here. So much rage. *So much.*

It's a blazing inferno, igniting across my skin.

"Get a room!" a man shouts as he shoves past us.

I rip my mouth away from Ian's, inhaling heavy, gasping breaths. I try to reacquaint myself with air, with the earth.

"What the heck was that?" I snarl.

Ian looks over my shoulder again and his eyes light with satisfaction, a small smile curves his lips. My stomach drops, and the inferno turns to ice. I whip around, yanking free of Ian's grasp.

It's Josh.

He's across the street, nearly a block away.

People, buses, taxis, fire hydrants, a newsstand, separate us. But it's like none of that is there and I'm standing right in front of him. I can see him perfectly.

To   say   that   he   looks   stunned   would   be   an understatement. To say that he looks devastated would also be an understatement.

He looks like I just tore out his heart and threw it down into the subway grates to be run over by a speeding express train.

Do you trust me?

I did.

No. No, no, no.

"Josh," I say, even though I'm certain he can't hear me over the beeping car horns, the construction noises and the traffic.

I lift my hand, "Wait."

He looks at me a moment, and it feels like a last sort of look. A goodbye sort of look. He's in one of his comic book t-shirts and a pair of torn jeans, his hair is messy and even from here I know he has ink stains on his hands.

A small sound escapes me. I look up at Ian. He's smiling. He's smiling at Josh.

Rage.

Boiling, steaming hot rage.

He did this.

He said I'd thank him.

He did this.

He knew Josh was there. He kissed me knowing Josh would see.

"Why?" I ask.

But then, it doesn't matter why, because Josh has turned. He's not coming to confront me, or yell at me, or even to punch Ian. He's leaving.

"Josh!" I yell.

Josh pauses, his back stiff, his fists clenched.

"Josh!"

But then, like he's decided that he's had enough, that he's

tired of a fiancée that doesn't love him, seemingly doesn't *want* him, he keeps walking, turns the corner onto the side street and disappears.

There's a subway entrance down the block. He could be gone in a second. Down the stairs, into the tunnel, on a train.

No.

All the emotions.

All of them flood me.

I have to stop him.

I have to talk to him *now*.

Not later.

Not tonight.

Not tomorrow.

Now.

To think that I was worried I'd feel nothing with Josh is laughable. The spinning, the tilting, it unlocked a hidden door and I know, I know without a doubt that I love Josh. No matter what has happened, no matter what's gone wrong, I love him.

It only took Ian fricking Fortune tonguing me on the street for me to figure it out.

I take off at a run, darting toward the street.

Ian grasps at my arm and I twist and slip free of his hand.

"Gemma! Stop!"

I won't. I'm blind to him. I can't see anything but the image of Josh disappearing.

"Stop!" Ian yells.

I sprint into the street. My feet slap against the hot pavement and my heart pounds in my ears. There's a screeching noise. Horns. I hear Ian behind me. Yelling.

I don't care.

I dart toward where I last saw Josh.

Then I hear another noise. Something besides Ian shouting and horns honking.

It's screeching.

The inhuman shrieking noise of tires trying to brake. And failing.

It's the sound everyone hears and then waits, breath held, for the sound of a crash, crunching metal and breaking glass.

I turn.

Find the source of the noise.

It's a bright yellow taxi.

It's fishtailing. Gravel spits up from the tires, hitting me, like little angry bullets. It's a funny thing, it looks like there's smoke coming up from the tires, screeching against the ground.

I can see the driver perfectly. The whites of his eyes, large and frightened. His hands gripping the black leather steering wheel.

He's going to hit me. We both know it.

He can't stop.

And I can't move fast enough.

The last time I was certain that I was going to die, I had a million thoughts. This time, I only have one.

I'm sorry.

I flinch, my body instinctively bracing for impact and I close my eyes. I don't want to think about how thin my skin is, how breakable my bones are, how fragile my organs are.

The impact hurts. I'm hit so hard that I fly through the air. My breath is ripped from my lungs and I'm catapulted off the ground.

But something's not right. Because I'm catapulted *forward*.

Across the street, toward the curb.

The impact came from behind, not from the front.

I hit the pavement, my teeth clatter together at the force,

the skin on my hands tears away, I skid across the street, my jeans ripping, the skin on my knees and legs ripping too.

The burn hurts.

But it's nothing. It's nothing.

Because as I'm sliding, I hear it. The tire screeching stops and then there's the noise.

The horrible, crunching *thud*.

The sickening *thwack*.

For the rest of my life I'll never forget that noise.

I try to make my lungs work, they're seizing up, not pulling in air. I let out a sob, exhale, and then finally, finally, I'm able to draw in breath. I shove myself up onto my burning knees and wrench myself around. Back toward the street and the taxi.

The driver's already out of the car. Yelling.

All the traffic has stopped.

People are running.

Someone grabs my arm, "Are you okay?"

I shake them off.

Crawl back toward the taxi.

"Call 911!" I scream. "Call 911!"

It's Ian.

He's the impact I felt. He pushed me out of the way. He ran after me into the street and shoved me out of the way.

Why did he do that?

A desperate animal sound escapes my throat.

I half stumble, half crawl back toward the taxi.

Stupid. Stupid, selfish, stupid, self-serving jerk.

"What were you thinking?" I cry. "Why did you do that?"

I kneel next to him. There are so many people around. Too many people.

The driver is still yelling. Why is he yelling?

Ian lies on the ground, half under the front of the taxi. His right arm is broken, the white of his bone sticks out of his arm. Nausea rockets through me and I think I'm going to throw up. I've never seen someone's bone sticking out of their skin.

Then I notice the blood. It's hard to see, because Ian's shirt is black. But it's there, on his chest, forming a quickly spreading circle. I slam my hands over it, pressing down. His shirt is sticky and warm. I push harder and Ian grunts.

"Easy there," he coughs.

I let out an involuntary sob. The sound of ambulance sirens picks up in the distance. They're not far. Please let them not be far.

"I told you..." Ian says.

"What?"

"Told you...selfless...never in a man's...best interest."

I stare at him in mute horror.

He's grinning at me. Ian grins at me. Okay, it looks more like a white-toothed grimace, but he's trying.

His face is deathly pale. His arm is broken. He's bleeding like a poked water balloon. Who knows what else is wrong. And he's making a joke.

"I hate you," I cry, the words fall out of me, bounce around us.

I can barely see him anymore because my eyes are so full of tears, and I can't wipe them away, because my hands are trying to keep his blood inside his body, but I think his smile grows even bigger.

"I really, really do. I hate you." I press harder, keep the blood inside.

"Good." He coughs. Spits out blood. Focuses on my face.

"Don't leave me," he begs quietly. His eyelashes flutter.

Then, on a wheezing exhale, "Please. Gemma."

Before I can answer, his eyes roll back, his head falls to the pavement and he's gone.

Unconscious.

Dead.

I don't know.

I scream. I think I scream.

But maybe I don't, because that shrieking, deafening noise is the ambulance pulling up beside us.

22

"You get back exactly what you put into the world."

I RIDE IN THE AMBULANCE, GRIPPING IAN'S LIMP HAND.

"I can't leave him," I tell the paramedics. "He said don't leave him."

I'm calm. At least on the outside I give the appearance of calm. I don't think I'd be allowed to sit in the ambulance if I didn't have this numb expression covering the raging storm inside.

"He said not to leave him. We're together," I tell them.

And they take that however they want. Girlfriend, fiancée, wife, friend, sister, cousin, whatever. I'm none of those things. Former employee. Yes. Former girlfriend. Sort of. Current...I don't know. Not friend.

"We're together."

The two medics work with swift efficiency. The man has the hulking build of a former wrestler, the woman is broad shouldered and works with fast, sure movements. We're stabilizing him, the woman says, we'll be at the hospital in three minutes, she tells me.

Ian's still alive. Passed out from trauma.

"I'm here," I whisper to him. "I'm here."

And I imagine that the reason he asked me to stay isn't because he wants to love me, but because he doesn't have anyone else.

He doesn't have a single person in the whole wide world who would care that he's gone. He'd rather have me, a woman who says she hates him, than be alone.

I crush his hand in mine, thinking about the fact, that if he died, his mom probably wouldn't even realize that he was gone.

That is a horribly depressing thought.

"I'm here," I say again.

FIVE HOURS PASS IN A NUMB, JUMBLED UP SORT OF BLUR.

When we get to the hospital Ian is rushed to surgery. I'm shuttled to another room. All I can do is ask about Ian. Is he okay? What's happening? Will he live?

Apparently, I was covered in enough blood, my own and Ian's, that an ER nurse told me to sit down, be quiet, and let them do their job.

Which basically involved the painful process of flushing half a city street's worth of gravel out of my legs, hands and arms. It took nearly two hours to rinse, pick, poke and tweeze out all the dirt, rocks and shards of who knows what from my street burned skin.

I've had rug burn. This was like that, but a thousand times worse. The top layers of skin on my palms, thighs, and knees is gone. All that's left is a red, shiny, streaky layer that stings like an army of ants gnawing on a fiery hot sunburn.

The nurse coated it with an antibiotic and a numbing agent and then wrapped gauze and medical tape over the top.

One of my knees had a deeper cut, a gash from a piece of glass lodged in my skin. It needed stitches, but instead of thread, they used medical-grade super glue to hold my skin together.

The nurses also took my vitals (old hat for me) and the doctor assessed me for internal bleeding, broken bones, contusions, etcetera. I was sent off to have an x-ray, "just in case."

After hours of care, I'm covered in gauze, tape and dried blood, and there are purple and blue bruises poking out from beneath my bandaging. I've made a statement for the accident report, although I don't remember what I said. It all sort of blurs together.

The clock on the wall says seven, but it feels like only five minutes has passed since I ran after Josh.

I lean back in the plastic chair, groan at the pinch of my raw skin, and drop my chin to my chest.

Ian is quiet in the hospital bed next to me. The nurse said he'd wake up soon.

Hours ago, when I was waiting for him to get out of surgery, I told my nurse Ian and I were together and that I had to be there when he got out of surgery. They found his wallet with his ID and insurance card, so they all know that they're caring for the most hated man in the country.

I don't care what they think of him as long as they take care of him.

His tally of injuries includes a broken arm, two broken ribs, a deep laceration in his upper right chest, and a whole lot of bruising.

He looks like crap, all except his face, which somehow defied injury and still looks picture perfect.

I glance at the round white, institutional-style clock. Seven fifteen. I realize, stupidly and suddenly, that Josh, my mom, neither of them have any idea where I am. The last time my mom saw me she expected me home shortly after lunch. The last time Josh saw me...I was kissing Ian.

"Crap."

You'd think that the first thought you'd have after an accident is to call your family. It wasn't. In fact, I don't know that I had any coherent thoughts for hours and hours.

My purse is on the ground near my feet. It's a leather hobo bag and survived my skidding across the pavement admirably. I glance at Ian. He's still out.

We're in a tiny private room, it's about eight by ten and has the beige linoleum and chipped gray paint of an overcrowded, overwhelmed New York City hospital that's a hundred years old and has seen better days. Hospitals in the city are often maxed out, with patient beds double lining the hallways, and ERs with beds crammed into every available space. Forget privacy, you're having your organs discussed six inches from the next person.

Private rooms come at a premium, so even though Ian's room looks like an interrogation chamber from Soviet Russia, it's a luxury. Heck, it even has a window. It faces a six-story concrete parking garage.

I guess when the staff found out their patient was Ian Fortune, they decided that the most hated man in America probably needed to stay away from others.

I let out a long sigh and pull my phone out of my bag. The screen has a star-shaped crack, probably from when I slammed into the ground. It's still powered off.

I press it on and wait while it loads all my missed texts and calls.

Three missed calls.

A slew of missed texts.

I open Josh's messages.

There's the first from this morning, the one I never read: *Morning. You should've woken me up. Sorry about last night, I didn't know Lisa was coming here. She's fine. Are you alright?*

My heart skips over itself and clatters around my chest.

His next message is from a half hour later: *Hey. You okay?*

There's another message a few minutes later: *Tried to call. Your phone's turned off. I'm guessing you went to therapy early. Call me.*

An hour later another message: *Hey. I might have to go to LA tonight. Call me.*

Then, a half hour later: *Your phone's still off. I'm coming to The Whittcombe. Be there in a few.*

I realize that I'm gripping my phone really, really tight, so much so that my raw skin aches even with all the numbing cream and painkillers.

There are a few messages from my mom: *Hey honey. You're late getting back. Josh is heading your way.*

Then, at five: *Sweetie. Call me when you get this. Josh is heading to the airport. I'm with Hope 'til you get home.*

My heart, still clattering around in my chest, goes still.

My hands shake. I open my voicemail and listen to the messages. There are three. The first is from this morning at eight.

It's Josh.

"Hey. Didn't see you this morning." His voice is warm and has that sleepy quality that means he hasn't made it to his second cup of coffee yet.

For some reason my eyes feel itchy and my throat goes sore. "Sorry about last night. I tried to wake you but you were completely out."

I remember the blanket I woke up with, the one he must've covered me with before heading to bed. "I didn't know Lisa was coming by. Sorry it was a shock."

He pauses and I close my eyes, trying to block out the words. "I wish you hadn't left before we could talk. You looked...I'm worried. Call me, okay?"

My lips tremble and I press them together, biting down on my bottom lip. The message beeps and then the next starts to play.

"Gemma, it's Mom. Where are you? Hope is teething, my oh my, she's cranky today. Do you know where that nubby teething toy is? Oh never mind. I just found it in the freezer."

There's rustling and I hear the freezer door shut.

Then, my mom says in a chirpy voice, "I'm checking in because you're an hour late and Josh says he hasn't heard from you. But he's headed down to check so I'll just... hmmm...okay."

There's another beep and the final message begins. It's from three fourteen, long after Ian started surgery, yet while I was still having gravel scraped from my legs.

"Hey. It's me." Josh pauses. His voice is no longer morning coffee warm, it's cold and distant.

He clears his throat, then says, "I see you're still not answering your phone."

My chest burns hot then cold. "I, uh...obviously I saw you with Ian. And the fact that...the fact that you're not calling and that you're still not home...Gemma, what are you doing?"

There's a rustling noise on the phone. Wind blowing into the receiver. "Okay. So, I have to head to LA. We have to put out this fire, rewrite the last episodes, they want to include a surprise pregnancy. Yeah...anyway. I was going to delay until tomorrow, but I think I better just go tonight. Your mom is going to watch Hope until you get home. Can you...dang it."

He sighs and the wind muffles his voice, but I can still hear him clearly enough when he says, "I'll be gone a couple days. Let's not talk until I get home. I don't want to do this over the phone."

The line disconnects.

I keep holding my phone to my ear even when the messages stop and the line goes silent, not quite sure I heard right.

No, I heard right. I'm not sure I understood right. Because I think what Josh is saying is that he doesn't want to tell me that we're over on the phone.

I squeeze my eyes tight and concentrate on the burning in my palm, the fiery pain on my legs. After all the fear, all the panic is pushed back by the pain in my legs, I open my eyes. Then I dial Josh's number.

It goes to voicemail.

At the beep, I start, even though I don't know where to begin, "Josh. It's me. I'm…" I don't know what to say, my mind is a blank chalk board, all the writing half-erased and mixed up.

I look at Ian, at his stupid, beautiful face, I grasp onto that. "I'm with Ian. I can't leave him."

My voice comes out in a horrible half-sob. "Josh."

The room tilts a bit and I think I might be hyperventilating. "I didn't mean to kiss him. Please call me. Okay? I told Ian I'd stay with him. Please call me."

My hands shake as I disconnect. I don't think I made any sense. I know I didn't. I'm shaking all over. I still need to get ahold of my mom. I don't think I can call her. Instead, I open up my messages and send a text.

I don't want to worry her, so I write: *Can you please stay with Hope tonight? Am with Ian. Very Important. Don't know when I'll be home.*

My mom texts back within seconds: *Ian Fortune? Your ex-boss? That horrible man? Why?*

I look over at Ian, his thick black hair stark against the white hospital pillow. There are small veins in his eyelids and dark blue smudges under his eyes.

Yeah. Him. I write back. *I'll be home as soon as I can. Can you stay?*

Her response takes a little longer, and when it comes all it says is: *Okay. I'll give Hope dinner. Take your time.*

I close my eyes, so grateful for my mom.

IAN WAKES UP. I'M NEARLY ASLEEP WHEN HE DOES, COMPLETELY exhausted by the day. But when I hear his voice—"They put us in the Ritz, didn't they? Spare no expense"—I jerk awake.

I'd like to say that I have a witty reply, but instead I say, "You're awake."

He smiles at that and then flinches, "Wish I weren't."

He stretches, gingerly testing his mobility, "Remind me to never jump in front of a car again. It was a bad idea."

At that, it all comes back. "Why did you? You're such an idiot. What were you thinking—"

"You know, for a moment, I thought you might be grateful." He lifts an eyebrow. It's ridiculous, because he's stitched up, bandaged up, lying in a hospital bed, yet he still manages to look sardonic and mocking.

"If you hadn't kissed me," I say, "none of this would've happened."

His eyes go to my mouth. "Good point."

Then his gaze flicks over my hands, my torn jeans and the bloody and bruised bits still showing beneath the gauze. "You look like hell, by the way."

I stiffen under his perusal and my eyes burn. I don't just

look like hell, I feel like hell. I need to go home. I reach down for my purse. Time to go.

"Well, in that case, I'm glad you're awake, I'm—"

"Thank you," he interrupts. His voice is soft and sincere, a tone I've never heard from him.

I stop. He's looking at me with something like...fondness. The tightness in my shoulders melts and I drop my purse back to the ground.

"For what?"

He reaches over with his good arm and touches the back of my hand, on top of the gauze.

"I felt you in the ambulance. I could feel you holding my hand."

My breath is tight in my chest. "Okay."

He drops his hand. "Thank you for staying."

His fingers are long, fine boned, like a pianist's. His eyes are shadowed and wary. I've seen a thousand faces of Ian Fortune, and I have no idea which one is the real one. Or if any of them are.

"Why did you kiss me?"

His dark eyebrows rise high. He wasn't expecting this question. He shrugs, then gives a grunt of pain.

Finally, he says, "Would you believe, that in my head, I thought Josh would see..."

His eyes narrow in thought. "That he'd charge over like an angry man bull, punch me, flashback Hamptons style, and then he'd carry you off into the sunset. And you'd live happily ever after." He looks up at me, a lopsided smile on his face, "For as long as you both live."

I stare at his smile, stunned. "What?"

"The flaw is, I didn't realize Josh would walk away." He frowns. "Faulty reasoning on my part."

"You kissed me so that Josh would get jealous?"

Ian looks up at the ceiling beseechingly. "Keep up, Gemma. I certainly didn't do it so I'd end up here." He grimaces at a large brown water stain on the ceiling tiles. "As lovely as the accommodations are."

"I don't understand."

He's saved from answering though. A hard-eyed nurse, a resident in baggy teal scrubs and the attending physician, a bald man with a mole on his nose and a long white coat, crowd into the room.

The space is suddenly much, much smaller. I scoot closer to the bed and tuck my legs under the plastic chair, trying to stay inconspicuous.

A good ten minutes passes while Ian's checked over, debriefed and told that he'll likely be discharged in the morning.

He's a lucky one, the nurse says in a tight voice. And he doesn't deserve it, her eyes say. It's clear she knows who Ian is, and she doesn't like him. Not at all.

Neither does the resident. She's late twenties, red haired and green eyed, cute, obviously smart. Basically the demographic of all the women who hate Ian. When she talks to him, her mouth twists like she's chewing on dirty socks, and when she looks at him it's like he's that bloated, dead rat that you'll often see tossed out on the city sidewalk next to the trash.

My back goes straight, and I feel an angry, protective instinct for him.

I fume in silence.

When they've gone, Ian studies my face, then quirks an eyebrow. "What?"

"They all hate you," I whisper.

It's awful, because when he smiles at me, it's sad and self-aware.

"You noticed that too, huh?"

My shoulders slump. There's not really anything to say.

"Here," Ian says. He holds out his hand.

"I don't want to hold your hand." I stare at his long fingers, the veins in his wrist, the blood flowing there.

I think about how only hours ago, I was trying to keep all that blood inside him.

He scoffs, "I'm about to tell you my life story, and you won't even hold my hand."

I give him a skeptical glance. Then, I look at his hand and say, "Josh doesn't want me anymore."

Ian's lips tighten. I think he's trying not to say something biting.

"Hold my damn hand, Gemma."

I narrow my eyes. "This doesn't mean I like you," I say, but it lacks conviction.

I drop my hand into his and his eyes light with wry humor.

"Did you know I grew up on an ashram?"

His hand is loose around mine, he's gentle, barely cupping my fingers. I think he's being careful of all the gauze and the street burn.

I take my eyes away from our linked hands and say, "That's not in your bio."

He gives a short, cut-off laugh. "You believe my bio?"

I think back to it. Born poor. A waitress mom. A chronically unemployed dad. Never enough to eat. Young Ian always had a drive to succeed and change the world. Excelled in school. Full scholarship to college. Graduated top of his class.

It was the whole rags-to-riches kind of story. An inspirational one. His first job after college was at the same company as Josh. That's where he stole Josh's journal. Obviously that bit wasn't in the official bio either.

But, come to think of it, his bio was full of a lot of glossed over clichés about pulling himself out of poverty and becoming the man he was meant to be. Living his best life. It could easily have been bogus. Which I guess it was.

"No...I guess not." I shrug. "I wanted to believe it."

He nods. "Me too."

That surprises me. He takes in my expression and says, "I'm not saying I didn't like the ashram. I loved it."

He tilts his head back in the pillow and stares at the stain on the ceiling.

"Where was it?"

"Upstate."

He sighs and I get the feeling I'm the first person he's ever told this story to.

"I was born here in Brooklyn. My mom was a yoga instructor, my dad was an art dealer. When I was three, they decided they were sick of the city and wanted to reconnect with their inner truth."

He looks back at me, an ironic gleam in his eyes. "People do this, you know? My mom taught yoga classes there, my dad painted. We had this little cabin on the property. Every day I played drums for meditation, chanted, practiced yoga. There's this type of yoga, it's service based. Basically, you serve others, sweep up, cook, clean. I was really good at that."

Shivers race across my skin and goosebumps rise on my arms. His expression is far away, like he's back Upstate, seven years old, sweeping up a yoga studio.

"All our meals were communal. Vegetarian. I liked the people that came up. They were nice. Sometimes families brought kids for the retreats and I got to play with them. I was homeschooled. My mom was a good teacher. Really patient. Some days I just wanted to roam the woods. Find bugs and toads. That sort of thing. She didn't mind."

He looks over at me, his brow wrinkled.

"You were happy?"

He nods. "Very much."

He's quiet. I sit still, my hand a heavy weight in his. Something happened between the happy kid at the ashram, the sweet boy his mom remembers, and the Ian of today.

"What happened?" Because something had to have happened.

His eyes shift to mine and his lips quirk. "I grew up."

I don't answer him, and when he sees that I'm not going to argue, he sighs.

"When I turned eleven, my parents decided that we'd go to the city for my birthday. They were going to treat me. I'd get to see Coney Island, Broadway, the Natural History Museum...do it all."

I remember how Ian said that he doesn't ever celebrate his birthday and suddenly I have a heavy, leaden feeling in my stomach.

"We didn't even make it to the George Washington Bridge." He looks away from me, out the window. His hand falls open and I can pull away, but I don't. Ten seconds pass. Twenty.

"Why not?" I finally ask.

"A Volvo station wagon. It was blue. Like a tank. It slammed into us. Police said they were going ninety. Shoved us into the metal barricade. We flipped over it."

I bite my tongue. I think if I start crying for the little boy that Ian was, he'll stop telling me his story.

"Your mom?" I ask.

He turns back to me. His eyes are watery and his jaw is

tight. For a second, I can see all the pain still wrapped up inside him.

"That's right," he says. "Traumatic brain injury. She never recovered. Her memory span is five minutes. She doesn't recall anything after my eleventh birthday. It was hard in my teens, my twenties. She didn't know who I was. Sometimes she was scared of me. Now, it's better. She thinks I'm my dad. I look almost just like him. I don't know what will happen when I get older."

His eyes cling to mine, as if he's daring me to look away but desperately wanting me to keep ahold of him.

"What about your dad?"

His mouth turns down and his eyes go dark. "I broke my leg in the crash. He had thirty-seven stitches. His arm went through the side window."

"Where is he now?"

"Remember how I said a lot of relationships don't survive brain injuries?"

Back when I was still an inpatient at The Whittcombe, he'd said that Josh and I wouldn't make it. That he knew from experience.

"I remember."

He nods. "Sometimes the people in the relationships don't survive either. It didn't take three months for it all to fall apart."

Ian looks away from me. Out the window again. I close my eyes.

"I'm so sorry."

He looks quickly back at me and then scoffs at my expression.

"Typical Gemma. You're making me out to be some misunderstood sap. Next thing I know you'll be telling everyone that I'm not really awful, I actually have a tragic backstory and a bad guy persona that hides a heart of gold. Don't be so predictable."

I glare at him. When he doesn't relent I reach over and flick his ear. "Stuff it."

He winces and then scowls at me. "Really?"

I shrug. "You deserved it."

He grins. "Probably."

I smile back at him, pulled into his ability to smile in such a grim situation.

"What happened to you after that?"

He lifts an eyebrow. "I went into foster care. Trust me, Gemma, an eleven-year-old raised on an ashram does not fare well in foster care in New York City."

"How do you mean?" I ask, even though I'm pretty sure I don't want to know.

"You don't want to know," he says, confirming my thought.

He winces and then shifts in his bed. "I think the painkillers are wearing off. Hurts to breathe."

He glares at me, like it's my fault. Which it sort of is.

"So then you graduated, became an evil mastermind and took over the self-help world?" I ask, trying to summarize the next fifteen or so years.

He snorts and gives me a sardonic look. "Not even close."

"Really?" I ask. "I thought you were doing really well with your villain origin story."

I give him a tentative, teasing smile.

Thank goodness he appreciates it. His fingers brush gently against my hand. "Stop talking, Gemma."

"Okay," I say, folding my lips together.

He shakes his head and tries to suppress a smile.

After a heartbeat of silence, he says, "I got passed around a lot. Sometimes I was able to visit my mom. Sometimes not. When I was fourteen, three years in...my mom snapped when she saw me, clawed my face, hit me, thought I was some hoodlum come to hurt her. She didn't recognize me anymore."

Ian's jaw clenches. I want to ask more, but I told him I'd stop talking so I don't. He stares at me to see how I'm taking this. I nod at him to continue.

"I realized then...I realized that the whole reason my dad was dead, the whole reason my mom didn't know me, the entire reason that I was in a foster home, despised and hated was because of that blue Volvo station wagon."

He looks at me to see if I understand the importance of this realization.

My heart beats loud, thudding in my chest. A drop of sweat collects on my chest and then snakes down my skin. I squeeze his hand gently and the gauze scrapes against my red, burning skin.

"I remembered the couple in the Volvo. A husband and wife. The wife was driving. They walked away without a scratch. My mom lost her life. My dad took his own life. I lost everything and they walked away without a scratch."

The tiny hospital room feels even smaller under the weight of his confession. The noises from the hall are loud, a busy hospital on a busy night. But there's a bubble around Ian and me that feels impenetrable.

"I went to my dad's grave and I swore to him that I'd find that couple and I'd destroy them, just like they destroyed us."

I hold my breath, fighting back tears, and the noise that's building in my chest.

"You understand?" he asks.

I nod, let out my breath in a shuddering exhale. Wetness falls over my cheeks.

He notices the tears and lifts an eyebrow. "It wasn't hard to find them. The husband from the accident, the man, he sent flowers to my mom every week. In fact, he sent them once a week for nearly twenty years."

There's simmering rage there in his eyes. "Can you imagine? You take someone's life and you think *flowers* is enough to make up for it?"

I shake my head. I can't imagine.

He shrugs. "It's how I knew he'd finally died. The flowers stopped coming."

He sits with that for a moment. "It's hard to say this, but I was sorry that he was gone. I didn't realize how much I'd come to depend on him remembering my mom until he wasn't there anymore."

He pulls his hand from mine and wipes it across his face. I hadn't realized he was crying. Except I don't think he is. He drags his hand over his cheek and pulls at his dark stubble.

"So you didn't destroy him?" I ask. I can't keep quiet anymore.

Ian looks at me from the corner of his eyes, an indecipherable gleam in their depths.

"No. I did. In a roundabout way." He doesn't sound sorry about it either.

He drops his hand back to the bed. Mine is still there, and he picks it back up again, looking at me to make sure it's okay. I nod.

He seems to find this amusing because he gives a short huff.

"Anyway. I did some research. I found the man's address. He lived in some Podunk town in Upstate. So one Saturday, I used all those five-dollar bills I'd saved up from my visits to The Whittcombe." He lifts an eyebrow and I smile.

"That's right," he says, confirming my suspicion that this was the five dollars he got from one of the patients there, "and I bought a round trip train ticket. I didn't have a plan. I just wanted to see where they lived."

He turns away from me and stares up at the ceiling again. The air conditioning kicks on and the breeze blows a cold draft over me.

"I hated the town," he says. "It was like a sitcom, perfect Americana. The train station had red benches and red, white and blue ribbons, the city park had some berry festival going on, the houses all had flowers out front."

"Sounds like where I grew up."

He looks back at me. "Indeed."

I shiver. The cold air blows over my bare arms.

"I walked to the address I had. Careful not to draw attention to myself. Not that the couple would've recognized me. Still, I was a skinny, dirty teen from the city with an old backpack, a ripped jacket, torn jeans, a black eye and scratches on my face. I didn't fit in this clean, shiny world. So I stayed out of sight. Slunk behind a tree and watched the house. Waited for something. I don't know what."

He swallows. Traces his fingers over mine. I wonder if he realizes what he's doing?

"Anyway. An hour later the man pulls up into his drive. I recognized him. He still looked the same. The wife wasn't there. But his son was. I hadn't realized they had a son. I was even more surprised that he looked the same age as me. That's where the similarities ended though. That kid was happy."

Ian's fingers stop moving and he looks at me, like he's trying to tell me something vitally important. "The dad laughed. The kid smiled. I hid behind that tree and I watched them, like they'd stolen my life, the happiness that I'd had."

"Who were they?" I ask.

"You know."

I swallow and shake my head. "I don't."

"Coward."

I press my free hand to my stomach. Bile rises in my throat. "He never did anything to you."

"I know."

I stare at Ian, still not quite able to accept what he's saying.

"Josh?"

He nods, slowly, firmly. Yes.

"Mr. and Mrs. Lewenthal. Drivers of the blue Volvo. Parents to Josh Lewenthal."

Ian's lips turn up, but it's not a smile. "It was easy after that. I decided I was going to destroy their son's life. His mom died a few years later. I went to the funeral. Mr. Lewenthal recognized me. He didn't even seem surprised I was there. I asked him where his son was, and he told me that his son didn't know his mom was dead. Can you believe it? Then he asked me not to tell Josh if I ever ran into him. We shook on it. Can you imagine? We shook hands on it."

Ian gives me an incredulous look.

I can't imagine. I really, really can't. I know for a fact that Josh doesn't know his mom is dead. He has *no idea*. I didn't know until this very moment.

Josh's mom left when he was eight. He hasn't seen her since. I have no idea why three years later his dad and mom were driving together in a blue Volvo, and I bet Josh doesn't know why either.

"Years later, when we were at college, I asked Josh if he ever went looking for his mom. He said, 'She doesn't want me, why should I want her?'"

My insides turn to ice. Does he still think like that? Will he think that about me?

"I didn't tell him she was dead."

Ian looks at me to gauge my reaction. When I don't say anything he shrugs.

"So, Josh and I went to college together. I became his friend, worked to find a way to hurt him."

He nods to himself, going back through the closed drawers of his memory. I think about Josh going off to college too. How I lost my virginity to him in my parents' garage at his high school graduation party. How he said he'd miss me while he was away. I think about how soon after that he met Ian.

"I liked him," Ian says. "That's the worst part. I wanted to hate Josh, but he's...he's too good of a person to hate. It felt like a betrayal to my parents. My dad was gone. My mom had started to believe I *was* my dad. Being his friend felt wrong. My life...it went on. Everything went on. Then I found Josh's journal. He told me he was going to make something of it. Something big. He had plans. I figured this was my chance. I'd take it. I'd steal his everything, and I'd make it my own."

Ian shrugs again. "So I did. I became a superstar. Loved by millions. And Josh took years to recover. Working minimum wage, writing his comic. Going nowhere. I did that."

He looks into my eyes. There's no pride, no joy in his voice.

Ian shifts, winces, so I reach over and mound up his blanket and then gently move his broken arm to rest on top of the pile. When I take his hand again he looks at me in surprise. Like he didn't expect me to want to voluntarily touch him ever again.

I shrug. "Yeah, yeah. You're a horrible person. I get it."

He blinks, unsure how to take my statement. He watches me like he expects me to get up and leave. And I might. I haven't decided yet.

"His dad died. The flowers stopped coming."

I nod. "I know."

Ian's jaw clenches. "I watched them bury him. Mr. Lewenthal. I stood at the edge of the cemetery."

I close my eyes, blocking out this news. Ian squeezes my hand and I look at him again.

"When he died...before he was gone, I'd planned on stealing you away from Josh, I'd wanted to find a way to ruin the burgeoning popularity of his comic. Then...Mr. Lewenthal was gone. And. Look, I watched them lower his coffin into the ground and I thought...this is it. Everyone that was in that crash is dead. Mr. Lewenthal is gone. Mrs. Lewenthal is gone—killed by her own alcoholism. My dad's dead. My mom doesn't remember anything. I'm the only one left. I'm the only one left hanging on to it. Everyone else moved on. Josh doesn't know. His dad's dead. I realized that his dad was my only connection to the past. He was the only thing keeping my parents alive. Then he was gone. And there was no point anymore. Not a one."

"I'm sorry," I whisper. "I'm so very sorry."

"I told myself I was going to stop. I didn't want to be the only person living in the past. Trying to get revenge on a friend who didn't even know what had happened."

Ian sighs and all the vitality, all the spark goes out of him. "Remember one of my more popular quotes? *You get back exactly what you put into the world*?"

I nod.

"Well. I spent twenty years putting hate into the world. I'd say that I've gotten it back a thousand-fold. All those people I've never met who hate me? I'd say that's karma finally catching up to me."

"I don't agree."

That implies you don't have the ability to learn from your

mistakes. We all should have the opportunity to make things right.

"Gemma. I grew up on an ashram. I know about karma."

I smile at him. "Fine. You're right. Being the world's most hated man is your karma."

"That's better. Now you're getting it."

I look at him, broken arm, broken ribs, stitched up chest. "I think, though, maybe you've paid enough."

He reaches up and taps my nose. "Of course you do."

I frown at him. "Did you really mean it? You want to love me?"

He gives me an innocent expression. "When have I ever lied to you?"

"Ummm. Always?"

A bright smile grows on his face. "When I saw you at The Whittcombe..."

He stops, shakes his head. "When you woke up, I decided I was going to make sure you were okay. And I was going to make sure that Josh was okay."

I raise my eyebrows.

He shrugs. "I was his friend once."

I don't have anything to say to this, so instead I ask, "If Josh doesn't want me and if everything falls apart, what'll you do?"

He stares at me, traces my lips with his eyes. They tingle under the heat of his gaze. "I'll find out where that kiss was headed."

"That's what I thought." He looks back up at me and I swallow. "Which is why I definitely, one hundred percent, have to make sure Josh and I stay together."

He flashes a delighted grin my way. "You'd be easy to love."

I shake my head. "I'm going home."

I move to stand and Ian stays me with his hand.

"Gemma. What'll *you* do if Josh doesn't want you and everything falls apart?"

I take a moment to consider my answer. What would I do? I'd have Hope. My family. But there'd be a hole in my heart, so big that everything else would just fall through. It hurts to think about it.

Ian watches the expressions on my face, patiently waiting for my answer.

Finally, I lean close and whisper, "If Josh leaves me, it'll be your fault. So I'd become an evil mastermind and destroy you."

He likes that. I can tell. "Does this mean we're friends?"

"No," I say, but I smile at him and he knows that I'm lying.

"I'll check on you tomorrow," he says.

"Don't bother."

I grab my purse and stand. "Get better."

Then, before I leave, I reach down and put a hand to his cheek. "Thank you. Thank you for saving me."

His eyes are sad and lonely. "Is this where I'm supposed to say something cliché? Like, I didn't save you, you saved me?"

I bite my lip. "Save it for someone who'll believe you."

"You're right." His eyes clear a bit, then he says, "You know, I don't think I'm ready for love, but I am ready for a friend."

"Is there a difference?" I ask.

I'm still learning about love. I realize now that before all of this, I really, really didn't know much about it at all.

"I'm not sure," Ian says.

I take my hand from his cheek. "See you tomorrow."

"Goodnight."

He closes his eyes and I walk out.

23

*"A single moment can have
a thousand truths
with none of them intersecting."*

IT'S NEARLY TEN O'CLOCK WHEN I MAKE IT HOME.

There were plenty of taxis in front of the hospital, so finding my way back was easy. It's dark, but the purple-gray kind of dark, where the city lights keep total darkness at bay.

When I climb out of the cab, my knees pinch and throb and I wince at the icy hot feel of pain.

I gingerly step across the sidewalk as the cab pulls away. The street is almost deserted. It's a residential side street, so that's not unexpected, but the quiet strikes me as sad.

The lights are on in the living room and through the window I can see my mom on the couch reading a book.

I breathe in the warm summer air. The sidewalk is lined with gingko trees, their heart shaped leaves shiver in the night breeze. There's a small flowering tree in front of the building, and its white frothy flowers smell musty, like wet cardboard.

I pause for a moment, feeling the quiet of looking outside in. I wish Josh were here. It feels harder taking those steps to the front door, knowing that when I go inside, he won't be there to say hello.

I take out my phone and send a quick text: *I'm home. I wish you were here. I need you.*

I have so much I need to tell him. We have so much to talk about.

I feel like I've been living in a house my whole life and someone just informed me that there's an entire floor that I've never seen before. I thought my house was two stories, when in fact, there's a third floor, a basement, and an attic, and it changes everything.

Or it doesn't change anything. I'm not sure. I have to explore it, see what it all means.

Today was a day of revelations. But the biggest revelation for me was that I've been wrong. I thought I couldn't feel love anymore. But that wasn't the case at all. I just wasn't feeling the same love.

But I think love comes in a million different forms and one isn't better or worse than the other. Just because I used to feel like I was flying when I looked at Josh, just because loving him felt like lying in the sun and eating ice cream on a summer day, doesn't mean that loving him can't feel like other things too.

I want to explore them now. All the millions of ways that love can express itself.

He's right though. This isn't really something we can discuss over the phone. Especially because for all I know, he's with the mother of his baby, and all he knows is that I'm with Ian Fortune. It's a mess.

The text message I sent is marked as unread. I didn't expect anything else. He probably won't land in California for another few hours.

I drop my phone back in my purse and head inside. When I open the front door, my mom looks up.

There's a beat of silence, then she drops her book and gasps, "Gemma, what happened!"

Fifteen minutes later we're on the couch, my mom has entered full mother hen mode.

She's set up a tray with hot tea, milk and honey, a bowl of tomato soup and a crisp grilled cheese sandwich.

I'm in pajamas, having gratefully peeled off my ripped, dirty, blood-stained clothes. The blood and medical ointments had dried and formed a brown crust on my jeans and top, so I decided to donate them to the trash can.

I'm looking forward to a hot shower, but I think my mom's head would've exploded if I'd taken longer than ten minutes to change.

"I can't believe *that man* saved you," she says again.

I give my mom a fond look. She reserves *that man* and *that woman* for people who shan't be named. Mainly, my ex-husband's wife, Ian Fortune, and one of Dylan's ex-girlfriends, a closet kleptomaniac who over the course of three months stole about five thousand dollars' worth of jewelry, cutlery, and art from my parents' house.

"You can call him Ian," I say. "He did break an arm and two ribs for me. And he lost a lot of blood. I think he can be Ian now."

She flinches, probably at the reminder that it could've been me with the broken bones. I told her the bare minimum, that I'd not looked before crossing the street and that Ian had shoved me out of the way of an oncoming taxi. I left out the kiss, that Josh had seen us, and Ian's confession.

"Well, I can't believe that *Ian* saved you." She grimaces when she says his name.

She likes him about as much as the rest of the country, which means, not at all.

"We're friends," I say simply. Funny enough, that feels true.

My mom frowns and looks over my bandages and bruises with a little less anxiety than when I first came in.

"Ian and I are friends," I say again.

She tilts her head, thinks this over for a moment and then says, "In that case, I'll bring him a few dishes tomorrow. Does he like chicken noodle soup? Or hmmm, what about meatballs? Or chicken tetrazzini?"

I shrug, I have no idea. "He likes submarine sandwiches with pickles and onions," I say, which is about the only thing I've seen him eating in the past few weeks. I think back. "Oh, and sushi."

My mom considers this, and I can see her drawing up a menu. One of my mom's favorite things is to plan menus. If there's a wedding, a funeral, a church potluck, a holiday, or someone in need, the first thing she'll do is marshal up the kitchen forces and make enough casseroles, pasta dishes, breads, meats, and desserts to feed an army.

"Subs and sushi. Hmm. What is he doing now? Does he have another job?"

I shake my head. "Not sure. He volunteers a lot." Sort of.

"Well. Hmm. Volunteering is nice. Caroline Kramer's daughter, Sue, she's a paralegal, remember her, she graduated a few years behind you, she just went through a nasty break-up and—"

"Mom."

"I bet she'd love to meet—"

"Mom."

I need to put the kibosh on this before my mom decides that Ian Fortune and Sue Kramer are going to get married, have babies, and eat her famous barbecue wieners and lime Jell-O at their wedding.

"What is it? Are you in pain? Should I get something?"

I shake my head. Then I ask what I've wanted to know since I got home, "Did Josh say anything before he left?"

The oven beeps in the kitchen. "That's your tater tots," she says. "And I threw in a green bean casserole."

I nod. "Sure."

Of course she did. I'm surprised there aren't cookies baking too. It only took me ten minutes to change, but that gave her ten full minutes to cook.

The oven beeps again. She reaches out and tugs on a lock of my hair. "He didn't say anything. Should he have?"

I shake my head. "No."

She hurries to the kitchen to retrieve the tots and the green beans and I discreetly check my phone. My message hasn't been read.

When I hear my mom's footsteps, I slip my phone between the couch cushion and my leg. She sets the plate full of potatoes and green beans next to my grilled cheese.

"Eat," she demands.

I pick at the cheddar cheese dripping from the edge of the sandwich. I should be starving, since I haven't eaten since breakfast, but I'm not. I'm just really, really tired.

"Didn't Josh find you at The Whittcombe?"

She settles next to me on the couch and grabs a tater tot. "I thought he went to tell you that he had to head out to LA? When neither of us could get ahold of you—" She pops the tater tot in her mouth and then waves her hands in front of her mouth. Yeah, those things are always lava hot.

I shake my head, "No. We didn't...we didn't connect."

She swallows, then says, "That's okay, sweetie. He seemed happy when he left. He was all smiles, seemed in a really good mood. Like the old Josh. He played patty cake with Hope, she giggled. He blew on her belly, it was very cute."

My stomach roils at this news and the smell of the green bean casserole, covered in mushrooms and cream, turns my stomach.

I've come to learn that the more Josh is hurting, the happier he looks to the outside world. My mom doesn't know that he'd just seen me kissing Ian and that he might be considering ending things. To her, he looked happy.

I let out a shuddering breath.

My mom doesn't notice, she keeps on, "He'll be back in no time. Did you want to try calling him? Let him know you're okay?"

I shake my head. "I don't want to worry him. I'll wait until he's home."

There's something in my voice that alerts her. My mom looks more closely at me.

"Everything okay, sweetie?"

I shake my head. "No."

"Want to talk about it?"

I look down at my gauze-covered hands. "Not really."

She scooches closer to me. My mom is petite, like Leah, smaller than me, but even though I was taller than her by the time I was twelve, she's still my mom, and I look up to her. She strokes my hair.

"Mom?"

"Hmmm?"

"Did the lingerie work? Are you and Dad okay now?"

Her hand stops mid stroke. She pauses for a second and then starts rubbing my hair again, just like she did when I was little and had woken up from a nightmare.

"I'll spare you the details"—her voice has a smile—"and merely say that your father is taking me on a month-long trip to France. We're doing a cooking vacation."

I look over at her and take in her pink cheeks.

"Really?"

She hums under her breath. "It turns out, your father is quite the romantic. And apparently, so am I. After thirty odd years, I'm finally finding this out."

I nudge her shoulder with my own. "I could've told you that. Nobody that isn't a romantic could make such delicious food."

She laughs her happy, chortle laugh and then kisses my cheek.

"Eat your dinner, Gemma."

"Yes, mother," I say, smiling at her, glad to have her mother-henning.

I pick up the grilled cheese and take a big bite and manage to eat the whole thing while my mom tells me about France. She says they'll wait until I'm better to go, but she's excited.

When I've eaten enough to satisfy her and my eyelids are starting to droop, she says, "Go on to bed. I'll manage Hope when she wakes."

"You'll stay the night?"

"I'll stay until Josh gets back."

I give her a quick, impulsive hug.

"Thank you." I bury my face in her shoulder, smelling her familiar perfume. "Thank you so much."

She pulls away, holds me at arm's length and studies my face. "Gemma dear?"

"Yeah?"

"I love Josh. He's been like my second son for years now."

I nod. It's true. He's been a part of our lives for a long, long time.

"Because of that, I see more than you think."

"Okay..."

She reaches up and pats my cheek. "When you were in the coma, I broke down one day. I was in your hospital room just falling to pieces. Josh found me there. He sat down next to me, and he stayed there for a whole hour, not saying anything, just...sitting with me. Then when I was done crying he looked at me and said, 'Don't worry, it'll all work out. She loves us too much to stay away.' Hope was still in the NICU then. Josh was exhausted. It was only a month into it all. But he believed in you."

"I..." I can't say anything, my throat hurts too much.

"He believes in you, Gemma. I know this has been hard, I know this is the hardest thing you've ever done. But try not to let him down."

I close my eyes. "What if I already have?"

"Well, try again then. Pick yourself up and try again." She squeezes my shoulder. Then says, "Go take a shower and head to bed. You look terrible."

My lips wobble and I try to smile at her. "Thanks, Mom."

She kisses my cheek and sends me to bed.

My phone chirping pulls me out of a deep sleep.

I flail around on the bed and kick the sheets aside, trying to find my phone. The first thought that enters my sleep-crusted mind is—Josh. The bright light, it must be late morning, accosts my eyes.

I snatch my phone off the nightstand and answer, "Josh?"

"Really, Gemma? After all I've done for you? *Josh*?"

I sit up in bed and rub at my eyes, they're gritty and puffy. "What time is it? Why are you calling me? Gah, you're the devil. Did I mention I hate you?"

Ian chuckles, and I can tell he's back to his usual self, "I'm outside your front door. I brought coffee."

"Ack!"

"Not the welcome I expected."

I scramble out of bed. "Why are you here?"

"Coffee," he says, like it's completely natural that he'd be here, bringing me coffee.

"No."

I hang up on him and throw my phone across the room. Of course, as soon as it lands in the laundry pile it starts to ring again.

I stare at it like it's a cockroach on the kitchen counter. If only I had a shoe, I'd beat it. Instead, I ignore it and throw on a loose sundress. It hurts too much to have jeans or shorts rubbing against my cut-up skin.

I look in the mirror. Yeah. Pretty much what I expected.

My legs and hands look like ground hamburger, my bruises are purple and green so I amend my analysis to expired ground hamburger. It's pretty gross.

I put my hair up into a loose bun on top of my head and smack my cheeks.

"Okay, I'm awake." I blink my eyes and bounce a bit on my toes, trying to get the blood flowing and the synapses firing.

My phone starts to ring again. I glare at it.

The problem with cockroaches is, they don't go away. The darn things can survive on toenail clippings and book glue.

I grab the phone and pick it up.

"What?" I snap.

I may sound even more frustrated than the last time,

because before I answered I saw that Josh still hadn't texted me back.

"I have egg sandwiches," Ian says. "Your favorite."

My stomach rumbles. I hang up again. Then I wander down the hall to the kitchen.

My mom's there. Her book is open on the counter, and I see she has a pot of chicken soup on the stove. The clock says eleven. Hope is in her swing, and when she sees me she lets out a happy babble.

"Morning, baby," I say, a smile coming over my whole body. "Morning, Mom. That soup smells good."

She taps a wooden spoon against the pot. "Why is Ian Fortune standing on the sidewalk?"

I look out the kitchen window. He's holding a brown paper bag and a tray full of coffee cups. It's actually impressive because one arm is in a cast and he's slightly hunched over, probably because his ribs hurt. He's unshaven, and since his beard grows in thick, his face is shadowed by dark stubble. He's back in sweatpants and a ratty t-shirt.

"I don't think that's Ian. Looks more like a vagrant." I suppress a smile.

My mom comes up next to me and stares at him. He finally sees us looking. He holds up the coffee and then gives me a look like, "Oh, come on!"

"I'm pretty sure that's him," my mom says.

"I don't know..."

But the jig is up. Ian marches over to the intercom at the building's door and a buzzing sound fills the apartment.

I go and tickle Hope under her chin. She giggles and I kiss her on her nose.

"You should let him in," my mom says. "This soup is for him."

I walk down and press the buzzer to unlock the building

door. Then I open our front door and stand there, arms folded, listening to Ian struggling down the hall, trying to carry coffee and sandwiches with a broken arm.

When he sees me standing in the front door, scraped up legs in full display, he stops and gives me an evil grin.

"Josh wouldn't want you here," I say.

I don't think he considered this, because suddenly he looks really pleased with himself.

"He wouldn't, would he?" His eyes crinkle and he pushes past me into the apartment.

"I don't want you here."

But before he can respond, my mom bustles into the living room, wooden soup spoon in her hand. She waves it at Ian.

"You saved my daughter. I've made you soup."

Ian stops and stares. I think he's surprised to see her. He probably wasn't expecting anyone to be here but me and Hope.

My mom has on a lace-trimmed apron, a dress, and her hair and makeup are perfect. In a nutshell, that's my mom.

"Err. Hello?"

Ha. He's speechless.

But my mom's not done. "I've been told that you are Gemma's friend. But I've also heard on the news that you're a nasty piece of work. If you hurt my daughter, I'll chop off your testicles and cook them in my soup pot."

Holy crap.

Ian coughs. Chokes on his breath. Wheezes.

I smirk at him.

"Ian. Meet my mom."

He clears his throat. "Pleasure."

She smiles at him. "You brought coffee. How sweet. Come to the kitchen. I made chicken noodle, you like soup, right?"

He turns to me, eyes wide, like he's trying to telepathically say, *heeeeeeelp*.

But I'm definitely not going to help him. He's the one who showed up uninvited.

"Come on. You can take the soup and go."

"I don't think I want the soup," he whispers.

I hold back a snort.

In the kitchen, Ian puts the coffee and sandwiches down on the table.

I go over to the baby swing, unstrap Hope and pull her into my arms. She's warm and smells like baby shampoo and bottle.

"Hope, meet Ian. He's a terrible person."

She waves her arms at him and bats her eyelashes, flirting baby style. Apparently she's completely smitten by his appearance. Ian has always had that effect on females. I guess even baby females aren't immune.

"Why is she looking at me like that?" Ian asks.

He has that sort of I've-never-seen-a-baby-in-my-life, keep-it-away-from-me look on his face.

"Because she likes you," I say. Then I add, "Probably because she doesn't know you."

She squeals and Ian takes a step back.

I hold back a laugh. I've never seen him so out of his element.

My mom is busy laying out the sandwiches Ian brought, scooping up soup, and putting the coffee into actual mugs.

When she's done she pats me on the back, "I'm going to go call your father."

We're quiet as she walks to the living room. I wasn't expecting her to leave. I glance at Ian, feeling incredibly awkward. Not even Hope, blowing spit bubbles at Ian, can cut the tension.

I clear my throat. "So, you got discharged."

"I'm not here to seduce you," he says.

I cough. "Yeah. I figured that." Then I say, "Why are you here?"

He pulls out a chair and sits at the table, blows on my mom's soup and then takes a sip from the spoon.

"Good," he says after a moment.

I lift the egg sandwich off the plate and take a big bite. The fluffy egg and cheddar cheese is beyond delicious.

"Thanks for this." I take a sip of the coffee.

"No problem. Stole it from the nurses station when I left the hospital this morning. They get busy...leave their food unattended. What's a guy to do?"

I spit the coffee back into the cup.

Ian laughs and takes a bite of his egg sandwich.

"Kidding," he says, mouth full. Then, "Actually, I'm not."

"Your morals are broken."

He shrugs. "My morals are flexible."

"I thought we talked about this."

His eyes spark with something close to glee. "I told you my life story, I didn't tell you I was going to become a saint."

"But how will karma ever stop catching up to you if you keep doing bad things?"

He takes another big bite of his sandwich and chews while he thinks this over.

"Maybe I like being punished?"

That sounds a little too much like a truth, so I dip my head and take another bite of the sandwich. Stolen or not, it's good.

"Don't worry, Gemma. I bought all this from the vendor at the subway stop."

I look up quickly. "Really?"

He shakes his head. "No."

I laugh, surprised at how funny I find this. I'm not sure which story to believe, but I bet he didn't steal this coffee or the sandwiches.

Probably...

Ian gives me a pleased smile then stands. "I'll be going."

"Why did you come?" I ask again.

He shrugs, "You're one of four people on earth who doesn't hate me. I figured it'd be nice to have a meal where someone doesn't try to throw food at me."

He's lonely.

He's hiding it, but there, right there in his voice, in his expression, I can see it.

He's lonely.

"Me. Your mom. The cardsharp. Who's the fourth person?" I ask.

He smiles at me and tilts his head, taking in the apartment, the sunlight spilling over the countertop from the window, the wooden IKEA table, the ink drawing of a rocket ship, framed, hanging on the wall.

Ian nods at the drawing, so obviously one of Josh's.

"Josh is the fourth person. He never had it in him to hate me. Even after it all. Although maybe that'll change."

He's right. Josh never hated him. Although, I don't know how he feels now.

But Ian's wrong about one thing.

"There are five people," I tell him.

"Really? Five?"

I nod and point at Hope.

He gives a surprised laugh. "Fair enough. The leaky, slobbery baby likes me. Wonderful."

"Idiot," I say.

He grins at me.

His smile pulls me in, and I lean toward him, take a

minute to study his expression. I think back on all I know about Ian, all the years I worked for him, everything I thought I knew about him.

"Question."

He lifts an eyebrow. "Answer."

Which in Ian language means, maybe I'll tell you, maybe I won't.

Still, Ian talking about how Josh could never hate him has made me curious.

"Last year, when I quit...everything you told me, all that about inventors stealing ideas to make the world a better place, all that about the ends justifying the means, that was a lie? It was never about taking initiative? That wasn't the truth? It was always about your..." I trail off as Ian's smile slips and his eyes darken. "Family?" I finish.

He blows out a long breath and pinches the bridge of his nose.

"Gemma, haven't you heard? Truth isn't a flat piece of paper with truth written on one side and lie on the other. A single moment can have a thousand truths with none of them intersecting."

He flicks his eyes to me. "Mind you, there can be just as many lies. More. But don't think that just because one thing is the truth, something else can't be as well."

And that just about sums up the complicated state that we all know as life.

He grins at me. "I'll be going."

But before he can leave, my mom rushes into the kitchen and packs him a bag full of chicken noodle soup, spaghetti and meatballs, chicken tetrazzini, green bean casserole, and a tin of meatloaf. She's been busy. If I had to guess, I'd say she's been cooking since sunrise.

Ian watches my mom with a bemused expression.

I shove him out the door, and my mom tells him to come by anytime, and I tell him to *not* come by anytime. He likes that.

LATER, MY MOM RUNS TO THE STORE TO PICK UP DIAPERS, formula, and ingredients for dinner.

She cleared out the refrigerator cooking piles of food for Ian. While she's gone I spread a baby blanket on the floor and lie next to Hope, counting her toes, kissing her fingers, and making her laugh with funny faces.

Now, it's nearly one, the afternoon sun is bright, and Hope and I are snuggled under a blanket on the couch. On the side table, Josh left one of his sketchbooks open.

"What's this?" I ask her.

I lean over and lift it up. I smile at it, at the drawing of a little girl with pigtails in New York City, "I think it's a children's book. Did your daddy write this for you?"

She makes a noise, which I take as a yes.

So I read it to her. And it makes my heart hurt.

It's a love poem. And I don't think Josh wrote it for Hope. I think he wrote it for me.

The little girl is lost in New York City, she let go of her parents' hands in Times Square, and she can't find them. Somehow she has to find her way home.

Through crowds, and a maze of streets, bus routes and subways, she has to get back home. I flip the page, hoping she does. But there's nothing there. He never finished it.

I squeeze my eyes shut tight.

Hope reaches up and pulls on my hair, making my scalp sting. I open my eyes and look at her, her brow is furrowed and she looks like she's working herself up to a good cry.

Her face is turning red and the little strawberry birthmark on her forehead is getting darker. I know just how she feels. I'd like to work myself up to a good cry too.

Unfortunately, I can't. But Hope does. For the next hour, she's inconsolable. I try giving her a bottle, patting her back, changing her diaper, walking back and forth with her in my arms, rocking her, running the vacuum, singing, running a bath. Nothing works.

For an hour, Hope cries and cries and cries.

It's *horrible*.

When my mom gets back, groceries in her arms, she sees me and says, "She needs a swaddle."

My nerves are as sharp as the end of a needle, I'm low level panicky from Hope's non-stop crying.

"A what?"

My mom hurries to the nursery, grabs a blanket, takes Hope and wraps her like a little baby burrito. Almost immediately Hope's cries fade to whimpers and then her eyes drift closed.

I let out a painful sigh. "Jeez."

My mom pats my back. "I'll go put the groceries away."

I collapse into the rocking chair, Hope in my arms. She's nodding off.

Finally, after an hour, tears come to my eyes.

"You know what I've realized?" I tell Hope.

She doesn't answer. Her eyes drift back open at my voice, but then close again. I push the rocker back and forth and study her face.

"I realized that I have a whole lot of guilt. Everyone knows you. Your dad wakes up at night to feed you. He knows how to make you laugh. Your grandma knows how to soothe you. What do I know?"

She's asleep. She lets out a little squeaky snore.

"I wanted you so bad. I wanted you for so long. And now that you're here, I'm so busy trying to get better that I don't know you. And I've been waiting to feel that flood of love for you. I feel so guilty that I haven't. Like, what's wrong with me?"

I trace my finger over her cheek. Trace her jaw, so reminiscent of Josh's.

"But I realized, you don't need me to love you like I think I should. You just need me to be here. You don't know the difference between the love I imagined and the love I can give. I think, this is love, right?"

I rock her, and sniff back my tears. "If you can forgive me for not being perfect, I'll try my best. I'll do the best I can for you. Okay? And when you're grown, I hope you look back and are glad I was your mom."

I lean back in the chair and close my eyes. The nursery is quiet, the only sound is the creaking of the rocker and the hushed sound of our breathing. I hold her close and feel the night starting to recede, the sun is that much closer.

I pull my phone from my pocket and take a picture of Hope. I text it to Josh: *We miss you.*

I stare at my cracked screen, waiting for his response.

I let out a painful breath when his return text pops up: *How is she?*

My heart thuds in my chest. What should I write back?

She's good. She's napping. I didn't know she liked to be swaddled. Did you know that? I read her a board book. She was more interested in chewing the pages than hearing the story.

I think about what else to type, should I tell him about the kiss, about Ian, about the hospital? Should I ask about Lisa? But before I can write, another text pops up.

Okay.

I stare at the word. *Okay.*

Never in his life has Josh been so short with me. He's frequently in his head, he often needs a long time to figure out what he wants to say, but he's never been...this.

Is this really it for us?

The heck with it, I dial the phone, waiting while it rings. He doesn't answer. His voicemail picks up. I cringe when I remember my last message. I don't recall exactly what I said, but I have a feeling it was probably a train wreck and left him thinking I was shacking up with Ian.

"Hey. It's me. I know you said you wanted to save this conversation for until you got home, but I just wanted to let you know that...I miss you. A lot. There's a whole bunch you don't know, and a whole bunch I guess that I don't know. But there's this really wonderful guy, his name's Josh Lewenthal, maybe you know him?"

I smile. "Anyway, he once said, the best gift someone can give is love. I never realized that love came in different sizes, and packages, and even had different wrapping paper."

I pause, "Okay, that metaphor got weird. Maybe you can say this better. If you agree with me, that is."

I bite my lip, feeling a little stupid spilling my heart to Josh's voicemail. "If you want to call me, I'd like that. Or if you want to wait until you get home, that's okay. But I hope that you don't think I've let you down. I told you everything I've done is to get back to you and... Okay. See you soon."

I hang up. Wait for a moment for Josh to call back. Text. Anything.

He doesn't.

The echo of what Josh told Ian all those years ago bounces around in my head. *She didn't want me, why should I want her?*

24

*"How can something fly
if you're holding onto it?"*

IT'S SATURDAY. JOSH ISN'T EXPECTED BACK UNTIL TOMORROW night. So, instead of sitting around worrying, moping, or imagining worst case scenarios, I decide to throw a party.

There are a few things in life guaranteed to cheer people up: shopping, chocolate, and parties.

I don't especially enjoy shopping, and I've already eaten two chocolate bars I found in the back of a cupboard (they didn't help). I can either spend the day obsessively staring at my phone or I can try to have some fun.

The Fourth of July has come and gone and my mom didn't have her annual party this year. So, we decide to throw an impromptu post-Fourth gathering in the grassy park down the street.

At seven in the morning, I send a text to everyone—my dad, Leah and Oliver, Dylan, Hannah, Brook, and Carly.

Then my mom and I spend the next five hours in the kitchen, juggling Hope with preparing the post-fourth of July picnic to end all picnics.

I have to be honest, my mom took care of nearly

everything. After I scorched the potatoes and added a cup of salt instead of sugar to the cupcake batter, my mom decided that I might not be ready for kitchen prime time.

"You'll get there, Gemma," she said, patting my arm.

I used to be a whizz in the kitchen. I might have felt sorry for myself, but I was reminded of Ian's book inscription—this is your life, live it. So I accepted the fact that cooking and baking weren't so simple anymore and just let it be.

Now, we're at the park, setting down a plaid blanket and pulling our feast out of the picnic basket. Corn on the cob, deviled eggs, Grandma's potato salad, barbecue wieners, watermelon, stars and stripes cupcakes, and a red, white, and blue Jell-O mold (of course).

I'm in a red dress and Hope is in a blue checkered romper. The two of us together look like a flag. I set her in my lap, take a selfie, and then send it off to Josh.

I'm saved from worrying about the fact that he doesn't reply by Colin, Sasha and the twins rushing across the grass toward our blanket.

"Auntie Gemma! Grandma! Baby Hope!"

I grin and wave as the Four Horsemen of the Apocalypse race toward us. Sasha skids onto the blanket, baseball style, and reaches for Hope. She's the oldest, and definitely baby crazy.

The kids all talk at once, and it's hard to separate the strings of their conversation, but it doesn't feel like overload anymore. It's been nearly a month since I've seen them and this time I can just sit back and enjoy them.

"Where are your parents?" my mom asks them.

Colin points to where Leah and Oliver are lugging a soccer net, a ball, a kite, and a large red cooler across the green grass.

Behind them, I see my dad, Dylan, and my friends.

I stand and wave. It's going to be a great party.

"Did I mention Ian is coming?" My mom asks.

I glance sharply at her. She's staring at the park entrance, her eyes on my dad.

"What? Why?"

"He called your cell while you were in the shower. It's rude not to answer when someone calls. Then I invited him to the picnic. It came out when he thanked me for the soup. I'm going to drop some hints about Sue. I spoke to her mother last night, she's very open to dating."

"Sue or her mother?" I ask.

"Hmmm?" My mom isn't listening anymore. She's straightening her hair and adjusting the collar of her dress. My dad's almost here.

I've changed my mind. This party is going to be terrible.

"TELL ME AGAIN WHAT HAPPENED," LEAH SAYS.

Her nose is already pink from only ten minutes in the full sun.

A little bit ago my dad, Dylan and Oliver moved our picnic blanket, food and coolers to the shade of one of the old trees lining the grassy field of the park. We have a nice area, it's free of dirt, cigarette butts and trash. Just grass.

I pluck at a piece of grass and spin it for Hope. She reaches up and tries to grab it.

"There's not much else to tell," I say, glancing over at Leah.

She's asking about the gruesome (her words) looking scrapes on my legs. When she saw them she freaked out.

"I didn't look when I crossed the street, Ian pushed me out of the way of a taxi."

We both turn and stare at him. Leah's kids are completely enthralled with him. Colin wanted help flying his kite—Ian purposely let it loose to fly away. When Colin got upset, Ian said, "You wanted it to fly, didn't you? How can something fly if you're holding on to it?"

Being a thinker, Colin figured Ian was right and also a person of *great* wisdom.

Then Mary asked Ian to help her find the best cupcake. He took the uneaten cupcake from my mom's plate and gave it to Mary. "Everything is better when taken from someone else. The grass is always greener, etcetera, etcetera."

All the kids were shocked, you could tell they'd never met anyone like him.

Now they're all playing soccer. Ian is the goalie.

Which basically means he's standing in the portable goal, letting the ball whack his shins. When he sees me staring he sends me a long-suffering look.

"He's corrupting my kids," Leah says.

I shrug. "Mom invited him."

She snorts. "Mom would invite a fox into a henhouse if she thought there was a chance for dating."

"What are we talking about?" Hannah sits down on the blanket next to me.

She lowers herself slowly and carefully because she's reached that point in pregnancy when bending over becomes really difficult.

When my friends got here they immediately descended on the homemade potato salad and deviled eggs like a swarm of tourists descending on buy one get one Broadway tickets. My mom has a gift.

Brook drops onto the grass nearby, she has a plate full of deviled eggs.

"Tell me we're talking about Lisa Perry. Because I've got a

few things to say. None of them complimentary." She shoves a whole egg into her mouth and chews angrily.

Carly bends down and gives me a kiss on each cheek.

"Where's the baby?" I ask Brook, trying to distract her.

"You're not going to distract me," she says. "Where's Josh? I saw the articles. What's all this about?"

"We're talking about Ian Fortune," Leah says, pointing to Ian standing in the soccer goal.

Everyone talks at the same time.

"Okay. I'm distracted. Why is the creep of America here?" Brook asks.

"Ewww, Ian Fortune," Hannah says. "What a slug."

"Why is that man here?" Carly asks. "And can he leave?"

They all start arguing at who should go over and demand that he leave the vicinity. Brook is winning. Apparently she has a brick in her purse.

I flinch on Ian's behalf. "He's not a creep," I interrupt. "He's my friend. I invited him."

Everyone stops talking. Hannah frowns at me and I get the feeling she's trying to read my aura. Carly lifts a perfectly groomed eyebrow.

Brook's mouth drops open, and I get a view of chewed up egg.

"Are you kidding me right now?" she asks.

They all stare at me.

I realize that as far as anyone knows Ian is a womanizing, workplace-harassing fake. The scum of America.

"Technically, Mom invited him," Leah says.

My friends ignore her.

Brook says, "Gemma. I've represented career criminals that have more of a soul than Ian Fortune. Why is he here?"

"Honestly," Hannah says.

A cold prickly discomfort coats me.

"He's not a creep." Usually it's Ian that makes me angry, now I'm angry on his behalf. "He's not a creep, he's a human. And humans make mistakes and humans say stupid things. Okay?"

He's lonely. He's lost. He's in pain and he made mistakes. But he's not a monster.

I stand up, slapping the dirt and grass off my dress. Brook stares at me, speechless.

"Gemma?" Hannah says hesitantly.

"I thought we were all on the We Hate Ian Fortune team?" Carly asks.

Slowly, Leah shakes her head no.

All of them look at me like I might break apart or explode any second.

"What?" I frown at them, then look over at Ian. He's still letting himself be used as target practice for my nieces and nephew.

"I'm going to go...check..." I shrug and then scoop up Hope. "I'll be back in a second."

I walk across the grass, avoid the soccer ball flying across the lawn, and stop next to Ian.

"Having fun?" I ask.

He *oofs* when Sasha hits him in the knee with the soccer ball.

Then he glances at me and says dryly, "The delights of this afternoon are beyond description."

I grin at him. "My nieces and nephew like you. That means your list is now nine people big."

He looks up at the denim-blue sky and ponders this number.

When he turns back to me he says, "Did you know that your mother made a Jell-O mold in the shape of George Washington's head?"

I smile at him, "She got the mold same-day shipping just for this picnic."

"That makes complete sense," he says.

Not to be outdone by soccer balls and Jell-O molds, Hope squeals and reaches out to Ian. He frowns at her, which apparently only encourages her, because she laughs and blows spit bubbles at him.

My mom joins us at the soccer goal.

"Gemma? I noticed we're out of eggs. Would you pop back to the apartment and grab the other tray? I'd go, but your father..."

She trails off and looks at Ian, then back to me, her cheeks pink.

Ahh. I guess my dad is putting on the moves and she's embarrassed to say so in front of Ian.

"Sure. That's fine."

I don't mind. The apartment is only a few blocks away, it'll take less than fifteen minutes to get there and back.

"I'll watch Hope," she says, holding out her arms.

Ian *ooomphs* again when the soccer ball hits him in the thigh,

"Oi!" he yells, turning to the kids. "That was playing dirty!"

They all giggle and run the other direction.

Ian turns to me. "I'll go with you."

I shake my head, about to tell him no, but then I realize there isn't really anyone here that wants him around. My mom doesn't count, the kids just want to kick the soccer ball at him, and I'm about to leave him to fend for himself.

"Alright. You can carry the eggs."

He looks down at his arm in its cast and lifts an eyebrow.

I laugh. "You'll figure it out."

As we're walking out of the park, Dylan jogs up next to me.

"Gem, hey. Can I talk to you a second?" He looks meaningfully at Ian and says, "Alone."

Whatever he has to say, it seems pretty urgent. Before we started to leave he'd been happily sitting with Oliver, talking about his promotion, and eating plate after plate of barbecue wieners and corn on the cob. Last I saw, he'd been inspecting the tray of cupcakes. For Dylan to postpone cupcakes...he must think this is important.

I step aside with him, off the path and about ten feet from Ian.

"What?"

I haven't seen Dylan since he stopped by and spoke to Josh. He doesn't know that I heard him tell Josh to leave me and I'm not really sure how I want to address it.

"I don't think you should be hanging around Ian Fortune," he says.

His shaggy hair pokes out from under his baseball hat, and he looks earnest and concerned.

Which, honestly, isn't what I need from him.

I put my hands on my hips and glare at him. He doesn't notice. He's completely caught up in his role of big brother protector.

Dylan turns and sends a dark look Ian's way.

Once when I was in fifth grade, a boy, Reggie Wingheimer, decided he wanted to pick on me—he called me Chubby Tubby Gemma. That nickname lasted exactly half a day, until lunch, when the sixth graders joined us and Dylan heard the news.

He marched over to Reggie, said, "Nobody says crap about my sister," then he tackled Reggie like a pro linebacker. No one ever picked on me again.

Here's the point. Dylan is sending Ian the same look he gave Reggie right before he sent him flying over the lunch table.

"What if Josh finds out?" he asks, still glowering at Ian.

My face flushes hot and I poke Dylan until he looks back at me. "*When* Josh finds out, he'll listen to what I have to say, and he'll understand. He'll be happy for me."

Dylan snorts and shakes his head. He doesn't believe me. Right then, I know exactly how I'm going to address this.

"Dylan, I'm going to be Ian's friend. There's nothing you can say or do to stop me."

Dylan holds up his hands. "Whoa, Gemma. Not a smart choice."

"But it's my choice," I say firmly. "And it's my life. Not yours."

The concern in Dylan's face fades, and I'm left with his disbelief. He tugs his baseball hat lower.

"You've changed. And not in a good way. The old Gemma didn't purposely hurt the people she loved."

I flinch. If I let myself think about it, his words would hurt, so I don't think about it.

Instead I say, "The old Gemma also said that my life isn't a sitcom that my big brother gets to direct. I make my own decisions. That's still the same. You should trust me to make the right ones."

Dylan looks over at Ian and whatever he sees has him scowling.

"Whatever. Just try not to get hurt. And try not to hurt my best friend." He turns back to me and his expression has gone back to earnest and concerned.

I flick the brim of his hat. "You're kind of an idiot, you know that?"

He frowns, considers this, then, "Sure. Do you think there's any cupcakes left?"

I shake my head and walk away, leaving Dylan to ponder desserts.

Ian catches up to me, his long stride easily keeping up with my quick pace. We cross the street at the crosswalk, heading back to the apartment.

"I've been thinking about what you said—moving to another state and changing my name," Ian says. "You were right, it might be nice to start over."

"Probably a good idea," I tell him.

We leave it at that.

I PULL THE WHITE CERAMIC TRAY OF DEVILED EGGS OUT OF THE fridge. They're pretty little egg boats full of fluffy bright yellow yolk sprinkled with red paprika. My mom put toothpick flags in each egg to make them look like sailboats.

Ian leans against the kitchen counter, his long legs out in front of him. He seems satisfied staying quiet, just watching. I lift an eyebrow then put the tray on the counter next to him.

The apartment is cool and soothing compared to the muggy bright heat of the afternoon. I reach up into the cupboard and pull down a glass for some water.

"Do you want any water before we head back?"

He shakes his head no. Ian's back in workout clothes. Probably because it was too hard to put on anything else with a broken arm and cracked ribs. I turn on the tap and stick my hand under the spray of water, waiting for it to turn cold.

I'm pretty certain Ian realizes that Dylan was warning me to stay away from him. As I've seen, he's not oblivious to the generalized hate directed his way.

"Sorry about my brother," I say.

The water's cold, I stick the glass under and watch the air bubbles in the water rise to the top as the glass fills.

"He's not wrong," Ian says.

I flip off the tap and turn around. Ian's smiling again, his chin dimple in full evidence.

"You don't even know what he said."

He shrugs. "I can guess."

I lean against the counter next to him and take a sip of my water. Even from the tap, it's cool and delicious.

Ian watches me from the corner of his eye.

"You really want to leave New York?" I finally ask, not believing that he'll ever really leave the city.

He narrows his eyes, like he's trying to envision that future. He'd be away from New York, his mom, his past.

"I don't know. Maybe."

I set the glass down on the counter and say, "I want you to tell Josh what you told me."

When Ian raises an eyebrow, I say, "He deserves to know. Especially about his mom. He deserves to hear it from you."

Ian scoffs and shakes his head. "Still trying to be my conscience?"

I rub at the condensation forming on the edge of my glass.

"No. I think you have one of your own." He grins at me, so I amend, "You just choose not to listen to it."

"Too right."

Then he tilts his head, like he's listening to something. Maybe the angel/devil on his shoulder.

"Will you tell him?" I ask.

Suddenly Ian straightens, shedding his lazy smile. The kitchen feels smaller, because the humorous, sardonic, self-deprecating Ian is gone. The charming, confident, slick superstar is back. His eyes gleam, backlit by some internal purpose, and he takes a step toward me.

"What?" I ask.

I stand my ground. I'm not sure how I spent seven years thinking Ian was attractive, but this smarmy self-help guru smile is not for me.

"Remember how I said I wanted Josh to be happy?" he asks.

"Yes."

His lips curl into a wry smile. "I lied."

He stares at my lips and I curl my right hand into a fist. "Kiss me again and I'll break another rib."

He grins. "I don't think it'll take kissing. But I would like him to suffer, just a little longer."

What does that mean?

He steps forward and puts his hand on my shoulders. "This is me saying goodbye, Gemma," he says in a quiet voice.

Then I hear it, a noise in the hall, hurried footsteps and then, "Gemma. I'm back, I'm sorry, I couldn't stay—"

Josh.

I try to step around Ian, he catches my arm, and gives one, subtle shake of his head.

I can't see around Ian's bulk, but I know that Josh has stopped in the entry to the kitchen. It's only a second, but it feels like an eternity. In fact, it feels just like when Ian kissed me in the street, and Josh stood on the other side, silent and stunned.

"You have two seconds to let go of my fiancée and get out of my house," Josh says. His voice is tight and furious.

My heart kicks around in my chest and somersaults over my ribs. He's here. He's back. He's here.

Ian looks down at me and smiles. "That's more like it," he says in a voice so low only I can hear it. Then, "Bye, Gemma."

And I think this is it. This is goodbye for good. Maybe he really is going to another state, changing his name, and he's not going to tell Josh anything about the past.

"Tell him," I mouth.

Ian shakes his head no.

"Get out," Josh says. "Now."

Ian winks at me.

And I realize that when he tilted his head and I thought he was listening to his conscience, he'd actually heard Josh coming in the front door.

Whether he wants Josh to suffer, he's trying to make Josh see the error of his ways, or a mixture of both, I'll never know. I'm not sure if even Ian knows.

All the same, Ian lets go of my arm and takes a step back. For a minute, he lets the charming guru persona slip and he sends me a fond look, one of thanks, and a shared past, and an apology too, then he closes that off and turns away.

Now that Ian has moved, I have an unobstructed view of Josh. I drink in the sight of him, like he's that cold glass of water on a blazing hot summer day.

My whole body tingles at the sight of him and there's a happy, joyful feeling sparking to life in my chest.

He's doing that to me. Josh.

He's tired, there are bags under his eyes. His hair is messy, like he ran his hands through it a thousand times on the flight back. His stubble is dark, his t-shirt is wrinkled, and my favorite part, there's a smudge of ink on his jaw. I know that happens when he has ink on his hands, and then he rubs his face when he's deep in thought. I used to laugh and wipe it off for him.

My chest gives a little pulsing squeeze.

Josh hasn't looked at me yet. I take in a shaky breath and his eyes flick to mine, just for a second. He looks away so quickly that I don't know what he's thinking, what he's feeling.

Ian steps forward. "Josh. Good seeing you again."

Josh's shoulders stiffen, he stares at Ian, and I think he's deciding whether or not he's going to punch him in the nose.

After five long seconds his shoulders relax, he nods and says, "Right."

I hold my breath, waiting for Ian to say something taunting or idiotic, something to goad Josh into punching him, like in the Hamptons.

Instead Ian says, "We're even now. It's settled. I'm done."

Josh watches him with wary eyes. "I have no idea what you're talking about. I'd like you to leave."

Ian nods. Then he turns back to me, lifts his good arm in farewell, then strides out of the kitchen. Josh and I stand silently until the front door clicks shut.

I feel short of breath and dizzy. Josh is here. He's only ten feet away from me, but he isn't looking at me, or touching me, or talking. His eyes are closed and he's pulling in deep breaths.

"Josh?" I whisper.

I step across the kitchen toward him.

"Where's Hope?" he asks, still not looking up.

"She's with my mom. We're all having a picnic in the park." I start to ramble, "We invited everyone. Leah and Oliver, the kids, Dylan, Mom and Dad, Brook and Hannah and..."

I trail off because Josh is looking at me, and his expression is stunned, "Gemma. What happened? What..."

He grabs my hands and flips them over, showing the scraped pink skin and the scabs. His touch is hot ice, licking at my wrists.

I close my eyes and feel the sensation. His touch is like

the pain of touching a hot stove. I don't want to pull away, I want to keep my hand on the stove. It hurts, but only because I'm waking up again.

His thumbs stroke the underside of my wrist and then I hear him suck in a breath, "What happened to your legs?"

He kneels down and I open my eyes to stare down at the top of his head as he inspects my legs. He rubs his hands over the back of my thighs where my skin is untouched, his fingers hover over the newly forming scabs on the front of my legs.

They're still bruised purple and blue and yellow, with red and pink scrapes and newly formed scabs. It looks like someone dragged me across a mile long piece of sandpaper.

Josh's shoulders shudder and he finally tilts his head up, "Gemma?"

It's hard to think when he's looking at me, I reach down and brush his hair back from his forehead. It's soft and fine, and I smooth out the mess. Josh furrows his brow, "Gemma. What happened?"

A tight ball of nerves solidifies in my chest. "The day you saw Ian kiss me?"

He nods and his jaw tightens. He looks away from me, but his hands tighten on the back of my thighs.

"I ran after you."

Josh quickly glances back to me. He hadn't realized. It's obvious in his expression that he thought I hadn't cared that he'd walked away. His eyes flicker with something. Hope?

I rest my hands on his shoulders, my fingers brush the material of his shirt. I concentrate on the feel of the fabric scraping the cuts on my hands, so I don't have to hear the sound of the taxi brakes screeching.

"I didn't see you," Josh says.

I shake my head and squeeze his shirt in my hands. "You wouldn't have."

I swallow, my throat is swollen and sore, and there are tears buried inside that are trying to break free.

"I didn't look when I ran after you. There was a taxi."

Even though Josh knows I'm okay, he's right here with me after all, his face loses color and his fingers tremble on my legs.

"I was going to be hit," I admit. "For some reason, when I saw it coming, I froze. I was certain that this time, I really was going to die."

He shakes his head no, like he's denying my words.

"Ian shoved me out of the way."

I flinch at the memory of the sound of the taxi hitting him. "I ended up with scraped hands and legs. He ended up in surgery, a broken arm, broken ribs, blood loss."

I shrug, which I suppose is something you do when words can't express how much something means. "He saved my life."

Josh's eyes are cloudy, like a storm before the rain.

"Why didn't you tell me?" he whispers.

I shake my head. "I was in the ambulance, I thought Ian was going to die, then I was in the hospital, it took them two hours to get all the gravel out of my..."

I cut off at the horrified look on his face, "I didn't think. It took hours for me to start thinking straight again. That's when I left you that first message."

He closes his eyes and nods. "The message where you said you couldn't leave Ian."

"Yes."

He swallows, "I thought you were leaving me."

His voice breaks at the end of his sentence and I glance quickly at him and I see behind the worry and fatigue there's pain and fear.

Josh drags in a deep, shaking breath and I realize how it

must have looked, sounded, felt.

I sink down to the floor, bring myself level with him, look into his eyes and shake my head, "No."

He sits back and pulls me onto his lap. "Can I?"

I nod and lean my head into his chest. His heart thunders under my ear, faster by far than his usual calm, steady beat.

"I thought you were leaving me," he says again. "When you didn't answer my texts or calls, I grabbed the excuse to go to LA. I was scared if I was here you'd leave me, but if I left, you wouldn't...you wouldn't leave me until I got back. I was giving myself time to come to terms with it."

Jeez.

Jeez.

"That's not..." I can't finish the sentence, so instead, I reach up and rub at the ink stain on his jaw. It won't budge, so I lick my thumb and rub at it.

Josh eyes warm as he watches me wipe away the ink, a familiar ritual.

"Then you left that voicemail and started sending pictures of you and Hope, and texts, and I thought"—he glances at me and lifts the corner of his mouth in a small smile—"I told myself that you wouldn't be sending those if you were planning on leaving me."

I rest my hand on his cheek and he leans into my fingers.

"But then I thought, well, Gemma's nice, even if we aren't together she'll want me to stay involved with Hope. So then I wrestled with myself, in a mental cage fight sort of way, will she or won't she."

He shrugs, and I see the agony in that shrug. "Finally, I decided it didn't matter. I didn't need any more time to come to terms with you leaving, because I'd never come to terms with it, not even if I had all the time in the world. So I grabbed the first flight home."

He reaches up and starts to stroke my back, his fingers trailing up and down my spine, the same way he does after we make love. When he reaches my neck, his fingers play with the ends of my hair.

"I'm glad you did," I say. "I missed you."

His fingers still. "I know you don't love me anymore. I know you don't want to touch or kiss, so when I saw you with Ian, I came to the logical conclusion that you felt something for him. Was I wrong?"

I look up at him. There's *so much* wrong with what he said. I know this only happened a few days ago, but so much has changed in those few days that it's like *everything* has changed.

"I didn't kiss Ian," I say. "He saw you across the street and he kissed me. To goad you."

Josh's eyes flash at that and I get the feeling he's considering chasing down Ian and punching him after all. But then he looks at me, and I guess he decides it's better to stay right here.

I try to make it really, really clear. "I didn't want Ian's kiss. I don't want him. I want *you*."

Josh watches me, and my words sink in.

"You want me," he repeats, testing out the words.

I nod. "I need you."

He swallows, "You need me."

I nod again. "I was terrified before that I wouldn't feel anything when you kissed me or when we made love. I'm not scared anymore. I want...will you..."

Josh sucks in a harsh breath and his cloudy eyes clear and turn dark.

"One request," he says.

"What?"

"Call your mom and ask her to keep Hope until dinner."

25

"There isn't darkness without light, and there isn't light without dark."

JOSH CARRIES ME TO THE BEDROOM. AS SOON AS I PUT DOWN my phone he scooped me up, one arm under my knees, the other behind my back.

Sometimes, I forget how strong he is.

I stopped seeing him as the sexy, toned, irreverent ladies' man a long time ago and started seeing him as my Josh. Artistic, kindhearted, loving. It's times like this though, when he easily stalks down the hall with me in my arms, that I remember, he's also that sexy, irreverent man.

It's what made all the women fall for him for years.

He kicks open the door to the bedroom.

Thinking of the Josh of years past makes me think of the reason that Ian kissed me and the other reason that Josh went to LA.

The thought of it niggles at me, like a rock in my shoe, and when Josh sets me gently onto our bed, I sit up and say, "Josh? About LA."

"Don't really want to talk about LA, Gemma," he says.

He lifts up my foot and pulls off my shoe, throwing it toward the closet.

"I know, I just thought..." A flicker of panic burns in my gut.

"Hmmm?" He pulls off my other shoe and tosses it toward the first.

"How's Lisa?" I ask quickly, before I can regret it.

I'll regret it more if we make love and then I find out that he has a baby on the way and he's planning on flying back and forth to see Lisa every other weekend.

Josh frowns, "Lisa Perry?"

I nod. Who else would I ask about?

He shrugs. "We rewrote the final two episodes to include a pregnancy. She's happy, the producers are happy. Everything worked out."

Everything worked out?

"But..."

"What?" He reaches forward to brush my hair back over my shoulder.

"Are you the father?" I ask.

His fingers stop and he stares at me in shock. "Am I what?"

Okay, I didn't expect him to look so shocked, or so offended.

"The father?"

He pulls back. "What?"

I sit up on the bed and clasp my hands together. I'm not sure how I can ask more clearly, but from Josh's stunned expression, I'm guessing that he never thought that I'd think he was... "Her baby's father?"

He takes a step back and then runs his hands through his hair, messing it up again.

"Gemma? Didn't you hear me the other night? Or Lisa?"

I think back to the night she showed up. I remember they were talking to me, but I don't remember what they said.

I shake my head. "I couldn't think. I couldn't hear anything."

His face goes white. "I guess that explains some things."

His hands clench and then he loosens them. "You thought I was the baby's father? That, what? Lisa and I slept together?"

When he says this, my lungs feel tight.

"I didn't know what to think. I figured..." I clear my throat. "I knew it was bad while I was in the coma and Hope was in the NICU. I thought, if Lisa offered you some comfort, helped you through or helped you stay strong, then I would be glad that you found help however you could."

Josh stares at me like he's never seen me before in his whole life.

"You'd be okay with me sleeping with another woman while you were in a coma?"

Well, when he says it like that...

"Jeez, Gemma." He moves across the room, unable to stand still.

Then he turns back to me, "You may be okay with it, but I wouldn't. I wouldn't be okay with it. Not at all." He says this vehemently, his words convicted.

My lungs loosen, and a heavy weight that I didn't know had been pressing down on me lifts and sets me free. I let out a long, clear breath.

"Lisa has a boyfriend. She told you that when she apologized to you the other night. Okay? Remember? Do we need to call her so you can hear it again?"

I grasp the comforter in my hands. Josh didn't cheat. The sky didn't fall.

"Why are you smiling?" he asks.

"I was just thinking, if Ian knew that, he'd never have kissed me. All his idiocy was for nothing."

Josh makes a low sound in his throat. "I'm not going to share you. And I thought you didn't want to share me."

I nod and let go of the comforter. "Yes."

"I thought I made myself pretty clear when I told you I'd love you as long as there's a sky above."

I nod, because my throat is so tight and so full of emotion I can't say anything else.

"Can I make love to you now?" he asks.

I lock eyes with him, and there in their depths is the smile and the we'll-get-through-this-together look that I love.

"Please," I say, because right now, I'm only able to manage single words.

He seems to understand, because he smiles, that Gemma-is-my-playground smile, and I know I'm in good hands. Then he steps forward and tugs at the ribbons on my shoulders and loosens the bows. The straps fall and my bodice drops. I'm in a strapless, lacy bra, it's red, just like my dress, and see through. When Josh sees it he lets out a soft curse.

Then he reaches forward and brushes a finger over my nipple. The lace rubs across it and I'm so sensitive that I let out a small moan as it puckers under his touch.

His eyes flash up to mine. "Okay?"

I lick my lips, nervously, then nod.

When I do, he kneels in front of me, takes me by the hips and pulls me to the edge of the bed. Then he puts his mouth over my sheer lace bra, right over my nipple and sucks. There are icy pricks as he bites down, and I cry out at the clenching in my abdomen.

His eyes heat and he moves to my other nipple, biting down on it, and sucking, hard. I let out a startled sob at the tight throb that echoes through me.

He reaches around my back, and unclasps my bra. He drops it to the floor and then leans back on his heels, and looks at my bare chest, a worshipful expression on his face.

"It's been too long, Gemma." He glances up at me. "You have no idea how hard it is to take this slow."

"Then don't," I say, finding my voice. "Don't take it slow."

He shakes his head and then tugs at my dress, drawing the cotton fabric over my hips and carefully over my legs. He drops it on the floor next to my bra.

"I've fantasized for months about making love to you again. I can wait a little longer."

It's then I notice that I'm sitting on the bed, naked except for my red lace thong, and Josh is still dressed. Even his shoes are still on. He smiles when he sees my realization.

"I've always wanted to draw you like this," he admits.

He watches me carefully, taking in my reaction. The thought of lying here on the bed, naked, with Josh taking in every detail of my bare skin with his pen and ink, seeing myself as he sees me, is the most erotic thing I've ever heard. I want him to draw my breasts, my nipples, my thighs, me touching myself.

"I want that," I say.

He gives me a smile that makes me feel like I just won a gold medal.

"Then that's what we'll do." When he sees my look, he adds, "Next time."

Then he rocks forward on his heels and slips his hands under the edge of my thong and pulls it down my legs. I shiver at the cold air and then Josh slips a finger inside me and I gasp. Still kneeling, he smiles up at me, and then drops his mouth over my clit.

Oh my word.

He sends his tongue over me, tastes me, and as his finger

works inside me, my mind goes blank. Not the bad kind of blank that has happened so much recently, but the good kind of blank, where I can't concentrate on anything at all except the sensation happening right now. Right here.

I let out a startled sob, and he lifts my legs over his shoulders, angling me so that his finger hits me in exactly the right spot. My abs clench, my thighs shake, and I think I'm crying please, please, please.

He pushes in another finger and I clench around him. I think I'm going to crawl out of my skin, I think I could walk on the ceiling if I tried. He scrapes my clit with his teeth, just as he hits the back of me with his fingers, and I let out another sob.

He works his fingers, tugs me closer, and I feel him shaking as he clenches my thigh with his free hand, tugging me closer. I want to squeeze my eyes shut, block out every sensation except the feel of him, but I don't want to miss anything.

He kisses my clit, he licks my wetness. His head is bowed, his hair is messy, his stubble marks my inner thighs, and his shoulders are tense with emotion. I lean up, grab his t-shirt and pull my legs free.

"I have to touch you," I say.

I haven't touched him in so long.

"I have to kiss you," I tell him.

I haven't kissed him in what's felt like years.

I need him. How could I have thought there wouldn't be any emotion? I'm drowning in it. It's blazing bright, a liquid sun, and I'm drowning in it.

"God, Gemma." His eyes are glazed, his cheeks are red, and I've never felt so in love in my whole life.

I tug him to me and catch his mouth in mine. When our mouths meet my heart beats wildly, and there are bright flashes and flickers, like fireworks. I whimper. I want to crawl inside him, I want to have every part of us touching, I want to press every part of me against him so he can feel everything that I'm feeling on the inside.

But then he lets out a ragged noise, grasps my hips, and I have a feeling that he knows exactly what I'm feeling.

I whimper and grab his jeans, tug down his zipper with shaking hands. He comes free, silken skin over hard flesh. I grasp him, rub my hand over his length. He shudders and lets out a ragged breath. I clench in response and rub my hand up and across his tip. He's wet there. He swears and murmurs a plea against my mouth.

"Please." I lie back on the bed and guide him to me. Rub him there. Heat sizzles through my blood. Bright and hot.

Josh drops over me, bracing his arms on either side of me. His eyes catch mine, and I can't look away. There's so much love there.

They say the universe was born in a bright, hot, explosion, and I think that there also had to have been love there, because right now, I see a whole universe being born in his eyes. It's a whole universe of love. And it's as bright as a supernova.

I feel the answering light in my own heart.

I arch my hips up, meet Josh. He slides inside me, fills me with a swift, desperate thrust. I cry out at the feeling. Not just at the feel of him inside me, but the feeling of love.

"Gemma," he says, over and over and over.

I grasp his shoulders, rain kisses over him, like stars coming to life across the universe. He murmurs pleas, praise, words of love.

The whole while all the love, all the happiness, all the joy in the world fills me. And I clasp them to me, gather them up, and hold them all in my heart.

"I love you," he says. "I love you so much."

At his words, I clench around him, and a bright burning sun races through me and an orgasm explodes over me. Grabs my whole body and crashes through me. I cry out, pulse around him, and hold onto him as I'm carried up and up and up. He thrusts harder, faster, buries himself in me, and then I hear him shout and feel him lose himself in me.

I grip his shoulders, pull him onto me, and let the weight of his body bring me back to earth. He kisses my cheeks, my eyelids.

"I love you. I love you," he whispers as he kisses me.

I'm so overwhelmed, so taken by the tsunami of emotion, that I don't understand he's pulled out and is sitting up, until I feel the weight of him leave me, and the warmth turn cold.

"Gemma?"

There are tears on my cheeks. My face is wet with them and I realize that I'm crying. Really, really crying. I didn't cry when I woke up, I didn't cry when Josh left, I didn't cry when I realized I'd missed the first three months of Hope's life.

Before Josh left and he asked me why I was crying, I hadn't realized that I had been. This is the first time since I woke up that I've truly cried. Really, really cried.

"Are you okay?" he asks.

I shake my head no and cover my face with my hands. Wipe at my tears and hold back my sobs.

I'm not okay. But I will be. I finally realize that I will be okay. We all will be.

It wasn't making love that brought back my emotions or love. I know that. They've been coming back for a while now. Especially the happiness and love I feel for Josh, for Hope and for my family. I now realize that they weren't ever really gone, they were just waiting for me to find them again.

I was searching for that great big soaring feeling I'd

always had with Josh. It made me blind to the other ways I love him. The little ways as well as the big ways.

I love the ink on his fingers. I love how he's patient and kind. I love his sense of humor and his unwavering faith. I love that he's obsessed with kaiju and classic comics, and that he has forty-seven (I've counted) graphic t-shirts.

I love how he taught himself to be a dad, without me being there to help. I love how he makes pancakes and always makes sure I have a cup of coffee first thing in the morning. I love how he sits with me at night while I read and he draws.

I love how when he smiles at me, it feels like he's giving me a gift. I love how when he touches me, I feel like I'm glowing, and when he says he loves me I feel like I'm burning as bright as the sun.

I look up, I have to tell Josh, I have to tell him that the dark is gone and everything is going to be okay. That I love him, that I've always loved him, it just took me a little while to find my way back to him.

He's pulled himself together. In fact, he's so put together that I wouldn't know we just made love, except for the fact that I was a part of it.

He's dressed again, standing at the doorway, his face wiped of emotion. I realize I must've been crying for a good five minutes, which was enough time for Josh to come to his own conclusions.

"I thought I could do this," he says, his words sound as if he's forcing them out one by one.

"Josh?"

He shakes his head and suddenly I'm cold. I sit up straight and wrap my arms around my chest. Something's changed for him too. I have a feeling it wasn't the same joyful revelation I had.

"I'm sorry, Gemma. I told you I had enough love for the

both of us, but that's not true. I can't love enough for the both of us. I can't. I love you so much, but—" He shoves his hand through his hair and shakes his head.

"Josh, I'm not—"

"Let me say this," he says. "I spent my whole childhood waiting for my mom to come home. You saw how that worked out. No matter how much I loved her, or wanted her to come back, she didn't. I can't make someone else love me. No matter how hard I try. I learned that lesson years ago. I just forgot it with you. I see my mistake now. It's clear."

There are tears again, trailing down my cheeks. And then that panic, the horrible, awful panic reaches up and closes my throat. I feel the darkness, the pinch of breathlessness. The grip is so tight that I can't say anything back.

Josh waits for a second, then when I don't, can't say anything, he nods, and says, "It's okay, Gemma. I understand. I just. I can't."

He nods again, like he's confirming his decision to himself.

I shake my head no.

"If it's okay," he says, "I'm going to take a night or two. Head up north. I'll be back to see Hope. We can talk about everything then." He waits a moment for me to respond. I can't push the words out. His shoulders fall. "You know, it's lucky we already have that visitation contract from when we were just friends. It'll make things easier."

Holy.

Hell.

Then, I know it really is over, because Josh gives me that smile. That the-world-is-my-playground, I-don't-have-a-care-in-the-world smile, and that's when I know, I've broken his heart.

I've broken him.

He turns, shuts the door behind him.

The blackness threatens to overwhelm me. I shove at it, try to fight through it, then struggle with shaking hands to yank my dress over my head. Finally, I tug it on, then I pull open the door and race down the hall.

"Josh!"

I sprint into the living room, check the kitchen, run back to the nursery. Finally I decide that he's actually left, I pull open the front door, run down the hall, out the building door and stand barefoot on the sidewalk, looking right and left and across the street.

But Josh isn't there.

He's gone.

So, I go back inside, and this time, I let myself feel all the emotions, I let them all crash over me. I lie on the couch, Josh's sketchbook, with the little girl lost in the city wrapped in my arms, and I cry and I cry.

And when it hurts even more than I thought it would, I'm glad, because that means that there isn't darkness without light, and there isn't light without dark. And that's how life should be. Right?

Which reminds me of Ian, *this is your life, live it.*

Which then reminds me that Josh was wrong. He spent his whole childhood thinking his mom didn't want to come back, but it's not that she never wanted to, it's that she couldn't.

Hours later, when my mom bustles back into the house with Hope, and Dylan and my dad are carrying the picnic basket, the cooler and the blanket, I've showered, dressed, done my hair and makeup and I have a suitcase packed.

"Where are you going?" my mom asks.

"California?" Dylan asks hopefully. Apparently he didn't get the memo that Josh is back.

"Where do you want the cooler, honey?" my dad asks. As usual, he likes to concentrate on the immediate tasks at hand.

I smile at them, hoping my eyes aren't puffy and bloodshot.

"Hope and I are coming up to stay for a few days."

Dylan's face falls.

But my mom likes that news. "That's perfect! Any reason?"

I nod. "So I can marry Josh."

Last year, when I wanted to tell Josh I loved him, my whole family drove me in a van down to New York City. In fact, to this very apartment. Now, we're headed back to my hometown, and I'm hoping Josh is where he said he'd be.

So that I can tell him that I love him and that I want to marry him and that I want to spend the rest of my life with him. He doesn't have to love enough for the both of us.

My mom rushes forward and hugs me, pressing Hope between us.

My dad drops the cooler on the floor and says, "Good. Excellent. I'll need to tinker with the gazebo a bit though."

Dylan stares at me a moment, then shakes his head. "About time, Gem." Then he turns to my mom and says, "Did you save any food for the road?"

I grin as I take Hope from my mom. I press a kiss to Hope's head and say, "Love you, baby. Love you so much."

26

"*Forever.*"

THE MOON HANGS LOW OVER THE LEAFY TREES, THE NIGHT IS SO dark that the leaves look black rather than green.

The crickets hide in the grass and sing a high, droning song. It's nearly eleven at night and the heat and mugginess of the day cleared hours ago, leaving behind the coolness of evening.

When you're in New York City long enough, you forget how many stars there are in the sky. It never gets dark enough in the city for the light of the stars to reach you.

Here though, in my small hometown, everyone turns off their lights by ten, there are only a few streetlights, and the stars glow bright in the dark.

I crouch down to the sidewalk and pick up as many pebbles as I can find. The sidewalk is cool and rough, and my shoes scuff against the concrete. The cracks in the sidewalk are filled with weeds and short tufts of grass.

The shadows play in the dark and the street is quiet. Most of the houses are dark except for the porch lights. I stand up and step into the grass of the lawn. There are lights on in this house.

In particular, the bedroom light is on.

I stand for a minute, the grass tickling my ankles, just watching Josh.

He's in his childhood bedroom, sitting at his desk in front of the window. His head is down and it looks like he's concentrating on something. His shoulder and arm move, so I think he must be drawing, or writing.

Suddenly he stops, drops his head, and then wipes his hand over his face. Then he drops his head in his hands, his shoulders slump, and I decide I've seen enough.

I take a pebble, a tiny little jagged rock and I toss it at his window. It hits with a sharp ting. I hear it crack against the glass, but Josh doesn't move.

I choose another pebble, one slightly larger, and throw it harder. It plinks against the glass.

Josh looks up, tilts his head and then looks around his room.

I smile and decide that this isn't the time for wimpy throws. I launch all the pebbles in my hand at the window. They hit all at once, at least a dozen rocks, cracking, pinging, and knocking on the glass.

Unfortunately, I didn't notice that some of the pebbles I chose were bigger than pebble size, and the window cracks.

Lines spread across the glass, a trail of spiderwebs. Josh stands, shoves back his chair, and stares out the window. It's bright in his room, and dark outside. I'm not sure he can see me.

But then, he does. Because his eyes widen and he leans forward and I see him mouth, "Gemma?"

I nod.

I think he says, *what are you doing here?*

I smile. I think that'd be obvious.

Slowly, I point to myself, then to him, and I make a heart with my hands.

He shakes his head.

So I try again, I point to him, then I point to me, and I make a heart. I hold the heart in front of my face and I smile.

He's running out of his room before the heart is even a second old. Josh flings the front door open and runs across the lawn. When he nears, he slows and then stops in front of me.

"What the heck, Gemma. You broke my window."

The shadows play over his face, and it's hard to see his expression in the dark, but I can't miss the grin fighting to come out.

"I was trying to get your attention."

I step forward, so that we're standing only inches apart. The smell of grass is kicked up, and little white night moths flutter up and away.

"You got it." He nods and then his happy smile fades and he says, "Why are you here?"

My chest sort of breaks open, and I feel my heart and all my emotions tumble out, and fall to the grass at his feet. It's all there.

"I came for you," I say. "You left..." I reach up and wipe at a tear that's escaped. "Did I ever tell you I'm glad you didn't sell your dad's house yet?"

He shakes his head no.

"Well I am. It made it easy to find you." I smile at him, then I reach up and push his inky black hair off his forehead.

His eyes search mine, then he says, "Gemma. Nothing's changed."

"I have something to show you. Trust me?"

He looks down at me, considers, then nods.

"You'll need to grab your car keys."

Fifteen minutes later, we're parked and walking through one of those cemeteries with the short golf course grass, flat plaques in the ground, and wreaths of plastic flowers.

I didn't talk on the drive, I wanted to keep all the explanations until after he saw.

Earlier, on the drive north, I texted Ian and asked a few questions. He had some answers. So here we are.

I walk down a long row, Josh's hand linked with mine. He's always been a good sport, willing to go along with almost anything, and he's been content to stay quiet, just following my "turn here, go left, turn right." Even when we pulled up to the cemetery he didn't say anything.

We're nearly there now.

Down the twentieth row, eight plots down, I stop in front of a flat plaque. It's too dark to see the name.

Josh peers at me. "I'm not really following, Gemma. What is this?"

I squeeze his hand, as tight as I can. "You said that no matter how much you loved your mom, it didn't matter, because she never came back. That you couldn't make her love you, and you couldn't make her come back home."

He stares at me, then looks down at the plaque. "Are you saying?"

"Maybe it's not that she didn't want to come back to you. Maybe someday she would have." I kneel down and look closely at the bronze plaque.

Josh kneels next to me, sucks in a breath when he sees the name. His fingers trace over the dates.

"She died when I was fifteen?" He looks over at me, and there's shock and grief and confusion written on his face. "Why?"

I shake my head. I don't know.

"I always thought she didn't come back, didn't look me up, because she didn't want me."

I squeeze his hand. His face pales in the moonlight.

"I stopped caring. I think, I was probably about fifteen, when I stopped caring whether she came back or not." He splays his fingers over the bronze slab.

"I remember."

Why should I want her if she doesn't want me?

"Sometimes, though, I wondered if I kept putting my name out there, pushing to make my name more known, more comics, more tours, maybe a movie, that if I made my name so bright she wouldn't be able to ignore me. Then, it stopped being about that too." His voice breaks and he pulls his hand away.

I lay my head against his arm. "I'm sorry. Are you..."

"I'm okay. I spent twenty-five years knowing she was gone. I've already said goodbye. Mourned her. This is just another kind of letting go. It's okay. It's almost...better in a way." His mouth twists. "That sounds terrible. Sorry."

"Don't apologize. You can feel grief and relief at the same time. That's okay."

He turns to me and lifts a corner of his mouth. "That doesn't make me a terrible person?"

"No. It just makes you a person."

He stares at me a moment, searching my expression. I think of all the people that witness their loved ones suffering before they die. They must feel relief and grief. It isn't a sin. I let this show in my expression.

Finally, he nods and looks over the wide, flat plain of the cemetery. "I wonder why my dad never told me."

There isn't any anger there. Josh always looks for the best in people, he doesn't expect them to be motivated by pettiness or anger. I imagine he expects his dad didn't tell him because of all the right reasons.

"I don't know," I admit.

Josh stands, pulls me up, and gently brushes the loose grass from the skirt of my dress. Then he stares at his mom's bronze plaque glinting in the moonlight for a good five minutes. He's quiet. There's just the heavy blanket of the night and our soft breath filling the silence.

Finally, he hitches his shoulders, brushes off the weight of it all, and says, "Thanks for telling me, Gem. But what I don't understand is, how did you know?"

WE'RE BACK IN THE APARTMENT IN THE BASEMENT OF JOSH'S dad's house.

It's just like I remember, plush carpet, comfy couch, dining table and chairs, small kitchen, a bedroom and bath off the main living area. Josh stayed here while he was taking care of his dad.

We're sitting on the couch, I'm in the middle, Josh is on the far side, like he's afraid to let himself touch me.

I want to tell him I love him, but I want to do it right, so there's no confusion and no doubt in his mind.

"Are you hungry?" Josh asks, he looks over at the kitchen. "I think there might be noodles and sauce in the cupboard."

I shake my head and smile. Reason number nine hundred and eighty-two that I love Josh—he always makes people food as a way to show them that he loves them. Even when they've hurt him.

"I just want to explain," I say. "You left before I could get it all out."

"Ah." He nods. "Sure."

It's silent for a second, the only sound is the ticking of the old-fashioned clock on the kitchen wall.

I bite my lip, praying I get this right, "When Ian was in the hospital he told me about his past."

Josh nods.

I scoot closer to him. An inch, barely noticeable.

"When he was eleven, he and his parents were in a car accident. His mom suffered a permanent brain injury and his dad died soon after." I watch Josh's expression carefully. This is the hard part. "The people in the car that hit them. It was your parents."

"What?" His frowns and shakes his head.

"Your mom was driving."

"My mom wasn't around, my dad and I had been here for years, she..." He stops, clears his throat, shakes his head again.

"I don't know," I say. "But for twenty years your dad sent flowers to Ian's mom. She's a permanent resident at The Whittcombe."

Josh lets out a long, shuddering breath. "Why..." He looks at me, his eyes dark. "No one ever said anything."

I scoot another inch closer. "Maybe your dad thought it best you didn't know. Ian, well, he decided when he was fourteen that he was going to make your family pay. So..."

I shrug. "You know the story. He becomes your friend, steals your journal, tries to make your life suck."

Josh's lips twist and he shakes his head, "He knew about my mom? That's how you found her?"

I move closer again. Now we're only a foot apart. "He was at her funeral. Your dad asked him not to tell you. He says they shook on it. For what it's worth, he said he was sorry when he learned of your dad's passing."

Josh pinches his nose and closes his eyes. When he does I

move closer again. When he opens his eyes we're nearly touching. He sees how close I am but doesn't move away.

"What a mess. The whole thing was a mess and I had no idea." He lets out a long, loaded breath, which about sums it up.

I drop my head to his shoulder and wrap my arms around his middle. He stiffens at first, then after a breath, relaxes.

"Would you have behaved any differently if you'd known?" I ask.

He's quiet. While he's thinking, his hand drifts to my arm and he strokes my bare skin, slowly, carefully.

Finally, he says, "No. I don't think I would have. I still would've been upset with my mom for leaving. I still would've been Ian's friend, in the beginning. I still would've started my comic. I still would've fallen in love with you. Still would've said yes to making a baby."

His hand stops on my arm. We both look down at him touching me. "I still would've ended up right here. Even knowing."

I know exactly what he means. I feel the same way.

Even knowing how hard the past months have been, how much it's hurt, I'd still do it again. "Even knowing everything."

His chin dips in agreement. "Yeah."

I'm so close I'm practically in his lap. I move even closer, trying to press all of myself against him.

"Something I've learned," I tell him, "is that sometimes things have to get really, really bad before they get better."

He reaches up and strokes my hair, pushes a strand behind my ear.

"You look beautiful tonight," he says. "I have to be honest, when you broke my window, I thought I was imagining you. Thought I'd lost my mind."

I stretch my legs onto his lap and try to bury myself in him.

"I was really scared when I woke up from the coma. I thought love had died."

He nods and his eyes dim. "I know."

"It was so dark." I look into his dark brown eyes, at the light shining in them.

"I'm sorry," he whispers.

He wraps me in his arms and I lay my head on his chest. My cheek presses against his soft t-shirt and I breathe in his smell.

"No. I'm glad," I tell him. "Before, everything in my life was so bright that I only noticed the big things. The big love. The big joy. The big happiness."

I rub my fingers over the stubble on his chin. It feels soft and scratchy at the same time. "But when everything went dark and quiet, there was room to notice the small things."

His hand moves to my back, and ever so slowly, he starts to rub his hand up and down my spine. My heart speeds up at his touch.

"It took me a bit," I tell him, "my eyes had to adjust. But then, with all the bright gone, I got to concentrate on the quiet, and the little, and all those things I'd never noticed before. Like...how you kiss me every morning on the same spot, on the right corner of my mouth. How you go out of your way to walk past me, just so you can trail your hands down my back. Or how you always make sure I have coffee, before I'm even dressed, and you always put in the perfect amount of cream. And how when we sit on the couch, and I read and you draw, you always put my feet in your lap. Or how you find the humor in nearly everything, and you always make me laugh. Or how I find sketches everywhere, on napkins, tissues, cardboard containers, socks, I mean, who sketches on a sock?"

Josh's mouth curves up, and his eyes are growing warmer and warmer, and he's watching me like he's reliving every one of the instances I'm telling him about.

"You can't go to bed without doing all the dishes, because everything has to be tidy, but then you draw on socks." I grin up at him. "And you always have ink on your hands, but you're careful to never get it on me. But sometimes, I'd really, really like you to get it on me."

"Gemma," he says, and my name comes out like a prayer. He reaches up and pushes his hand into my hair. "Tell me what you're saying."

"Isn't it obvious? I'm telling you that I love you. In a million little ways, in so many quiet, tiny, little ways, that they all add up to be greater than the biggest love in the whole world. I love you in so many little ways that it almost hurts. It almost hurts to love you."

He shakes his head, pulls my face close, and presses his mouth to mine. "I don't want you to hurt."

His eyes are raw and aching after all the revelations of the day. But still, it's *me* he doesn't want hurting. My Josh.

I reach up, hold his mouth to mine. "It hurts like it does when you see the most beautiful star-filled night of your life. It hurts like when something's so beautiful you can barely look, but you also can't look away. It's a terrible, wondrous, beautiful pain."

"Gemma," he breathes.

He pushes me back to the couch, and I fall into the soft cushions. He straddles my legs and presses his chest into mine. His hands run through my hair and his mouth devours my words. I feel wet on my cheeks, and I don't know if it's Josh that's crying or me. Maybe it's both of us.

"I can't be sorry any of this happened," I say. "Because it showed me how many ways there are to love. You said you'd love me as long as there's sky above. I want that. I want to keep exploring all the shades of the night sky, and the day sky, and sunset and sunrise. I want to find all the ways I can love you."

Josh stops kissing me, he pulls back and looks down at me, his hands thread through my hair.

His expression is cautious, wary. "You're saying that you love me?"

"Is that okay?" I ask him, nervous at the look on his face.

His lips lift up, and he has a smile on his face that I've never seen before. It's happy and sad, bright and dim, yearning and distant. He rubs his thumb over my cheek.

"It's been hell, Gem. You know that. I think sometimes you believe that it's easy for me to love. Easy for me to go through life. That it's all fun and games for me. But, Gemma, I get hurt just as deeply as the next person. You know?"

"I know." I've seen what's behind his smiles. I know.

He nods. "Just understand, you can hurt me more than anyone else on earth. That when I give you my love, I'm trusting you not to hurt me."

He reaches up and wipes at the tears on my cheeks.

"Don't cry," he whispers.

"I never meant to hurt you."

Then I remember, he said I left him, but he left me too.

"You left," I say. "I was panicking and I couldn't get the words out and you left." My voice breaks. "Why did you leave?"

He closes his eyes, drops his head. "I thought my world was crumbling. I was terrified. You were sobbing. After sex that for me was mind-blowing. That's when I realized I couldn't force you to love me. It would only hurt us both."

"So you left."

"I'm sorry. I'm not proud of that."

I reach over and touch his jaw. He shoulders shake, and he shudders as I settle my hand against his cheek.

"I thought we were over. I thought you didn't want me," he admits.

Like his mom.

This whole mess was a big, horrible repeat for him.

Except not.

Because...

"But I do want you."

He stares at me, taking in my features, like he's memorizing me in this moment.

"I love you," I whisper. And then I say it louder, because the words feel beautiful coming out of my mouth. "I love you."

He stops moving for a moment, a still life, caught in time. Then his eyes warm and he turns his lips into my palm, brushing his mouth over my hand.

"Gemma?" His voice is morning coffee warm.

I smile. "Yes, Josh?"

He kisses the corner of my mouth. "Do you remember when I said love is easy when everything goes well? It's the accidents and illnesses, the job losses and bankruptcies that show whether or not what you have is love or something else?" He presses a kiss to the other side of my mouth.

I remember.

"Do you think this is love?" I ask him.

He drops his lips to the center of my mouth. "You're here. I'm here. We made it through Gemma. I'd say this is love."

He looks down at me, drags a finger across my lips, down my chin.

"I'm not the same as I used to be," I remind him.

He gives me a surprised look. "I didn't ask you to be."

Still. "I can't cook anymore. Or bake. It's hard, my thoughts get lost in the kitchen."

He lifts an eyebrow. "I like cooking."

"I may never be able to go to Times Square again, or anywhere with a lot of stimulation."

"When have I ever wanted to go to Times Square?" he asks.

Which actually is a good point. Josh is more of a quiet night in kind of guy.

Still. I need to get all of this out there.

"I don't know if I'll ever be able to multi-task five things at once again, or have as many clients, or..." I shrug. "I don't know what my future holds."

He nods, eyes serious, then he takes my hands and threads his fingers with mine.

"If it's okay," he says, "we can find out what the future holds together."

"You don't need me to be the Gemma who danced in the rain?"

His eyes light with an ironic glint and he says, "As long as you don't need me to be Ian Fortune's best friend."

I laugh, just like he hoped I would.

"Fine," I say. "It's a deal."

"Seal with a kiss?"

"Wellll, I was going to say, we should invite Ian to our wedding."

Josh's face goes blank. "Oh yeah. When's that?"

"Tomorrow?"

He blinks.

"Or...not?" I say.

He shakes his head no. Definitely no.

"Well..." I don't know what to say. "Next weekend?"

He shakes his head no again. "I have a better idea."

"What's that?" I ask, hopeful at the happy look in his eyes.

"We'll spend the next bit making love, taking Hope around the city, going on picnics, doing all the little fall in love things you were telling me about a while back, and then when your appointments are done at The Whittcombe, we'll elope."

"Elope? Not a big wedding in my parents' back yard?"

He cringes. "That gazebo your dad built...it's an accident waiting to happen."

I think about the plans my dad printed off of the internet, the quick construction job, the potential for another wedding day disaster. I shudder.

"You're right. You're absolutely right. We should elope. I hear Fiji's nice."

He grins. "Now can we seal the deal?"

"With a kiss?"

Apparently, he has more than a kiss in mind. Thank goodness, because so do I.

JOSH HAS AN ARTIST PEN IN HIS HAND, IT HAS A POINT THREE millimeter nib with black pigment ink, it's waterproof and alcohol proof, which means it doesn't run and it's not coming off anytime soon.

I sit on the edge of his bed. It's a small room with light blue walls and a king-size bed that takes up most of the space. I really, really like the bed.

There's a bookshelf with a stack of graphic novels on it and some Toho collectibles. I push back the white comforter. I don't want to stain it. The little lamp on the side table spills off just enough light to make the room soft and intimate.

Josh watches me get comfortable. His fingers run over the pen's surface and his eyes darken.

"Are you going to draw me?" I ask.

He shakes his head, "No. I'm going to draw on you."

I flash a smile at him. "First the socks, now me."

I'm one hundred percent, completely into this. I pull off my outfit. When I do, the lingerie that my mom foisted onto me falls out of my pocket and lands in a pile on the ground. Josh and I both stare at the chain metal bra and the thong with a lock and key.

The silence is loud.

I clear my throat. It appears that Josh can't pull his eyes away from the medieval torture-themed lingerie I just dumped on the floor.

"Ummm, that was for if our conversation didn't convince you...I was going to..." I gesture my hands over my chest and the rest of me.

He lifts an eyebrow, then starts to laugh. "What? You were going to tie me up with your chain bra?"

He keeps laughing, and I cross my arms over my chest, but then I see that he actually, probably really likes the idea of my kinky lingerie.

"Josh Lewenthal. I think you like it."

He puts an innocent expression on his face and shrugs. I grin at him, and he suppresses a smile, but then he gives in and lets through the happiest, most carefree, pure Josh smile that I've ever seen.

Holy crap.

If I wasn't already in love with him, that smile would throw me over the edge and put me into a free fall.

"Lie down, Gemma," he says, voice low and hungry.

I scooch back on the bed and then lean back on my elbows, not willing to lay flat and lose sight of Josh's smile.

"You have to lie flat," he says.

"I want to watch you." The dark sheets are cool against my bare skin.

He hums in response, and I think that means it's okay. He kneels down on the bed, positioning himself over my lower half. In this position I can see how much bigger he is than I am, how much taller and stronger.

Then I'm distracted, because he starts to work.

First he picks up my right leg, cups my foot in his hand, and draws on the arch of my foot. The cold nib of the pen sends pinpricks over me. His thumb circles on my skin, and I can feel his concentration like a firm, sensual touch.

He works silently, drawing tiny stars up my arch, a little galaxy on my foot. Then he writes the words, "I loved you yesterday."

I read it aloud and he glances up at me. His hair falls over his eyes, and he smiles.

Then his warm hands move up, circle my ankles and stroke my calves. He watches my face as he touches my legs, and when I gasp at the sensation traveling up my legs and hitting me deep and low, he smiles.

Then he bends his head and starts to draw on my ankle. He draws a garden, a field of flowers, circling both ankles, and then he draws butterflies in flight, flying up my calves. His hands trail over my skin, and the pen feels like the wings of those butterflies, fluttering against me.

Then, he glances at me again, and in a long line, he writes up my calf, "I love you today."

I read it aloud, and he sends me a happy smile. His hair falls over his forehead again, and when he nudges it aside, he leaves a bit of ink on his face. My heart feels so happy, it's almost bursting.

But then, he strokes my inner thighs, circles my hips, and

pulls my legs open. He kneads the skin of my thighs, goes higher, higher. The room starts to spin and I'm lost in the sensation of his hands on me. I grip the sheets and watch as Josh's breaths come faster, shallower.

He looks up and his pupils are so big and so black, they've nearly swallowed the brown of his eyes. It's like his eyes have become the night sky.

"Josh."

His fingers grip my inner thighs, and he watches my face as I take in a ragged breath.

"Gemma?"

"Why haven't we ever done this before?"

He smiles at me, then I feel the sharp tip of the pen scraping over my skin. His tongue darts out, and he leans in and concentrates on drawing whirls and swirls and starry night stars all over my thighs, then he writes in a spiral, "I love you tomorrow."

He looks up at me, waiting for me to read it.

"I love you tomorrow," I say.

He nods. "Exactly."

Then he gently pushes me back to the bed and kisses my stomach. He draws a heart on my stomach, and next to it he writes, "I love your courage."

He brushes his hand over my ribs, and tingles and sparks rush over me. Every time he touches me, my body lights up and my blood fizzes with electricity.

He leans down, sucks on a nipple, kisses my breasts, then draws a flock of birds, flying over the clouds, and writes, "I love your heart."

He climbs up, over my body, wraps me underneath him, so that he can reach my collarbone. His legs enclose my thighs, his arms brace my middle, and his fingers drift over the place my neck and shoulders meet. It takes all my strength not to reach up and pull him down to me.

Every time his hands run down my neck and then back up again, I become more liquid, more sensation, and nothing else. My eyes drift closed. Josh leans closer, his breath tickles my skin, and the heat of him soaks into me.

He places a kiss on my collarbone, at the base of my neck, over my pulse. Then where his lips were, I feel the pen. He's gentle, it's barely there. In a moment, he's done. He's so still that I open my eyes. When I do, his nose is nearly touching mine, and he's looking down at me.

My heart tumbles around, and I reach up and grab his arm, steady myself. "What's it say?"

"Make love with me."

"That's not what it says," I say. But I reach down and unbutton his pants, pull them down his legs. He kicks them off.

"What does it say?" I ask again.

"I need to be inside you." His eyes flash and my insides clench in response.

"That's really not what it says," I say.

But I pull his t-shirt over his head. His abdomen is taut, and the skin on his chest is hot. He lowers himself onto me.

"Josh."

He smiles at me and bites the place on my neck where he wrote his secret message. "It says, 'I'll make you orgasm and you'll like it.'"

I laugh and shove his boxers down over his thighs. He springs free, and I take him in my hand. "Maybe it says 'Josh loves Gemma.'"

He grins at me, but I can tell he's struggling to stay focused. His eyes are glazed and there's a rumbly noise in his throat. I slide my hand down to his base and he makes a noise like he's in pain.

"Or it could say, 'Josh was here.'" I nod down between my legs.

He laughs. "That's exactly what it says."

Then he nudges my legs, spreads them apart, and runs himself over me. I grab him, wrap my arms around his back, and pull him as close as I can.

I focus on the weight of him on top of me, the heat of his body, the way all the sensations are pooling deep inside me, and when he whispers my name, and stretches me, fills me, I cling to him. Hold on.

It's not slow. It's not gentle. As soon as he's inside me, something turns on and we're both clasping each other. I'm tugging at him, begging, biting down on him, sucking.

He's making desperate noises, lifting my hips, burying himself deeper. And then he's lost his rhythm, his head is thrown back, and he's driving me higher, and his fingers are over my clit, stroking me, circling me, and when I feel him, feel him right there, I clench around him, pull him over me, and I cry out. Because I'm ruined. I'm done.

He collapses over me. Presses me into the mattress. His breaths are heavy, his skin is hot and sweaty. He pushes a hard kiss into my mouth.

"Goodness, Gemma."

He rolls onto his side and pulls me into him, starts to stroke my back.

I settle into the feel of him, into the feeling of this moment. It's warm, and beautiful, and bright, like lying in a field of wildflowers on a summer day.

"I love you," I say.

He smiles into the back of my neck and rubs his fingers over my neck.

Which reminds me. "What does it actually say?"

"Thank you," he says at the same time. He kisses me again.

I turn my face to him, and his eyes are smiling. "Thank you?"

He nods and presses a kiss to my nose. "Thank you."

I lay back down on the soft mattress and settle into his arms. Then I close my eyes and think about dreams, about how night is a wonderful time, because that's when we dream.

"I love you too," he finally says. Then when I think he isn't going to say anything more, he says quietly, "It says forever."

I fall asleep smiling.

27

"You're stronger and more resilient than you ever thought possible."
—Take 2

ON TUESDAY MORNING, JOSH COMES WITH ME TO THE Whittcombe.

Hope is strapped in her stroller, and I push her down the long hall toward the waiting room. We stopped for coffee and bagels on the way. While we stood in line, Josh softly pressed his fingers into my collarbone.

The ink washed off, but even so, I flushed, which made him smile. It's then I decided that next time, I'll be drawing on him.

"I shouldn't have had two lox bagels," Josh says, stepping closer to me as we pass an aide delivering breakfast to a patient's room. Even under the tray cover, I can smell pancakes and syrup and coffee.

I grin up at him. "You always say that. But it's not gonna happen. It's why I love you, you can't resist the lox."

He nods. "True. But this time I really—"

He stops mid-sentence. The smile drops from his face. And there, not twenty feet away, Ian has come around the corner, a bouquet of purple lilies in his hand.

Last time Josh saw Ian he didn't know about his mom, or Ian's family, or that Ian had saved me, or anything else. I wasn't sure how Josh would react if he ever saw Ian again. Honestly, I didn't expect it to happen so soon.

When Ian sees us, he stops. He drops his arm, and the bouquet hangs face down toward the floor.

He looks as if he's deciding whether or not he should turn around and leave, or if he should keep walking, which would lead him right past us. Then his shoulders drop, and I think he's come to the conclusion that he had when the women threw pie at him. You can't run.

I lift my hand and wave at him.

He shakes his head, and there's a slight smile there, as if to say, "you really can't stay away, can you?"

"I'll be right back," Josh says.

He presses his hand to my back and then strides down the hall.

Hope fusses when she sees her dad walking away, so I kneel down.

"Don't worry, baby, your dad just has to...say hi to Ian."

Which *could* be true.

I can't see Josh's face, but Ian looks like he's resigned himself to being punched. Josh stops in front of him. I strain to listen.

"Ian," he says.

Ian nods. "Josh."

I hold my breath. Josh lifts his hand and Ian braces himself. Then, instead of hitting him like Ian must've thought, Josh rests his hand on Ian's shoulder.

A gesture of solidarity. Forgiveness.

I let out a relieved breath.

They stand there, for a good five seconds, then Ian shakily exhales and jerks his chin, nodding.

"You've always been too good," Ian says. "It's your greatest fault."

I can tell Josh is smiling, even though his back is to me. "You said the same thing ten years ago."

"It was as true then as it is today."

Josh squeezes Ian's shoulder. "You know, you're just as much a selfish ass as you ever were. Come to think of it, there's a villain in my next comic with your name on it."

Ian gives the first real smile that I think I've ever seen. His eyes scrunch at the corners, and he grins like a little boy that just won a toy car. I've never seen him look so genuinely happy.

I push Hope's stroller next to them. Hope gives a happy gurgle when she sees Ian and starts to wave her arms at him.

"I'm going to head to my appointments. You're good?"

Josh drops his hand from Ian's shoulder and turns to me. He reaches forward and brushes his hand over my cheek.

"I'm good." He looks down at Hope and gives her that in-love-dad smile, then amends, "We're good. Ian and I are going to catch up. Grab a coffee."

"God save me from saints and do-gooders," Ian says dryly.

"Have fun," I say, smirking at him. I stand on my tiptoes, rest my hands on Josh's shoulders and brush a kiss on his jaw.

I'm not sure how long Josh and Ian will talk, what exactly they'll share, or if after today they'll ever speak again. But I do know that Josh deserves a chance to hear about his mom, and his dad, and Ian deserves a chance to talk about his own family.

As I walk away, I hear Ian say, in a deceptively honest voice, "Did you say coffee? You go on ahead. Let me grab those. I know the perfect place."

I shake my head, deciding that I don't need to warn Josh about Ian's coffee habits. He'll find out soon enough.

On the way to the waiting room, I see Dr. Matsos walking down the hall. She's looking down at her pager, chewing on her fire-engine-red lips.

"Dr. Matsos, good morning."

She glances up, brushes her curly hair out of her face.

"Gemma, hi. How are you? I haven't seen you in a while. Everything okay?"

I can tell she's in a hurry, she's probably on rounds, or on her way to check on a patient, or put in orders. I won't keep her, but I do want her to know something.

"I'm great. I'm really great."

Dr. Matsos tilts her head and takes in my dress, my flushed cheeks, my smile. "You look great."

"Thank you," I say. Then, "I don't know if you remember this, but shortly after I woke up, you said that a lot of people find out that they are stronger and more resilient than they ever thought possible."

Dr. Matsos nods, "Yes. I tell all my patients that. It usually comes true."

I'm glad. I'm glad she does. Someone needs to. Someone needs to be there to tell people when they've lost who they used to be, that they'll come out the other side, and they'll be stronger, and wiser, and more truly themselves than they could ever have been without.

I press my hand to my chest. "I didn't believe you at the time," I admit. "But you were right. So thank you."

Dr. Matsos nods, reaches out and presses her hand to mine. "It's my job. I come here every day hoping to help. Thanks for reminding me of that."

Her pager beeps, she looks down, and then an all-business expression comes over her face.

"Back to it," she says.

I lift my hand in farewell, then head to my appointments.

Three hours later, when I come out, I find Josh in the waiting room, Hope on his lap. I drop into the chair next to him. He bounces Hope up and down and she gives her baby belly laugh.

Josh grins at me as we both soak in her laughter.

"How was it?" he finally asks.

"Good. Really good."

Every day I work a lot harder to get a little less far. My therapist tells me that means I'm getting better.

I lean into Josh. He presses a kiss into my hair. He seems happy, content.

"Ian's gone?" I ask.

Josh looks off into the distance, like he's remembering something from their conversation.

"He claims he's moving to another state," Josh says.

He shakes his head, like leaving New York is unfathomable. Which it is.

He continues, "I told him that he couldn't disappear altogether though, since he's coming to our wedding."

I cough then start to laugh. The look on Josh's face is priceless.

"You did that just to taunt him, didn't you? Now he'll really think you're a saint. It'll drive him insane."

Josh grins. "Do you think I took the good guy thing too far?"

I laugh. "No." Then I reach over and brush the edge of Josh's jaw. "You really want him to come?"

He shrugs, "I want you to come."

I start to laugh again and he gives me his Gemma-is-my-playground smile.

"I love you," I say. "I really, really love you."

He reaches over and grasps my hand, "I never doubted it."

I scoff. "What? You did. You doubted it right up until the last minute."

He puts on a mock-offended look. "Gemma, didn't I ever tell you? Being in love means forgetting all past mistakes."

I laugh, "Who said that?"

He winks at me. "I did. Of course."

I stand, pull him to his feet, and strap Hope into her stroller.

"You also said everything's better the second time around," I remind him.

He considers me, his eyes warm. "I did, didn't I?"

I nod.

It's settled. Love is definitely better the second time around.

"How about lunch?" I ask as we walk out onto the sidewalk and into the sunshine.

"What do you think about lunch, baby girl?" Josh asks Hope. She doesn't answer, she's busy playing with her toes.

"We could get pizza, walk any which direction, find a dessert place before we're finished," I add.

Josh looks at me with laughing eyes, "Gemma, are you trying to fall in love again?"

"Maybe..." I give him an innocent look.

We stop walking and grin at each other in the middle of the sidewalk as people part around us. He reaches out and presses a finger to my lips.

"Alright. I'm in," he says.

Thank goodness.

I stand on my tiptoes, wrap my arms around his shoulders, and when he presses his mouth to mine, I forget that we're on the sidewalk, surrounded by people and traffic and tall buildings, and all I remember is the feeling of love.

And it feels really, really, really good.

28

She said, "We could walk any which direction."

29

He said, "Rendezvous?"

30

He said, "We dream at night."

31

"Ever after."

OCTOBER 12

IF YOU'RE GOING TO GET MARRIED FOR A SECOND TIME, FIJI IS the place to do it.

We're on the beach under a white fabric awning, tropical flowers twist around the poles, perfuming the salty sea air. The clear turquoise ocean water laps at the sand, only feet away. I'm barefoot and in a simple, short white dress.

I clasp Josh's hands. He's in linen pants and a buttoned shirt. We're a far cry from tuxes and ballgown wedding dresses. Did that already, got the t-shirt.

Speaking of t-shirts, Dylan, the best man, is wearing a t-shirt and shorts. All the guys, Dylan, my dad, Oliver, my friends' husbands, are all in beachy garb.

Even Ian is wearing shorts, a black t-shirt, and flip flops. Yes. He came to our wedding.

Probably because Josh really did make a comic book

villain based on him, and it made Ian laugh so hard that he decided he and Josh were better friends than enemies.

My mom and sister are here too. They're in matching coral and yellow sundresses. Hope is in a frothy pastel sundress that looks like sea foam.

My friends, Brook, Carly and Hannah are all relaxed, and enjoying the vacation—they all flew over with Carly. Hannah's baby is here, three months old, a boy named Phoenix. Brook's baby is coming up on one now, and a ball of energy, just like her mom. Luckily she has a police officer and a lawyer for parents, so their moxie can match hers. Brook claims the terrible twos will be no match for the NYPD.

Sasha, Mary, Maemie and Colin haven't been able to sit still since we got here. Apparently, the seventeen-hour plane ride was enough sitting to last years.

It's the middle of our wedding, and Maemie, Mary and Colin have all stripped out of their wedding clothes and are splashing in the ocean. Leah grinds her teeth, and I can see her visibly restraining herself from yelling at them. I catch her eye and wink. She shakes her head and rolls her eyes.

Sasha, being the oldest, is still in her dress, standing next to her mom, looking very grown up. But I can tell she really wants to run into the water and join her siblings.

Josh sees me looking at the kids and smiles.

"You okay?" he mouths.

I nod, I'm definitely one hundred percent okay. It's been three months since we agreed to elope. We did exactly what Josh said, we spent nearly a hundred days taking things slow, making love, noticing the little things, and falling in love again every single minute of every single day.

I finished therapy at The Whittcombe and I'm taking on clients again. I'm not the same as I used to be, I can't do the same things, and I don't think the same way, but that doesn't matter. I am who I am. I don't live in spite of what happened, I live as me because of what happened. I like who I am. This is me.

It wasn't love, or sex, or feelings that had some magical healing effect. No, it was just my brain, doing its thing, slowly repairing itself. But I have to admit, love didn't hurt the process. It was that star that pulled me through the darkness and led me back to myself.

Late last night, Josh finished the first volume of his new web comic series. He'll be putting out new content every week for a whole year. He's going to show it to me later today. I can't wait. In fact, I can't wait to have a whole life together, seeing what he creates and what we do together.

I squeeze Josh's hands.

"Do you, Gemma Jacobs, take Josh Lewenthal to be your lawfully wedded husband? To have and to hold..."

You better believe I do. I smile at Josh as the officiant recites the wedding vows.

Josh watches me carefully, his eyes never leaving my face. Last time, when we were standing under the wedding gazebo, Josh looked worried, probably because I was about to collapse. This time, he just looks happy and like he doesn't want to miss a second of this.

"I do," I say.

Josh's smile flashes bright. And when it's his turn to repeat the vows, he says them in a firm, steady voice. The ocean breeze ruffles his hair, and I have the urge to reach up and brush it back.

"I do," he says.

At that, Josh leans down, grabs me under the legs, and swoops me up. I throw back my head and laugh and laugh.

"I now pronounce you man and wife," the officiant says. "You may now kiss your bride."

"Seal it with a kiss?" Josh asks.

"I had something else in mind," I say.

Josh grins.

Then we're kissing, and Josh carries me down the aisle, back to our honeymoon suite, a thatched roofed cottage on the water. And I'm waving at my family and friends, and Sasha runs toward the ocean, kicking up sand behind her, rushing to join her siblings, and Leah chases after the kids, mother-henning.

My dad dips my mom in a kiss, then he picks up Hope and bounces her in the air. I can hear her giggles even over Sasha's excited shrieking.

Brook hauls her daughter toward the water. Dylan heads to the buffet table, a smorgasbord of tropical fruits and desserts. He punches Ian on the shoulder as he passes and says something about Jell-O shots.

I smile at Josh and shade my eyes against the afternoon sun. The sky is so blue here and the sun so bright.

"They're all happy," I say, and there's happiness overwhelming me. It feels a lot like warm sand on my feet and cool breeze on my skin.

Josh nods at me, pushing aside palm fronds and fragrant fuchsia-colored flowers as he heads down the path to our cottage door.

"So are we," he says.

He's right.

He opens the wooden cottage door, steps over the threshold. A breeze blows through the open window, rustling the sheer white canopy of the king-size bed.

"Does that mean this is happily ever after?" I ask, comfortable in his arms.

I give him a soft, teasing smile.

He pauses, studies my face, taking in my expression. I

have the sudden urge to kiss him again and not stop for at least a day.

But then he says, "I think life would be boring if it were only happily ever after. I don't need a happily ever after."

Me either...but...

"What *do* you need?"

He kicks the door shut, crosses the teak floor, and drops me onto the cushy bed.

I sink into the thick down comforter and watch as he pulls off his shirt, revealing the heart that I inked on his chest last night.

He considers my question, eyes thoughtful, then he smiles at me.

"How about...and they lived ever after, together, sometimes happy, sometimes not, but always together. In love."

I grin up at him. "That's a little wordier than 'they lived happily ever after.'"

He steps out of his linen pants, kicks them aside.

"That's okay," he says, "because this next part doesn't require any words."

We smile at each other, in perfect accord.

Because he's right.

It doesn't.

But just in case we need a reminder, I reach over to the nightstand, grab one of Josh's ever-present ink pens, and write on his chest, inside that little heart, the words, *ever after*.

THE END

*ILLUSTRATIONS BY JOSH LEWENTHAL

ACKNOWLEDGMENTS

Not all books are based on life experience—this one is. My mom made me promise to put this book out there for all the people who have been in a coma, had traumatic brain injuries, and who have had their live's changed in an instant. Gemma's journey was truncated for the sake of fiction, the real journey lasts a lifetime.

If you're struggling—it's okay. If you make mistakes—it's okay. If you don't know if you're going to get through it—you will. It's okay. You are stronger and more resilient than you ever thought possible.

And...thank you Mom, this one's for you.

JOIN SARAH READY'S NEWSLETTER

Want more Josh and Gemma? Get an exclusive chapter from Josh's POV.

When you join the Sarah Ready Newsletter you get access to sneak peaks, insider updates, exclusive bonus scenes and more.

Join Today for Josh's Chapter:

www.sarahready.com/newsletter

ALSO BY SARAH READY

Stand Alone Romances:

The Fall in Love Checklist

Hero Ever After

Once Upon an Island

Josh and Gemma Make a Baby

Josh and Gemma the Second Time Around

French Holiday

Soul Mates in Romeo Romance Series:

Chasing Romeo

Love Not at First Sight

Romance by the Book

Love, Artifacts, and You

Married by Sunday

My Better Life

Scrooging Christmas

Stand Alone Novella:

Love Letters

Find these books and more by Sarah Ready at:

www.sarahready.com/romance-books

ABOUT THE AUTHOR

Author Sarah Ready writes contemporary romance and romantic comedy. Her books have been described as "euphoric", "heartwarming" and "laugh out loud".

Sarah writes stand-alone romcoms and romcoms in the Soul Mates in Romeo series, all of which can be found at her website: www.sarahready.com.

Stay up to date, get exclusive epilogues and bonus content. Join Sarah's newsletter at www.sarahready.com/newsletter.

CPSIA information can be obtained
at www.ICGtesting.com
Printed in the USA
BVHW051616291122
652939BV00002B/9